INTUITION OF THE NEWS

Intuition of the News

A Collection of Short Stories

by

ROBERT WEXELBLATT

Adelaide Books
New York / Lisbon
2019

INTUITION OF THE NEWS
A collection of short stories
By Robert Wexelblatt

Published by Adelaide Books, New York / Lisbon
adelaidebooks.org

Editor-in-Chief
Stevan V. Nikolic

For any information, please address Adelaide Books
at info@adelaidebooks.org
or write to:
Adelaide Books
244 Fifth Ave. Suite D27
New York, NY, 10001

ISBN: 978-1-951214-81-4

Printed in the United States of America

Contents

Acknowledgments

"Intuition of the News" first appeared in *Carolina Quarterly*

"Odo" first appeared in *Sou'wester*

"The Lenders' Dinner," "Our Rabbi," and "Inter Scoti et
	Scuti" first appeared in *Offcourse Literary Journal*

"Standards of American Measurement" first appeared in
	Apeiron Review

"Confessions of an Adolescent Arsonist" and "Sickness and
	Health" first appeared in *The Montréal Review*

"Crazy About Her" first appeared in *White Whale Review*

"Terminus ad Quem" first appeared in *Apt*

"Pornstar/Daredevil" first appeared in *Temporary Infinity*

"Thermal" first appeared in *Happy*

"Romanza" first appeared in *Amarillo Bay*

"A Laurel Greener" first appeared in *Otis Nebula*

"Harbor Islands" and "Last Poems" first appeared in
	The Write Room

Intuition of The News

It was Flynn's father's gun, a Smith and Wesson .38. When Flynn swiped it that morning he was probably more afraid of his father's finding out he'd sawed off the lock on the cabinet than of anything he might do with the gun. That's Flynn all over, I mean scared of the wrong things because he's scared of everything. He was scared of Geare and even more of Dooley, afraid of being dared, of being mocked. It's childish but then, at bottom, boys' bravery is always about being scared of something. Even Dooley, what you might call a *consummate* bully, even Dooley was terrified somebody might giggle at him. Well, not just somebody—somebody like me.

I used to look at myself in the mirror and imagine how the boys thought about what I saw. A girl. A pretty girl. New breasts, shapely legs. Clear skin, slim ankles. Bright bedroom eyes and semi-demi-quasi-innocent cheeks. Sweet waist and heart-shaped bum. Brisket. Sirloin. Chops. I could just contrive to see myself dismembered but the mystery eluded me and I know I was a mystery to them. A girl can tell and use it too. The simplest trick is just to keep your mouth shut. A surprising number of girls can't manage this and so they've no idea what an edge they're giving up. If you can be a blank blackboard they'll scribble all over you and you'll still be untouched.

If you can hold it in and look at them they'll bluster and strut and act tough like Dooley, but just get a girlfriend to look at them with you then turn and giggle behind your hands. Such brittle egos, little wine glasses that shatter just like (I am snapping my fingers). It's really no wonder they all dream of violence.

It was stupidity, mostly. Everything is, mostly. I can see it. Dooley pushing him in the chest, calling him Flynn-the-Fag, Geare going along, laughing.

"What the hell do you want it for?" he'd have pleaded.

"You getting it or not?"

"Yeah. Okay."

"I mean if you're *scared*, if you're going to be *faggy* about it, then forget it, Flynn."

"I'm just asking—"

Dooley would swagger with impatience and mockery, trying to look cool when he was scared, though of the wrong things. Dooley would come into a room and the first thing he'd ask himself was what he could grab to break the windows. As for Geare, he was just a good-looking jock. Physically he had it all—the cut pecs, straight hair, thick neck. Geare walked with the athlete's waddle, one powerful leg out, then the other. I disliked seeing him walk; it was as if his muscles ached and he was being careful that they shouldn't touch anything. Geare's gracefulness was in inverse proportion to his rate of locomotion. Running down the field he was a thing of beauty and a joy forever. In fifth grade Dooley persuaded Geare to jump out of his bedroom window onto an army surplus cot. Busted his arm. Dooley was insecure underneath but down there Geare was truly a sentimentalist; his roly-poly soul must look like a yin-and-yang of brutality and Hallmark mush. Dooley was stringy and wiry and looked almost fragile next to his sidekick

Geare, and you could already see how pudgy Flynn would be; but it was easy to tell which one was dangerous and who would cry if somebody he knew happened to get killed.

I used to have two fantasies. Fantasy's as good a word as any.

Fantasy the First.

Breakfast is done and my father is going to drive me to school. I am in second grade. He is wearing a suit and tie. I have on a plaid dress and patent leather Mary Janes. We are an exemplary pair, shiny and dutiful, diligent and proper. Mother looks us up and down with approbation and hands me my lunchbox, kisses me goodbye. She'd have kissed my father too but he is eager to be off.

"Let's get going," he says.

We drive in silence but only two blocks from the house he pulls over. He takes off his tie and turns to me with a mischievous grin.

"We're going to play hooky today, sweetheart. Do you know what playing hooky is?"

"Some kind of game? With sticks?"

He laughs and leans over and gives me this peck on the cheek.

We drive and drive. He turns on the radio and opens the windows. It's a spring day and you can smell the spring in the air rushing through the car. Spring springs from the dirt, he tells me. It smells good as it comes back to life. The ants are happy. The bees are happy. The worms are happy because it's spring.

"And you're happy too," I say experimentally.

Taking the wheel with one hand, he reaches under his seat and pulls out a box and hands it to me. Inside is a new pair of red sneakers, just my size. I put them on and they fit perfectly. They are far more comfortable than the Mary Janes.

We drive across a border. There's a sign. "Look," he tells me, "we're in another state." I like the new state and imagine it is quite another kind of place, with different ants and bees and worms.

"What's it called?" I ask.

"It's called the state of Freedom."

We drive to an amusement park. It's opening day and there are balloons and cotton candy and glorious rides. We go in a motor boat and through the fun house, throw rings and shoot at wooden ducks, go high on the Ferris wheel, and finally climb aboard the enormous roller coaster. Up and up slowly, rising action reaching toward a climax. I cling to him and shut my eyes and cling harder and squeal. He laughs. "We're playing hooky," he yells into my ear.

Fantasy the Second.

I am lying in bed thinking about how to become even more miserable; that is, I see myself tearing off the last veils over my misery, the illusions that hide misery from me and me from it. My father's long gone, remarried with a new daughter. He sends me inappropriate presents on holidays, a Barbie, a plaid skirt, moose hide gloves, a pair of binoculars. Every twentieth Sunday he phones, like clockwork. My mother repels me. First there was her desperation, which was bad, and then her bitterness, which is worse. I refuse to see things from her point of view and, despite the unfairness of it, I am certain this is perhaps my only healthy impulse. I'm in my last year of middle school, the purgatory to which they banish bad teachers. The boys are jerks of the Flynn, Geare, Dooley types or else little terrified boys, the smarter the more scared. The girls are sullen or brazen, depending chiefly on breast size and hair texture. I have no friends.

I don't belong here. The sentence is like a trumpet call. A clarion. The heavens open. It's clear as a new glass. I don't belong here, but somewhere else.

I go to the window and raise the sash. A spaceship about the size of a van is standing in the yard. It is dark silver in the moonlight, both the yard and the ship. I'm not in the least surprised. In fact, I nod, confirmed. Soundlessly a door slides open in the smooth side of the ship and a tall female creature glides out. She is wearing a silver bathrobe and holding a finger to her thin alien lips. She is dignified, old, and about seven feet tall. She looks at me hard, up in my window, and I can hear her voice in my head. It is a calm, placid voice with a slight accent, the way Canadians talk. She assures me that they'll return for me when my mission is accomplished. She says I am doing fine; they are all pleased with me but I must persevere.

I am in the vale of tears. I am on a mission. My sufferings are merely provisional. I am an alien.

To be an alien is even better than being an orphan.

When I entered high school I had the idea of training my mind by studying logic; I wanted to be sharper, a mistress of deduction who could penetrate the appearances of my errant senses. However, I soon discovered that logic cannot govern in any realm but its own, that it is at ease only in its own parlor, so to speak. For this world it is too brittle, too desiccated. Logic is like an old man living all by himself who painstakingly rearranges his memories, snapshots that have been boiled down to concepts. Possibly I think of logic this way because of a post card pinned to the bulletin board in my English class. It depicts the writer Hermann Hesse, author of *Siddhartha,*

Magister Ludi, Demian, etc., in his old age. He is so old he is hardly even Hesse. Seated at his desk he is writing with a fountain pen, completely absorbed and apparently unaware that his picture is being taken, let alone that it would someday wind up on a bulletin board in an American high school. Logic too must ignore a great deal to function. To me Hesse looks as if he is deducing the structure of an alternate reality, one where every detail may be deduced from certain indisputable, *a priori* propositions. "All men are mortal. I am a man. Consequently, I am mortal." This is very sad. Though knowledge cannot advance in this fashion yet the cobbler sticks to his last. I can see he has no cat and that he is wearing a suit and tie. I like that he dresses up to write out his dispositions and disquisitions. No stroker of tabbies he, no fancier of frigid feline pulchritude. The more you look at it, the more the candor of this photo looks false, the more it appears staged. The absence of cats only seems accidental but is actually premeditated. "If X is the same as Y and Y the same as Z, then X is likewise the same as Z." Only in his sealed-off study in hyper-secure Switzerland, only in such a well-pressed suit and decorous necktie could X really be the same as Y, or Y the same as Z. Elsewhere, amid the humid midden out here, they are distinct, isolated, lonesome. "All snakes are animals but not all animals are snakes." That's true enough, and a good thing. "All mothers are females but not all females are mothers." This is undeniable. I am a female but not a mother. "All french fries are potatoes, but most potatoes are neither French nor fried." Who could doubt these apodictic sayings? Though they only tell me what I already know, I am inspired to write these verses on Hesse/Logic's behalf:

> Lucidity that is as good as French
> relished while reclining on a bench

idly teasing pigeons, toting up the crowd
parading primly by, is never loud
or argumentative, each small insight
an aperçu whispered to the twilight,
for this world's poison the sovereign serum
pure as the Pythagorean Theorem . . . .

He writes it all out slowly, building up the particulars of his logical world; and because he is a virtuoso, he even includes certain conundrums for the sake of verisimilitude. "Say a room has six walls and two are removed, suddenly knocked down or burnt up. Is it now a room with four walls or a room lacking two?" As he piles concept atop concept I follow him with my eager mind, which yearns to become a steel trap to catch those around me once and for all. "All deserts lack water but water never lacks deserts." I am disappointed by logic. It cannot describe, let alone stand up to, the world. Dooley could bash in the old man's head with ease. The principle of identity dissolves before my eyes but the old man goes on writing at his desk, in his suit and tie, hard by well ordered Lugano.

That's logic for you, just a fancy form of interior decoration.

They are squatting down in the woods, in a clearing, wearing jeans and tee-shirts. Flynn, who sports a leather bomber jacket over his tee-shirt, takes the gun from his pocket. He shows it to Dooley, who doesn't take it from him at once. No, he lets Geare take it first. "Not bad," he says.

As he takes the gun Geare lets out an appreciative sigh and nods.

Flynn expands under all this understated praise. "It's loaded," he says as if he had himself invented firearms.

Geare holds the gun carefully by the barrel as though it were a snake, then hands it back with exaggerated nonchalance.

Only Dooley hasn't touched it. Dooley is undecided or perhaps he is biding his time; he rubs his hands on his jeans and gets to his feet.

Dooley hasn't any plan, nothing like a clear idea. He never has clear ideas. The woods around my hometown are the opposite of Lugano. Dooley aspires to be a bull in a china shop. His hatred of civilization is unfocused and contradictory; after all, only civilization could produce a .38 caliber Smith and Wesson pistol. Harnessed by pernicious idealism Dooley might have made a successful U-boat sailor or a willing suicide bomber. Without a theory his actions were bound to be petty, shooting cats with a bb gun, beating up the occasional ectomorph, dropping cherry bombs in toilets, goading Flynn into lifting his dad's gun. All his semi-understood impulses rest on a dogged resistance to restriction, to having the trackless wilderness of his psyche invaded by lawgivers and jailers. As for females, giggles that humiliate will later infuriate. It's not much of a prophecy to say that Dooley will someday beat women.

He walked to the edge of the clearing and peed against a pine.

Geare and Flynn didn't look at one another.

"Ever fire the damned thing?" Geare asks the grass.

"Sure," Flynn tells the sedge.

"Shitting me? At anything?"

"Target."

"Hit it?"

Flynn waits, considers. "Nah."

They chuckle, eyeing Dooley's nasty sixteen-year-old back.

I know. It's a kind of freshman ritual, rite of passage, initiation. First paper of the first year. Get them to write about what they think they know, then show them they don't know anything and can't write. Annihilate, but don't discourage.

Your assignment was to write about my hometown. "One-inch margins. 12-point font. Four pages *maximum*." That italicized maximum told me a lot about you, Professor.

Obviously I am submitting more than four pages. I wonder if you will read them all. Have you already stopped? Are you slashing these unwanted pages with a baroque diagonal of red professorial ink? Will you fail me? Alert the counselors? Or will you scrutinize my every word thinking "a promising student, talented, precocious even, but difficult, insubordinate, undisciplined and maybe a little twisted." I wonder, Professor, is it your professional opinion that no writing assignment ought to require a student actually to tell the truth?

So much depends on point of view, on perspective. You said so yourself. I began to examine my environment, my *hometown*, as an alien should if she is on a mission. The lights that illuminate the baseball diamond have to be outside it. When I was enmeshed in it all, when I thought I was of it as well as knee-deep in it, I couldn't muster much sympathy; but, once I felt myself to be the most outside of outsiders, I began to feel pity. Saints must be aliens. I saw that everybody suffered, had suffered, was going to suffer. Only when I ceased to consider myself human did I discover what *types* like Malraux and Sartre call *la condition humaine*.

I began to catch on not just emotionally but intellectually too. For example, I saw that the leading principle of life in town was division: classes, status, income, beliefs, being in or out, strong or weak, pretty or plain, loved or ignored, envied or despised. As with Zeno dividing up a race course, there was no end of dividing. Even in this putative democracy people found countless ways to distinguish nobles from commoners. The second thing I noticed was the human obsession with, need for, and endless consumption of stories. Human lives, it seemed to me, existed to provide material for stories to be told in movies, books, signs, newspapers, creation myths, gossip, dreams. I began to admire the storytellers, I mean the really great artists, but then I also had contempt for them too, or for the needs they satisfied. I went back and forth on this, unsure if the stories were ways of penetrating reality or simply evading it. What I liked least of all were the storytellers who didn't even know they were telling stories. Once I heard a friend of my mother's, a divorcée like herself, whine into her coffee, "If I knew the deal was going to be fifteen years of loneliness maybe I'd have tried a little harder." Everybody saw their lives as stories, epics crammed with episodes, stuffed with fascinating sex scenes and interior monologues, or long tales of woe and unmerited deprivation, injustice and rejection, novels with huge trajectories. Nobody could mistake who the hero was.

The story, I concluded, not logic, is the human weapon against meaninglessness.

If I were to become a professor I would like to teach a course about death. I would give my students multiple-choice examinations, which can be graded even more rapidly than four-page essays.

Comedy is to sex as tragedy is to
    a. solitude
    b. oversleeping
    c. death
    d. a lecture on tragedy.

Death is to beauty as logic is to
    a. the spin cycle
    b. hot coffee
    c. delusions of grandeur
    d. family therapy.

Which of the following are not mortal?
    a. filles de joie
    b. nuns
    c. Romantic poets
    d. your great-great grandson.

All comediennes are
    a. pregnable
    b. funny
    c. prone to being doomed
    d. two-legged.

    I thought of writing you a poem (four pages long) beginning with a description of the freak snowstorm that paralyzed and perplexed my hometown the first week of that April, the snow falling on it more like a judgment than a cold front. Here are the first two lines: *Privet hedges crushed under suburban schlag/depressed like badly wed accountants*
    . . . There seems to be a surplus in town of accountants who have married neither wisely nor well—also these accountants' spouses. However, I am not cynical. For me, all married couples are presumed to be happily married until proven otherwise. When I was being an alien, of course, I understood the purpose of marriage through its complex relationship with human biology. Frankly, I felt a little sorry for marriage, fighting out of its weight class. Still, I could see the sense in

the institution, in households, in mothers and fathers who manage to live together and children who grow up under their delicately interlaced, protective branches.

Geare's father is an accountant. He becomes frantic at tax time and irritable to the point of exasperation. The pettiness of his trade and his clients really ought to have spared him from tragedy. Yet even Mr. Geare once fell in love with Mrs. Geare deeply enough to court her. Adults can be mysterious even when they are predictable. My town is full of adults who have forgotten how much they would have liked to blow up their high school.

From the left rear pocket of his jeans Dooley took out a soft pack of Marlboros. He extracted a flattened cigarette and inserted it in the corner of his mouth before offering the pack to the others. Flynn took one, Geare refused. Being an athlete he only smoked at night, well after practice was over. Geare was a social smoker.

"Let me see that thing."

Flynn handed the gun to Dooley, handle-first. Holding it sideways, Dooley bounced it in his palm, testing its weight. He aimed it at a tree trunk. What went through his so-called mind, that generator of anarchic images as the charge of metal coursed up his arm? Potshots at squirrels? Killing his father? Smuggling it into school? Knocking over a gas station? Jacking a car? Showing off for somebody with curves like mine?

"Got a light, Flynn?"

Flynn searched the pockets of his bomber jacket and came up with a pack of matches. He lit his own cigarette first then held the lit match out for Dooley, cupping it with his hands. Flynn leaned forward on his haunches, Dooley did likewise and pushed his head toward the flame.

Geare was thinking about me in a halter top, about me in short shorts, perhaps about me in a white silk teddy. Geare had a thing for me, the alien. He had made this clear enough in the aggressively shy fashion of those with good physiques and no conversation. Like Dooley, he wanted to go out with me, which is to say he wanted to get his hands on me. It was the same sort of impulse that had once lead his father to court his mother in an ancient springtime without freak snowstorms, back before April meant only tax returns.

I presume the evolution of the neo-cortex was pleasing to the neo-cortex which, among other functions, longs for stories and, in general, new ways to kill time pleasantly. To function successfully, rationalization (the hedonism of the middle-aged) requires the insignificance of pure mechanism. Your soul is made of dendrites. *So long as we exist death is not with us; but when death comes, then we do not exist.* Fully functional rationalization is always negative and risk-averse. Pleasure is the absence of pain. To be good is not to break the law. Smart means not getting any answers wrong. To pray is to waste your time, unless you really enjoy it. Such logic is a colossal defense mechanism, a sort of vending machine which spits out invulnerability. I think aliens make good Epicureans.

Dooley, who instinctively knew he had no chance with me and expressed his baffled desire by calling me various unpleasant names, could not quite reach the match. He leaned further, extending the cigarette and the lips that held it well beyond his center of gravity. Suddenly he fell over, striking his right elbow on the ground. The shock caused an involuntary neuro-muscular contraction to shoot down his forearm into his hand, into his fingers, including the one on the trigger.

The noise was loud and echoed off the trees on which the first pale leaves had just begun to show.

The bullet went through Geare's left eye and straight into his neo-cortex, seat of logic and fantasy, of memory and deduction.

For an instant the astonished Flynn stared at them both on the ground. Then he ran. He ran to me, to me, to my house. He was in tears; his nose was running; he was almost incoherent. The snow from the freak storm having just melted, his sneakers left muddy tracks on the carpet. I put him on the couch, but he couldn't sit still. He ran to me as if I weren't the sexy detached girl around whose locker he hung but a mother, a nurturer, the BVM who forgives everyone for everything. I pushed him back on the couch. While he sat there crying like a defeated boxer I went to the phone and called the police of my hometown.

Odo

1.

Odo squatted under the thick fronds, a hideous satyr, his phallus mockingly upturned like a carrot on a college snowman. Mucus and excrement had dried in foul lava flows down his simpering face.

The silent forest smelled green and wet. Back in the village the Hamora would be sleeping off the ceremony, the women still quarantined; but even the insects and wind seemed to be snoring. The forest at dawn reminded Koplowitz of the enchanted one surrounding Sleeping Beauty, a barrier against motion and therefore stopping time.

He took off his backpack, stepped gingerly, placing his sneaker on the freshly trampled ground. He felt alert, crazy yet sure of himself, no longer dizzy from last night's harpoi. He cleared his throat. *Guilt is civilization trying to occupy the wilderness.* He chuckled, took one giant step forward and, aiming for Odo's flat nose, spat as well as a beginner could. Then Koplowitz relieved himself.

2.

In his careful way, the Dean had hit on the most decorous attitude. "Go on, Beth," he said encouragingly, but not without a whiff of judicial severity.

"Well, like I told Ms. Cianci," said Beth in her heartbreakingly breathy and by no means insincere voice, "he came up to me and, you know," here she slightly elevated her Platonic idea of an arm, "brushed against me. . ." Here she gazed demurely downward with both cerulean blue eyes, embarrassed. "Against my . . . chest."

Dan Schlesinger's knuckles got a little whiter, the Dean's jaw jutted out a smidgin further, while over in the corner Mr. and Mrs. Schrempf, a rather spiffy and youngish couple, looked by turns murderous, tearful, dignified, vengeful, concerned, outraged, sympathetic, hateful, and bored.

"What do you mean he *came up* to you?" Calipha MacPherson, by far the more aggressive of the two student members of the panel, wanted to know. "Weren't you both sitting down?" She looked at Beth with what seemed to Koplowitz precociously lawyerly hostility, but it might just have been the rimless spectacles and her penchant for frowning. Koplowitz knew her slightly. She had a reputation for combative brilliance. Calipha managed to give most white people the feeling she despised them. Perhaps she did.

Beth, as she always did when feeling challenged, ran her finger over her smooth and burnished hair, unconsciously teasing out split ends. With an aggrieved glance toward mom and dad, she went on. "We were both sitting down to *start* with, of course. But then he got up to make a point or get a book or something. Anyway, he crossed over to where I was and that's when it happened. I mean, I was there to talk about my *grade* and I got the *very distinct* impression that—"

Calipha interrupting, anything but satisfied: "Whose idea was it to talk about your midterm grade?"

"Whose idea?"

Calipha smirked, glasses glinting ferociously in the fluorescent glare. "Did you ask to see the professor to get your grade raised?"

Beth, all outraged virtue, looked witheringly at Calipha. She was so ticked off that for a moment she misplaced her Aryan victim face. Over in the parental corner, Mrs. Schrempf huffed audibly in her becoming pinstriped suit and whispered something to her husband who was pink with fury.

Here Muriel Schwartz, a no-nonsense mathematician with spotless professional and feminist credentials, cut in like an icebreaker through the Bering Strait. "I think we've established *that* already, Ms. MacPherson. The key question is obviously whether or not Professor Koplowitz said anything to suggest to Ms. Schrempf that her grade might be affected by her willingness to favor him," here she paused not quite half a beat, "to favor him *sexually*, I mean."

The Dean blanched at the word and seized the chance to be more catholic than the Pope. "But Muriel," he chided, "I'm sure you agree that the, the, um, *touching* alone would be sufficient grounds for a charge of harassment, or even assault."

"If you say so." Muriel raised her eyebrow, leaned forward, looked down the table at Koplowitz as if she were his aunt and it were Thanksgiving. "Well, *did* you brush up against her breast?"

In the close air of that room, even this brutality seemed refreshing to Koplowitz. "Not that I can remember," he said.

"Can't *remember*?"

"What?"

"Oh, *really*."

Beth looked triumphantly at the Dean, who made a note then nodded gravely, signalling her to continue with her evidence.

"Well, as I *also* told Ms. Cianci, Professor Koplowitz was always looking at me, you know, in a certain *way*. In class, before and after, whenever he saw me on campus. Anyhow, it was a way that made me *very* uncomfortable."

Calipha made an unpleasant sound and furiously scrawled something on her yellow pad.

Muriel Schwartz looked impassive.

Dan Schlesinger, professor of Byzantine history, persisted in looking paralyzed.

The Dean, decorous as ever, ruffled his papers.

There they were in the same conference room where Koplowitz had joked with colleagues at inane committee meetings, where he had committed the folly of making passionate speeches about trival policies. It was the same table over which he had so frequently slumped, the grain of whose wood he had often studied while stupefied by boredom. There were the seventeenth-century Dutch landscapes whose flatness he had identified with on late afternoons in November. Now the place had been transformed into a hearing chamber, a courtroom. A tape recorder had been set squarely in the middle of the table. Three small microphones, each on its little stand and linked to the recorder by a snaking black wire, had been meticulously disposed at precise intervals. The room felt costumed, a stage set, dramatic tension in every cubic inch of its dead air. The effect on Koplowitz was nightmarish because the setting was so familiar, not unlike a bad dream in which your high school algebra teacher turns up as a rhinoceros.

Koplowitz felt guilty. In fact, he had no difficulty believing in his guilt. There was no doubt Elizabeth Schrempf had it right about his looking at her, although one might ask who looked first or which of them was made the more uncomfortable by it. Yes, he had looked, but then he looked at all his students. In a way, he loved all his students, though he had not lusted after any of them, not even Beth Schrempf. But maybe it was only in his actions that he was not guilty, only in that thin stratum of consciousness at the top of the cortex. That sort of provisional innocence hardly rules out guilt. Guilt, he would have liked to leap up and announce to this drumhead court, is not an objective fact; it is not a sensation of remorse. At its purest guilt isn't even the emotional residue of a temptation successfully wrestled to the floor. Guilt is a punishment. It is an inquisitor complete with rack, press, and screw. Guilt is civilization trying to occupy the wilderness.

Koplowitz was chockful of wilderness, a guilty man whether or not he had–on purpose or with inadvertence, by chance or by design, in fact or merely in fantasy–brushed up against the, now that he really looked at it, unquestionably desirable breast of Elizabeth Schrempf, C- student in Zoölogy 101.

Mr. and Mrs. Schrempf would not look at him, but he found himself checking them out every few seconds. He could hardly take his eyes off them. They were about his own age.

3.

The only grant he could get barely covered a quarter of his expenses but Koplowitz was determined to go anyway. If not now, when? There would never be a better time to search out that viviparous lizard which Shaughnessy had written him about. Shaughnessy was an old Aussie sot and fellow zoölogist, a good old boy from Down Under. Anyway, the lizard, real or not, viviparous or not, made an excellent pretext and not only for a grant. Zoölogy, like any other art or science, can be escapist if the spirit's there.

Koplowitz did not, however, look for lizards on his way back to his camp. He was thinking of the women imprisoned in the huts and of good old Elfar, all skin and bones and wisdom, and of how Elfar would smile to see him spit and take a leak on Odo. Elfar knew nothing about postage stamps or telephones yet he could speak a pretty fair French; in fact, his French was a good deal less rudimentary than Koplowitz's. And how did the old savage learn the language of Rousseau and Gide? He had explained it himself, or halfway at least: "*Deux anthropologistes—homme et femme.*"

Oh yes, Koplowitz remembered that he had for a couple of years been married to a woman who, as a sophomore at Wellesley, took introductory anthropology to fulfill her social science requirement. That was the extent of his connection to anthropology. In several respects, he had liked being married, but all of the respects were wrong. They were too respectable. Marriage made him feel like a solid citizen, afforded him social standing, gave him the heady sense of an unequivocal adulthood. By the relatively simple expedient of marrying he had ceased to be a son and might become a father—even a grandfather, if he could keep it up. He was able to move with ease among married couples, handing around drinks and hors d'oeuvres; he could elbow other married men in honest goodfellowship; he could take out a mortgage, buy a lawnmower. Respectable hogwash, of course. His marriage turned out badly because it turned out to be a lie. Koplowitz, in fact, had come to believe that social life is founded on lying, candor being a peculiarly anti-social virtue, though he had adjusted to this lie, indeed, had done so with a rapidity and completeness that made him mistrust himself ever after. His wife, on the other hand, had initially believed in the marriage much more strongly than he, had stumped for it with a kind of *credo quia absurdum* argument, and had left her maidenhood to enter upon the wedded state as whole-heartedly and apparently finally as a parachutist leaves an airplane to enter the sky. Yet it was she who became increasingly frank about the marriage's shortcomings, which is to say his. They separated after a year, divorced a year later and exchanged Christmas cards for two years after that. So it had been a while since Koplowitz was socially respectable in any respect.

He wondered about "*les deux anthropologistes—homme et femme.*" Not about their fate—that he had figured out at last—but about them. For example, were they lovers or husband and wife? Did they find out things before things found them out? There in the jungle, did they miss *vin ordinaire*? If they were able to discover anything, did they get to write it up? Were they supported and edified by their work or did they merely hide behind it to avoid the pain of *la réalité contemporaine?* How much did they delude themselves? Why didn't they simply go away, back to Paris and its bistros? Did they see it coming?

Elfar would not tell *Monsieur Kopo* the story of the anthropologists although he spoke almost nothing but stories. For example, there was the epic fable of Kalah and Kataan, the folktales about Beilith the Fool and Poma the Dog, not to mention the climactic story, the history of Odo and the Other. To these tales Koplowitz listened like a child, a child still capable of guiltlessly walking into the woods, into the wilderness of stories.

4.

Outside, after another day of elucidation, the campus was falling again into darkness. The Dean's jacket hung over the high back of his chair; behind his glasses, his eyes were red. The large map of the Northwest Territory, the formal portraits of the last four deans in their regalia and chilly smiles, the out-of-place Cézanne reproduction in its golden frame—all hung unnoticed on the walls, fixtures, official witnesses.

They both knew it. Koplowitz had become a problem; he had been the occasion of things not going smoothly. All deans are averse to the unsmooth; they dislike problems, particularly those with tenure.

Taking a seat as far as possible from the decanal throne, Koplowitz entrenched himself behind the coffee table with its little fan of alumni magazines and the heavy pictorial history of the University, to await the verdict.

The Dean took off his glasses, released them over his blotter like a bomb, and rubbed the bridge of his nose. This, Koplowitz knew, was a prelude to sincerity.

"Look, Saul, let me give you some advice, okay? In case you haven't noticed we're living in litigious times. So in the future make sure your office door's open and for Christ's sake don't get *anywhere* near female students."

"Not guilty then?"

"Jesus, Saul. Of course not guilty. Unanimously, if you want to know, and in about three minutes flat. But the Schrempfs are pulling the girl out and they're making noises about suing."

"Suing?"

"Oh, don't worry. I'm pretty sure they won't actually do it. The case is pretty lame. Your record's clean, we gave the testimony a good going over and the machine's got every word. Hell, they saw it all themselves. No. In fact, I'd bet Ms. Schrempf isn't going to have a very pleasant ride home. What was it, anyhow? She out to get you over a midterm grade?"

Koplowitz didn't know. "I don't know," he said.

The Dean sat back, turned reflective. "It's damned scary really. I mean any time any one of these kids wants to they can file a charge, throw shit anybody's way."

"What if they're telling the truth? What if Beth was? What if I *did* look at her in a way that frightened her? What if I *did* brush against her?"

The Dean swivelled his throne and bent forward. This kind of talk displeased him. It was not what he was expecting.

Koplowitz knew he should hold his tongue but bubbled on. "Like discrimination, harassment doesn't have to be intentional, does it? We've learned that much, I suppose. All of us have unconscious impulses. It's what we *mostly* have. Aren't we responsible for them in *some* way?"

Frowning, the Dean made a dismissive gesture, as if brushing away a gnat. "What you call impulses matter only if we *act* on them. Which in your case you didn't. Right? Look, I can imagine you're feeling pretty lousy. An accusation like this, well it's just an incredibly terrible thing to go through. Really awful. Bad enough that other people think . . . you know. . ." The Dean trailed off, thought of psychology. "But aren't you just *internalizing* it, Saul? Just a *little* bit? I mean nothing *happened*. Officially it's a simple misunderstanding. Done, finished, and over with. So come on. What do you say? It's late. Time to go home." The Dean got to his feet. At the door he offered Koplowitz some more advice: "Have yourself a stiff drink; try to forget about it. And stop making things so damned am*big*uous. All right?"

5.

Koplowitz stretched out on his air mattress and gazed up at his green tent. Both he and the tent were sweating. How desirable, he thought, to be able to sleep as the Hamora sleep. They would do it anywhere, any time. To them sleep was holy, a gift to be accepted whenever bestowed, peopled by messengers, the dead, spirits both evil and good. The Hamora revered sleep as the most spiritual part of life. Elfar had lots of kennings for it: the road of adventures, the hour when truth blazes, dusk of mysterious shadows, season of warnings, bliss of reunions. Koplowitz had always felt a little stupid, a little cheated because he could seldom recall his dreams. He thought it was more from politeness than curiosity when Elfar asked about them: "*Et vos rêves?*" The question was, he soon discovered, the common Hamora greeting. Koplowitz was ashamed to confess the truth, that he was cut off from his dreams. Sure enough, when he told this to Elfar, the old man commiserated with him as with a double amputee. *Poor bastard, only half alive, aren't you?* Koplowitz had always yearned for dreams, always envied those who could relate even the most frightening nightmares. He seldom thought about dreams, but when he did it was the way a thirsty man thinks about water, which is with considerable precision.

Koplowitz's opinion was that when we dream, we go down a winding staircase from the neocortex with its Scandinavian furniture to the dark curling mahoganys below, hardwood from old jungles, through layers of evolutionary fear, plummeting into the serpentine, burrowing into the reptilian past and, if we are lucky, recollecting it all, transformed into human images. In dreams if nowhere else, he thought, ontogeny recapitulates phylogeny and evolution is not a trail but a map.

Reptiles had always spoken to his heart. Not only was he without prejudice against them, he loved geckos and snakes for being so clean and bright-eyed, certain and quick. He had always thought them magical and wise and, though he seldom quoted the Bible, he liked this verse: "Now the serpent was more subtle than any other wild creature that the Lord God had made." Why should subtlety be evil?

If there exists some terrifying race-memory in children of a murderous competition between the last dinosaurs and those furry mammals our distant ancestors, it had not lodged in little Saulie, who kept garter snakes and liked to stroke their heads. His grandmother, horrified by his fondness for these beautiful and harmless creatures, had written him a memorable letter while he was at summer camp, collecting samples. In this memorable epistle she carefully printed out—in Hebrew, as if he knew it!—the divine injunction to the serpent: "I will put enmity between you and the woman, and between your seed and her seed; he shall bruise your head, and you shall bruise his heel."

Why shouldn't lizards dream, he wondered. After all, the limbic system of the human brain is essentially the same as the reptile's. You could even say the reptilian brain lies in cold-blooded silence beneath all our hot-blooded noise. Research had found that discharges in the electrical flux of the limbic system may result in effects akin to those produced by hallucinogens or psychoses. To people like his Nana, the reptile is the abhorred Other, cold and emotionless, but perhaps deep in the lizard's brain are to be found feelings of terror and self-abasement, awe and hatred. Why shouldn't such feelings congeal into a rat snake's nightmare or a salamander's vision of bliss? Tickle the amygdala and even the most phlegmatic newt will erupt in frenzy; remove it entirely and even the passionless iguana can turn sentimental. Why should we boast that love is an invention of mammals when, on the reed-choked banks of the Nile, female crocodiles carefully scoop hatchlings into their mouths and bear them daintily to safety in the mother of waters?

The whole forest was dreaming. Only speculative Koplowitz, left behind with his bruises, lay awake.

6.

Well, he had had his bruise after all, though not quite on the heel. Old Nana Koplowitz had not cited scripture in vain.

It had curled up for the night in his sneaker, a perfect burrow, warm, dark, and close. He had been warned not only as a child and theologically, but more recently and with full local particulars, though, as an expert, he hardly needed to be reminded of the peril. Shaughnessy had gone on and on about the danger of snakes, what antidotes he should bring along, what to do if bitten. This was after Shaugnessy had gotten over being incredulous and indignant.

"You can't go out there on your own, you idiot. It's a flaming lethal place, believe me. Look, Saul, it's like swimming. You've got to have a mate, mate, if you're going to keep from drowning. Just give me a month, three weeks. I'll wind up my courses early. I can hand the damned journal over to Cochoran, and I my humble self will be delighted to accompany you. I'll even bring the beer. We'll have a high time and we'll find that sweet momma lizard, too. Your name'll come first on the article. Promise. What do you say? Just another three weeks?"

Damned stupid. He ought to have looked first, shaken out his shoes. The strike, though not deep, was quick and surprisingly painful. One perfect little pearly fang had broken off in the ball of his right foot when he pulled it out. Taking the heavy sneaker by the toe, Koplowitz hopped over to the brush, found a stick, and gently picked out a beautiful viper. With one fang gone, she slithered in among the ferns, unaware or not caring that she was more fatally wounded than the imbecile who had rudely awakened her.

Koplowitz hopped back to the tent and fetched out his knife. First he pried out the tooth then cut a cross deep into his foot. Not being a yogi, he could hardly suck out the wound, but he pushed out a lot of blood before slathering on antiseptic and binding up his foot. Infection set in by the following afternoon. The foot grew hot and swelled up as if it had been listening to Bruckner.

Incana and Intara, two young Hamora hunters, wandered into his camp a couple days later. They greeted him with what seemed like politeness, insisted on touching his foot, took a can of Mandarin oranges and his compass then, cheerfully chattering in unintelligible paragraphs, went away. A few hours later they showed up with old Elfar who saluted Koplowitz in French, stayed with him a week, and eventually cured his wound with herbs, incantations, and an impressive quantity of spittle.

"*Avez-vous rêvé?*" Have you dreamed? he asked each morning.

"No. None of dreams. And you?"

Elfar always answered earnestly though not at length. "*Moi, j'était sur la montagne et puis dans la grande mer avec les poissons.*" As for me, I went up in the mountains and then down in the great sea with the fish.

Koplowitz's French, a good deal shy of fluent, improved along with his foot, in both cases the old man being the cause of amelioration.

"Elfar," he asked on the third day, "what is it that which your French is so large when you do not have person in which to speak?"

The old shaman rose on his spindly legs and scuttled into Koplowitz's tent. He returned with a notebook which he held up like a prophet with an invitation to a Canaanite orgy.

"Hamora, they write nothing. Eh, good? You understand? *Rien*, understand? That is why it is that we remember everything. And so why is it that you do not dream, Monsieur Kopo? Is it that you write too much, perhaps? Or perhaps it is a punishment for some great sin?"

"Punishment? But Elfar, I dream yet I do not remember."

"If you dream and do not remember, how is it that you know that you dream? That is a punishment, is it not so?"

"Perhaps. But then I do not suffer from the . . . the . . . "

"You would say *cauchemars?*"

"Yes, that's it. *Pas de cauchemars.* No nightmares."

"Yes, but I do not understand *cauchemar. Tous les rêves sont bon.*"

The Hamora thought most lizards good, too—full of protein, or as Elfar put it, a source the most excellent of wisdom. You know what you eat.

In the course of his convalescence quite a number of the Hamora came to gaze solemnly at Koplowitz and to ask Elfar about him, or to ask him questions through Elfar, but never a woman, only men and boys. Elfar explained.

"It is simple, Monsieur Kopo. Women may not leave the village. Even under guard we would not bring them so far as this."

"Why?"

"So that they will not run off to *l'Autre*. Even so, there are those who do so. In my dreams of the mountains I often encounter those that have run off," said Elfar, that half-naked old boulevardier.

7.

Ellen McManus attracted Koplowitz without in the least caring to do so. She had red hair, pale legs, an air of intellectual sanctity. He liked her especially in green. In fact, he would almost have preferred dressing Ellen up—what terrible clothes she wore!–to undressing her. A velvet forest green evening gown, well off the shoulder, for example, would have been more than fetching, particularly if he could persuade her to have her hair properly done. Ellen had freckles, like his wife, who had likewise been Irish. Koplowitz wondered if some fatality attended his displaced Galician tastes, some culturo-pituitary quirk directing his eye Hiberniawards.

But it was an idle and fruitless flirtation, for there was something nun-like about Ellen, something of the closeted and pure. True, she consented to go out to a movie or a lecture with him once in a while and they had lunch together a couple times a month, but mostly she preferred sticking close to her lab and her mother, her twin devotions, the filial and microbiological.

It was over a Greek salad at the Omega that Ellen explained the obvious. She didn't even try to be gentle.

"You mean you didn't notice? The reason your enrollments are down, Saul, is that there aren't any women in your classes. I'm afraid you've got yourself a reputation. In fact, to be perfectly frank, if I cared two cents about gossip I wouldn't be eating lunch with you myself."

The world and his stomach filled up again with the peril Koplowitz thought was averted. Guilty, even though innocent; guilty, irrespective of responsibility.

"Do I have a nickname? Kop the Feeler? Sleazy Saul?" He wondered if the bitterness of his tone belied or confirmed his guilt.

Ellen without irony, delicately extracting an olive pit from her mouth: "I haven't heard yet."

"Great." Koplowitz rubbed his increasingly high forehead.

Ellen squirmed on her seat. "Look, when was your last sabbatical?"

"What? You think I ought to clear out until the smell goes down?"

She turned toward the window, toward the wide April world, and shrugged her lovely shoulders. It was painful to Koplowitz to see how utterly a matter of indifference the exile she was recommending would be to her. Ellen might have been handing him a pistol, averting her eyes as she admonished him to be a man and do the honorable thing. It was not the opinions of the Dean or Calipha or Muriel or the Schrempfs, but that shrug of Ellen McManus's that decided everything.

8.

When he was better, Koplowitz moved his camp closer to the Hamora. They interested him more than the elusive viviparous lizard. Elfar said this would be acceptable, so long as he pitched his tent at the prescribed distance between the village and the river. Then the old man surprised Koplowitz by inquiring whether he would like the loan of a woman, suggesting the daughter of his niece.

"But Elfar, I thought the Hamora kept their women under close guard?"

"Yes, very sure."

"But if you are so jealous, why would you loan one to me, a kinswoman?"

"Not jealous, Monsieur Kopo. You, you are not *L'Autre*. You will not take away the daughter of my niece, is it not so? You would not let her go away, surely?"

"Tell me about *L'Autre*, Elfar."

"Not yet." Elfar got up to leave. "I will send to you two men to help move your camp. Is it not good?"

"Thank you."

"And the daughter of my niece?"

Koplowitz considered whether he should risk offending the old man. "No, thank you much."

In a manner remarkably similar to Ellen McManus's, Elfar shrugged.

9.

Remember everything, record nothing. As conducted by Elfar, Koplowitz's education was a cycle of fragmented stories whose relationship did not become clear until all had been told, until the learner had organized and appropriated them, until he was able to tell them himself.

Gradually then, Koplowitz learned how the Hamora came to be, born of love and war, or the war that is love.

Once, said Elfar, there had been only women. They made their babies by spitting in a certain way on each other's private parts and they were content, watched over and provided for by the Nameless One. But then from the sea came Odo in his great canoe. Odo cleared land and planted crops and hunted animals. The women were frightened of Odo and beseeched their female god to send her dragon to kill him. But the Nameless One was not convinced.

"Has this Odo done anything to harm you?"

"No," admitted the women. "But he wounds the earth and kills the animals. He eats them and grows wiser than we."

"Tell me why you are afraid."

"Because he is not like us or you."

"Difference need not beget violence. Violence may not be the answer but gentleness and imagination."

"Not with him!" The women were even prepared to try insolent arguments. "If you do not send your dragon to kill him how can we feel safe? And if we do not feel safe, how can we worship you?"

And so, with an uncertain heart and mostly to quiet the women, the goddess consented to send her dragon against Odo.

They squared off in a clearing, the dragon with his teeth, Odo with his club. In the fierce battle that ensued, blood and spit mingled, frothed over the forest. This froth or foam congealed into the first men.

"*L'amour*," said Elfar with a smile, "what is it but a truce in the war that goes on perpetually? Is it not so, Monsieur Kopo?"

Odo was originally not a deity, merely a giant. He became divine when he killed and ate the dragon and when, with the aid of those men who were dear to him as children, he displaced the women's god, whose name it was forbidden to pronounce. Odo accomplished this latter feat by stratagem. First he sent men to the Nameless One with gifts of birds he had caught, crops he had grown, and harpoi which he was the first to ferment. The messengers apologized on Odo's behalf for the necessity of killing her dragon. They told tales of Odo's beauty and strength. They proclaimed his goodwill and the mildness of his intentions. In effect, they courted the goddess on his behalf until the Other longed to encounter this Odo who had frightened her adherents and had slain her dragon. Though she did not trust his men and could hardly abide their smell, she nevertheless accepted their gifts and agreed to meet Odo by the river, uncertain whether to humble him or to destroy him. But Odo the Clever had fashioned a strong trap for the goddess, a snare of vines hidden just below the water.

When the Nameless One came to the river, Odo stood naked and erect on the opposite bank. By turns he taunted her, boasted to her, offered her his love, threatened her, dared or begged her to come across to him. He too seemed indifferent as to whether she should fight him or love him. As soon as the goddess, infuriated yet perplexed by Odo's contrary speech, stepped into the river, Odo gave the signal and his men sprung the trap, ensnaring the goddess. Though she changed herself into a thin water snake and a slippery fish, no matter what form she took, she remained caught fast, so cunningly had Odo woven his trap.

Now Odo ordered the men to fetch the women to the river so that they might see in what manner he had vanquished the Other. When the women came and saw what had happened, they set up a great wailing and cursed Odo from their hearts. But the giant laughed at them and announced that from that day he would set the laws for all the Hamora [people], male and female alike, and that now he would be their god and they must worship him.

From the river the impotent goddess called him usurper and cursed him. She declared he had tricked her to the harm of all the Hamora. She said that he might become the god of the people but that his would be the responsibility for all the evils of the future, since it was through him that evil came into the forest. Therefore the Hamora would never love him as her innocent children had loved her.

Undaunted and enraged, Odo told his men to pull the goddess out of the river so that he could kill her with his club; but as soon as she was on dry land, the goddess changed into a parrot and, with an angry squawk, flew through the vines up into the mountains.

"And is that why the women wish to escape into the mountains?" asked Koplowitz.

"Alas, not just the women," said Elfar grimly.

"I don't understand."

"That is because you do not remember your dreams, Monsieur Kopo, and because you do not eat the right things."

A terrible idea suddenly struck Koplowitz.

"Elfar."

"Yes?"

"Is it possible that you would eat *me*?"

"Why should I do that when you know nothing I wish to know?"

10.

That night Koplowitz dreamed he was being pursued through the forest; the Hamora were right on his heels. At their head, holding high his shaman's stick, ran an amazingly spry Elfar. He encouraged the warriors in two voices, male and female: "*Aux armes, citoyens!*"

Koplowitz dashed through muddy pools full of lizards, salamanders, eyeless newts, splashed across the river where Odo had ensnared the nameless goddess, and fled into the dense bush on the other side. Here every tree was festooned with snakes, from tiny asps to enormous anacondas. In terror he brushed them away like heavy cobwebs, like fallen beams.

At last he came to a sunny clearing in which lay an enormous lizard, even larger than the Komodo dragon. As in his dream Koplowitz broke out of the thicket of reptilian trees, the lizard turned her hideous head, smiled maliciously at him, and hissed. Then, slowly, she opened her great jaws from which burst an unending stream of slithering, scuttling hatchlings.

Though Elfar didn't say so, Koplowitz believed it must be because he told his dream that he was invited to attend the night ceremony. "*Châque mois,*" Elfar cheerfully explained–regular as the menstrual cycle.

Koplowitz walked into the village at sundown. All the women had been banished to the huts. These were ceremoniously sealed with Elfar's copious spittle, though Koplowitz noticed that guards were also set.

Around the fire, the men were eating minced lizards, insects, and birds wrapped and roasted in leaves. They passed around the harpoi and caroused. Koplowitz sampled the fare and very nearly retched. His foot itched. Everyone laughed and spoke things to him he could not understand.

At around midnight the men took torches, organized themselves into two lines, and marched off into the bush on the side of the village opposite Koplowitz's camp. As they walked they made a noise that might have been drunken conversation or a disorganized chant. About half a mile into the forest they halted and Elfar went up to what looked to Koplowitz like nothing more than a thick patch of undergrowth.

With an effort, Elfar, unaided, peeled back the leaves and branches, revealing a hideous idol of grey stone, sunken into the earth. Torches were stuck in the ground on either side of the thing. Then, at a sharp command from Elfar, the men fell silent and formed up in the ranks of their hierarchy.

One by one each of the men stepped up to the statue, bowed, and declaimed a speech. Some spoke briefly while others went on like preachers or professors. Each address was patiently, even solemnly attended to by the others. When all had finished one or two of the men shouted, but Elfar held up his stick. He looked about and motioned to Koplowitz to come nearer.

Am I going to be killed now, Koplowitz wondered. Will I be eaten too?

The old rascal put his face right up to Koplowitz's. *"Confessez-vous,"* he whispered, his breath reeking of harpoi.

Koplowitz approached the statue. The Hamora remained silent, bored, respectful, drunk. "I am a lizard," he said in English, then he turned to Elfar. "*C'est tout.*"

The old man looked hard at Koplowitz, not through him but with a sort of avuncular good will. "*Bon,*" he said, then raised his stick and yelled.

Instantly the men broke out in wild imprecations, danced around, spitting on the idol, urinating on Odo in great harpoi-laden streams; they threw handfuls of dung, reviling the image of the usurping father-god, murderer of dragons and hunter of birds, pouring on his head their sins, in filth ritualizing their redemption.

Koplowitz stole back to the village. He thought for a moment of trying to overcome the sleepy guards, but then simply returned to his camp, packed up, and waited for the dawn.

The Lenders' Dinner

"Since his death in 1932, fifteen monographs and countless scholarly articles have been written about Guillaume Barrineau and his work. There have also been six biographies, four documentaries, and even a novel in which he appears as character—a rather disreputable one, I'm afraid, but then the novel, like Barrineau, is French."

She was good, this Millie Schonkenner. Though she looked young to be the curator of a major show, her self-assurance was without fissures; in fact, it was attractive and so was she with her red hair, designer dress, and good legs tapering down to spike heels. It was these stilettos I noticed first. While, to put it mildly, I can't afford such footwear, I have a thing for them, an aesthetic affinity, I'd say, not a fetish. I suppose some of the guests had identical feelings about expensive modernist paintings, except that they could own them. Ms. Schonkenner's shoes were distinctive. Not Prada or Manolo Blahnik, not Jimmy Choo; I had examined those catalogues the way some men do golf gear. These stilettos were jet black with curved straps, the usual pointed, closed toe; but the leather had some magical midnight-blue highlights and soles of the same jazzy hue. I found myself guessing: Gianvito Rossi? Brian Atwood? Gucci? Couldn't be Christian Louboutin; his soles are always red.

It was a happy crowd. They were pleased with themselves for being there, and Millie Schonkenner deftly reinforced the mood of self-congratulation. They rewarded her by laughing at her witticisms. She made them feel included, on the inside of something unimpeachable, culturally speaking, and that counted for a lot. I'd noticed that among the better educated populace of Los Angeles the yearning for cultural validation is endemic. Perhaps it's owing to living on the left coast instead of the right one. So Millie Schonkenner made these folks feel valued, like philanthropists and connoisseurs. Above all, they were being thanked which was, presumably, the chief point of the dinner.

I stood at the back, arms at my sides, leaning against the wall by the big doors. I looked at my black shoes, so practical, so hideous. I had to wait for the speeches to wind up and the guests to depart; then my colleagues and I would clear the dessert plates and the coffee cups. A waitress waiting, uniform on her back, Oxfords on her feet, arms at her sides.

"I had the idea for this show long ago, when I was still in graduate school," Millie was saying. "That's right, believe it or not. I fell in love with Barrineau's work and wrote my dissertation on him. I won't tell you the title but, in German, it could sink a heavy cruiser."

I touched the silk paneled wall, looked at the crystal sconces and beveled mirrors of the Bordeaux Room. The Beverly Wilshire Hotel is at 9500 Wilshire Boulevard. The Los Angeles County Museum of Art, LACMA, where Millie Schonkenner landed her dream job, is just a few blocks down, at 5905. The choice of venue for the banquet was obvious; and, given all the well-heeled Francophiles among the guests, it had to be the Bordeaux Room. The Beverly Wilshire has as many stars as you can get, five of them; it's like a pair of Giuseppe Zanottis, impressive and worth it, if you've got the dough.

"As we all know, Guillaume Barrineau was industrious, really prolific, yet his standards never slipped. His work is in museums all over the civilized world. Luckily, the University awarded me a travel grant so I was able to study a lot of his work by visiting museums. But, I'm greedy. I knew that the majority of Barrineau's output was in private hands. In *yours*."

I estimated the crowd at about sixty people, full capacity. The Bordeaux Room is multifunctional. It can be filled with tables, as it was that night, or chairs set in rows for presentations from the stage. Without all the chairs and tables, the place makes an elegant ballroom. The Bordeaux Room is French the way Grauman's Theater is Chinese.

Millie wasn't perfectly impeccable. She had a tendency to talk about herself when she shouldn't. I understood. She was only a few years older than I am, fresh from graduate school, while I'm still in it. My field is Early Modern Europe—think Charles V and Cardinal Richelieu. The hotel calls me when they need me, and the money comes in handy. Anyway, I talk about myself or my work at the wrong times. My advisor, Professor Rheinach, was probably right when he observed that, in our twenties, we really believe the universe is an infinite sphere and we're in the very middle of it. Professor Rheinach himself is over seventy and gets exasperated when he's asked about his retirement plans. He once told me he would like to expire in the middle of his lecture on the persecution of the Huguenots. He's a wise man who likes young people while many of his junior colleagues aren't and don't. I think he'd appreciate Millie Schonkenner.

"At my job interview, I told the Director about my idea for this show," Millie was saying. "He must have liked it because here I am and there you are. The administration must have thought I'd be able to pull it off—which means charm you into loaning us your pictures. And you agreed, bless you. I know it was more than the promise of a dinner at the Beverly Wilshire Hotel and admission to today's private opening. I believe we united in this enterprise because of our love of art in general and the astonishing work of Guillaume Barrineau in particular."

Replete with gourmet fare and perhaps a little fuddled with grand cru drink, everybody applauded Millie and, I suppose, themselves. If Barrineau was a great artist and they owned one or two or three of his paintings, then, to that degree, they were great too.

It was getting late and I figured things were wrapping up, but Millie didn't leave the stage. I was getting ancy. A paper on Huldrych Zwingli lay half done on the bridge table that served as my desk. I could see that my coworkers, comely one and all, were impatient too.

The applause stopped when Millie motioned for silence, palms down, as if bouncing a beach ball or landing a plane on a carrier. "I have a special treat for you all, a last-minute addition to the evening's program. We're fortunate to be joined by Mademoiselle Julie Prixendieu, who has flown in specially from France to be with us tonight. Mademoiselle Prixendieu is a direct descendant of the artist we are here to honor. She would like say a few words to you about her great-grandfather. Mademoiselle Prixendieu?"

A woman rose from one of the tables nearest the stage, the one with the museum's bigwigs. Her age was difficult to fix; it often is with the *bien soignée*. Thirty to fifty, somewhere in there, I guess. She was slim, dark-haired, tall, wore a striking violet dress with a fringed blue scarf, and sling back pumps that looked like the pair of Valentinos I'd drooled over in *Vogue*. She climbed to the stage gracefully, took Millie's proffered hand, but did so formally, then gripped the sides of the podium and began to speak in an enchanting accent and a bell-like voice.

"Yes, I am, to be sure, a direct descendant of Guillaume Barrineau—direct but not, *hélas*, legitimate. My great-grandfather had, so far as I know, three children but not even a single wife."

There was scattered laughter of the same variety evoked by Millie, more polite than sincere, companionable, not hearty. Mlle. Prixendieu looked sternly out over the tables, and the mirth quickly petered out.

"My own profession," she continued, "lies in the industrial art at which this city excels—that is to say, cinema. I do costuming and art direction. When it comes to the study of Guillaume Barrineau, I confess I am merely an amateur, albeit an interested one. I hope you will be kind enough to be patient with me. I was told by Kristin Scott Thomas that my English is not so bad, but that my accent is."

There were deprecatory noises from several men. I expect they were fascinated by this sophisticated, striking, and exotic woman while their insecure wives and girlfriends were trying to size her up.

"I was pleased and surprised to be asked to join you this evening. Not many people know of my connection to the artist, but then few know as much about him as Mademoiselle Schonkenner." Millie's surname she pronounced *ShowenkenAIRE*.

"I hesitated. It is a long way to travel but I am between films and the Museum generously offered to pay all my expenses. Did they do the same for you?"

This rhetorical question elicited a quantity of genuine laughter. I couldn't see Millie, who had returned to her place at the bigwigs' table, but I imagine she was blushing.

"As I say, I am no scholar. I have not even read much about Barrineau. Nevertheless, there are a few things I should like to say about my great-grandfather and his work. You must understand, though, that these remarks derive from family history, which is always an oral history and erected on shifting sands.

"I shall begin with something quite definite and that ought to be pleasing to devotees of Barrineau's work. For eighty years people have been saying that great-grandfather was under the influence of Fernand Léger, especially in what are called his *peintures mécanistes*, the ones mocked by a famous critic with a pair of glib and dismissive similes. I'm sure you know the sentence: 'His chrysanthemums look like buzz saws, his women like locomotives.' *Oui, ses femmes comme des locomotives!* To this he added the less famous but more interesting and perceptive verdict that Barrineau's art is 'full of tenderness and hatred.' It is easy to say Barrineau's mechanistic modernism was inspired by Léger's style, called, also disrespectfully, *le Tubisme.* This is simply because Léger was born in 1881 and Barrineau in 1893. But, according to my grandmother, the case was just the opposite. That is to say, it was Guillaume who influenced Fernand, the younger who led the elder. They knew each other well, of course, and were close until their friendship ended. The two shared a bond that made them equals. I refer to their service in the Great War. Léger was gassed at Verdun; Guillaume was three times wounded and, apart from periods of convalescence, in combat more or less continuously for four years.

"Grandmother once told me that no one can understand her father without grasping what the war did to him, what he lost, and how he was deranged by it. What he lost was what all France lost—his generation, all the dearest friends of his youth. There is a group of paintings done near the end of Barrineau's life which are considered by critics to be lyrical and serene, harkening back to the Impressionism of *La Belle Époque,* quite unlike the rest of his oeuvre. These are the plein-air landscapes done in 1930 and 1931. As Barrineau neglected to give them titles, the curators did so. They chose simple names: *Dawn, Sunset, Noon, Portrait of Zouzou on a Picnic, Monsieur Torquemal Fishing, Country Cottage Near the Escaut,* etcetera. Proper titles would have revealed their true significance: *Dawn over Verdun, Sunset on the Somme, Noon at Ypres, La Zouzou Picnicking at Paschendaele, Monsieur Torquemal Fishing in the Marne, Cottage at Cambrai.* All battlefields, bone yards one and all.

"Barrineau suffered from shell shock. What they now call PTSD. That is why he beat those two models, why he assaulted the teenage daughter of a gallery owner; it is behind all those barroom brawls and the infamous rift with Léger as well. Barrineau was tormented by dreams and memories like nightmares. Only through art was he able to achieve calm, relief, redemption. . . ."

Here Mlle. Prixendieu halted and looked over the audience of collectors, the plutocrats of whom, I later learned, her great-grandfather had said: "They are loathsome and absolutely vital." Everyone could see that she had been carried away, had all but forgotten about us; but she quickly recovered herself and concluded with just two more sentences.

"The same, it occurs to me, might be said of the twentieth century. *Merci et bon soir.*"

People clapped and Millie made for the stage, but Mlle. Prixendieu did not relinquish the podium. "I fear to detain you further, but I have brought with me from Paris an uninvited guest. He is, I believe, waiting out in the mezzanine. He too would like to address a few remarks to you."

She looked straight at me. "*Ma Chère,*" she said, "would you be so good as to summon him? His name is Laurens de Meester."

The lenders stirred; all faces turned toward me. At the bigwig table there was consternation. Millie froze halfway up to the stage, stilettos trembling beneath her. I had no idea who this Laurens de Meester might be, but evidently she did.

I stepped out to the mezzanine. There wasn't much going on at that hour. Plush carpets, piped Vivaldi, a few couples, a view of the lobby below. On a banquette across from the elevator I spotted a balding man, fiftyish. He was dressed in a well-cut tuxedo complete with patent leather shoes. His long, intelligent face was alarmingly pale, like a yeshiva scholar's. Seeing me, he leapt to his feet and smiled. It was a rather foxy smile.

"Mr. Laurens de Meester?"

"In the flesh, such as it is," he said jovially and in an accent I supposed must be Dutch. He leaned toward me conspiratorially. "May I go in?"

I held the high, padded door open for him, and Laurens de Meester strode into the Bordeaux Room with the confidence of Cary Grant or James Bond. Whatever was going on, it wasn't boring.

Mlle. Prixendieu motioned for him to join her on the stage. There was no need as de Meester was already making his way with brisk agility through the maze of tables. He bounded up to the stage, stopped for a couple deep breaths, then took Mlle. Prixendieu's hand. He bowed over and kissed it then conducted her to one of the chairs at the rear of the platform. The whole routine struck me as comical. Something's definitely up with these two, I thought.

Meanwhile, Millie had sought a safe haven back with the bigwigs, under the protective wing of the Director, so to speak.

De Meester made himself comfortable at the podium and offered everybody his cunning grin.

"For those of you unfamiliar with my name and reputation—and, in all modesty, I must suppose that at least a *few* of you will be aware of both—I am an art forger, a rather successful one, with the exception of one regrettable slip, a moronic error. Three weeks ago I was released from the Bijlmerbajes, Amsterdam's prison which, incidentally, is one of the few jails the Dutch government has yet to close for lack of trade. We Netherlanders are a law-abiding nation, a forgiving one too. I served only four years of my seven-year sentence. Good behavior after bad."

He pointed to his right cheek. "I regret to appear before you so pasty-faced. The sun and I have only just been reintroduced to one another. . . . However, to business—for it is on business that I am here, the business of Barrineau. I shall try to explain everything precisely. Then, should you have any questions, I shall undertake to reply with equal clarity."

He paused here and pulled up his sleeves to reveal his gold cufflinks.

"Now," he resumed, "I love many artists and, if I may be permitted to say so, with a greater understanding and a more profound intimacy than the most devoted scholars and collectors. Among my favorites is Guillaume Barrineau whose great talent, I am certain, no one here will gainsay. To paint a Barrineau is to feel his pain, his rage, his loss, his tenderness. I say this so that you will not mistake me for a mere common criminal. Criminality is a necessary attribute of the art forger but scarcely sufficient. Only those capable of an empathetic leap, only those who can feel the soul behind the brushstroke will achieve real distinction in the craft. Therefore, while I am ashamed of my past misdeeds, I am nonetheless proud of my work. Believe me when I tell you that I have embarrassed the foremost experts in Europe and America. . . . But, as I keep saying, I am here on business." Again he paused, looked left and right. "Excuse me. Would it be possible to have a glass of water?"

One of my male-model colleagues fetched it for him.

As de Meester took the glass he stared at the dude a bit creepily. "Thank you, young man. You know, you would have made a fine subject for Albrecht Dürer or rather, no, wait— I think rather Eustache le Suer."

He smiled his vulpine smile. He drank his water. We waited.

"To business, then. At last. A business proposition, that is. I almost regret to inform you that among the paintings you have so generously loaned to the magnificent Los Angeles County Museum of Art there is one that was not painted by the ancestor of Mademoiselle Prixendieu. It was created by yours most truly. Needless to say, were this provenance to become known, the market value of said picture would plummet the way your stock market did on the twentieth of September, 2008. However, if you will give me the paltry sum of $700,000 I hereby solemnly promise to keep the matter to myself. Forever."

The reaction was about what you'd expect. Howls, as they say, of indignation.

"Really," said de Meester loudly yet smoothly, "if you *all* contribute—and you should, as you are all running the same risk—the sum can be arrived at with minimal pain. Think of it as a one-time insurance premium."

"I'm calling the police!" an obese man shouted and took out his cell phone.

"This is not an affair of interest to the police," replied de Meester.

"It's a shake-down!"

"Extortion!"

"Not at all," said Laurens de Meester airily. "I have served my penitential time, more than half of it, anyway. The forgery in question has already been paid for—I mean by me and, of course, by one of you. You are familiar with the concept of double jeopardy, no? Moreover, I am truly a reformed man, full of amazing grace. Would you prefer me to confess the truth, then? To say which of your valuable paintings is not— valuable? I have violated no law this evening. I have simply proposed, as I keep reminding us all, a business arrangement among mutually interested parties. You are entirely free to turn it down. You are free to contribute or not, just as you wish."

"It's a goddamn outrage!"

Everyone looked toward the bigwigs' table where Millie cowered and the Director shrugged.

"I'll take my leave now and allow you to confer on the issue," said Laurens de Meer. "Mademoiselle Prixendieu and I will be easy to contact. We are staying upstairs tonight—in the Signature Rodeo Suite, isn't it, Julie?—thanks to the munificence of the Museum, for which we are both grateful. We will, I'm afraid, need your answer by noon tomorrow. I'm sure you understand; we have a flight to catch. Thank you and I wish you all a very good evening."

With that, he and Barrineau's great-granddaughter walked out of the Bordeaux Room.

My colleagues and I were dismissed, the tables still uncleared.

There never was an announcement about any fakes. The show of privately held Barrineaus proved a real draw for LACMA and, I presume, was a triumph for Millie Schonkenner. Perhaps the claim that there *was* a fake was the real fake. Who can say for sure?

I did manage to finish my Zwingli paper on time. Professor Rheinach gave it an A-. I was tempted to celebrate with a pair of Fendi pumps. They were on-line and on sale, but I really couldn't afford them. Besides, they might have been knockoffs.

Our Rabbi

Marriage

One of our rabbi's students had just become engaged. Forgetting himself in his joy, the young man asked the Rabbi about his own marriage.

"My marriage? All I know is that I'm a lucky man."

"What is a lucky man, Rabbi?"

"A lucky man. He is one who's resigned himself to the idea that between him and the world stand a thousand walls and perhaps just a single door and, though he isn't even sure that door exists, yet that's the very one he stumbles on."

Carrots or Parsnips

A journalist came to interview one of the former students of our rabbi. The man was now a rabbi himself with a large congregation and a big family, but in his youth he had been nearly destitute.

"When you came to the rabbi asking to study with him, what did he say to you?"

The man laughed. "I didn't ask; I begged. And I was dumbfounded by the way he received me."

"How's that?"

"I'd come from far away and arrived at dusk. At first he showed me into the parlor. He asked my name, about my family, the town I'd come from, the things I had observed on the journey. Then he invited me to follow him into the kitchen. His wife was preparing the evening meal. 'My dear, could you leave us alone for a few minutes?' he asked her. When she had gone he told me to peel a bunch of carrots that she had left in the sink."

"Carrots?"

"It was a long time ago. It could have been parsnips."

"But why the peeling?"

"Exactly what I asked myself. You understand, I was terrified so I just obeyed. I took up the knife the rabbi's wife had left on the counter. He stood behind me, looking over my shoulder. I worked slowly and carefully, bewildered but wishing to please the rabbi. During the ten hours on the bus I had been thinking of how the rabbi would examine me on the Talmud, test my Hebrew, or ask me to resolve some baffling ethical dilemma. But all he wanted was that I should peel these carrots—or parsnips. When I had finished the whole bunch, he took up each vegetable and inspected it closely, turning it in his hand. Only then did he say, 'Very well, you can stay.'"

"What did it mean?"

"I was too relieved to ask. Of course, I admit I was also a little disappointed. An obscure midrash I expected, but not root vegetables. I thought if I were able to distinguish myself a little he might tell me about the carrots, or the parsnips. And this I set myself to do."

"So you asked later? I mean about the carrots."

"Or the parsnips. No. For one thing, I didn't succeed in distinguishing myself. On the contrary, and that, in fact, is how I found out about the vegetables."

"How was that?"

"In those days the rabbi had a half-dozen of us studying with him. One morning he set us to discussing the meaning of Jacob's supplanting of Esau. Since I had suspected he would ask about this story, I had prepared myself. I wanted to shine. I longed to surpass the others in his eyes, to show myself more incisive, more subtle. The three who spoke before me stuck to the most conventional interpretations. When it was my turn to speak, I picked the story apart as if with tweezers. I diced the text like a radish and twisted it like a challah. I took up eight interpretations and cited authorities for this or that view of the story. All the while I was anxious about being interrupted, for the rabbi seldom let us go on for very long without posing a question and, when that happened, we were lost. But no, like a runner who leads a race, the way before me remained clear. The longer I spoke the more confident I grew. I must have spoken for half an hour. At last, having exhausted all my crammed knowledge, I concluded with what I thought was a particularly elegant exegetical flourish."

"And what about the carrots, or parsnips?"

"I'm coming to them. When I finally fell silent the rabbi politely asked if I were done. 'Yes,' I said, expecting praise to rain down on my head. 'Tell me,' he said, 'can you recall those carrots I asked you to peel the night you arrived?' As I say, they might have been parsnips."

"Yes, yes. Carrots or parsnips."

"So I told him I remembered. 'Good,' he said. 'You peeled them properly. So perhaps you can tell us the most important point in peeling.' I was still fixed on my speech and didn't know what to say. 'Come now,' he said to me. 'You know perfectly well what it is.' I felt my face grow hot. I looked at my feet. There was this terrible silence and then he asked the next student what he made of how Jacob had tricked his brother Esau."

"I don't understand."

"But it's quite simple and it was a lesson I've never forgotten."

"What was the lesson?"

"First of all, he was teaching me the difference between really knowing and merely showing off; he was making me see that virtuosity is unseemly when it comes to scholarship. And not only that. You see, the important thing about peeling carrots—or parsnips—is knowing when to stop. You have to scrape away everything that's dirty or inedible and leave all that's good and nourishing. If you go on because you want people to admire your peeling, then you'll be left with nothing at all. Neither carrot nor parsnip."

Teitelbaum

Our rabbi was an athlete in his youth. He played basketball, baseball, volleyball, soccer—anything with a ball and a team. When he took to study, however, his work made him solitary and he soon felt his double loss, of comradeship and exercise. He resolved to find some physical activity he could do on his own but that would lead him into contact with others. This is how our rabbi became an inveterate walker.

On one Sunday, Professor Teitelbaum, who taught philosophy at the university and specialized in German Idealism, was surprised to see our rabbi seated alone on a bench across from Aeropostale and Williams Sonoma. When Teitelbaum's daughter Leah was young he and his wife used to attend services dutifully and they sent her to Hebrew school. Now that the girl was in high school, the Teitelbaums came just on High

Holy days. They still came because when he was a little boy Teitelbaum's mother had said to him, "If we don't go, the Goyim won't respect us." Nothing else his mother said to him had left so deep an impression.

"Teitelbaum?" said the rabbi.

The professor was surprised to see the rabbi and embarrassed that he had not been to services for months. He decided to be disarming. "Oh, Rabbi. It's been too long since we've seen each other." He hoped the use of the plural pronoun would make it appear that the responsibility was mutual. "So, what brings you to the mall?" he added quickly.

The rabbi extended his hand. "It's nice to see you, Teitelbaum. Everyone well? Your lovely wife and charming daughter?"

Teitelbaum relaxed and sat down next to the rabbi. "They're fine. Leah was elected president of the Honor Society. We're pretty sure she'll make valedictorian. She's going to be in a ballet recital next week. A scene from *Coppelia*. Just now we're waiting for the scores on her SATs and the APs."

"That's good, Teitelbaum. Nice you should be proud of your daughter."

The professor smiled complacently. "So, Rabbi, what brings you to the mall?"

"Two itches. One in my legs and another to learn."

By now all the professor's embarrassment had evaporated. He had been right to put his absences on the table right away. He chuckled to himself. *Itchiness.* He thought the rabbi quaintly old-world with, for example, his habit of addressing all men by their surnames. Americans use first names or titles. A lot of people called him "professor," with a mixture of respect and irony. Who walks to a mall? Who comes there to learn?

"Then you're not shopping, Rabbi, only taking some exercise?"

"So much I needed to sit down."

"But it's such a lovely day. Why stay indoors? Why the mall?"

"You're an expert on philosophy. Wasn't Socrates once asked a similar question?"

Teitelbaum searched his memory and came up blank. What could this man know of Socrates that he didn't? "You got me, Rabbi."

"Oh. Well, it seems he once fell deep in conversation with one of those young idlers who attached themselves to him. Phaedrus, I think. Anyway, it seems the pair wandered away from the marketplace and soon found themselves in the suburbs. Socrates looked around and pronounced himself lost. The young man was astounded that a man three times his age who'd spent his entire life in Athens could become lost scarcely half a mile from the center of the city. . . . But you're humoring me, Teitelbaum. Surely you know the story?"

Teitelbaum shook his head. Was he being teased?

"Well, Socrates explained to the boy that rocks and trees taught him nothing while people in the marketplace taught him a great deal. So, isn't this our agora?"

Teitelbaum felt obscurely that he had been insulted. But he quickly decided he was not. And then he thought it odd that the rabbi should know something about Socrates that he didn't.

"Isn't Plato a little out of your line?" he asked.

"Oh, Socrates was a very great rabbi, no matter how Plato tries to make use of him."

"Really? And may I ask what you learn from Socrates, Rabbi?"

"To avoid a rabbi's worst temptation."

"And that is?"

"To give the conclusions without first giving the arguments."

Teitelbaum, who prided himself on his lectures, who relished speaking in auditoriums full of students whom he didn't know but would grade, was again vaguely troubled by what the rabbi said. He quickly excused himself and headed for Macy's.

Leibowitz

Our rabbi, out for one of his walks, ducked into a used furniture store. There he found Leibowitz, the owner, arguing with a man the rabbi had not met.

"Hello, Rabbi," said Leibowitz, looking irritated. "I'm a little busy at the moment."

"This your rabbi?" said the other man. "Well, Rabbi, this no-good here cheated me. He sold me a chest with a cracked back. He concealed it, put paste over it so I wouldn't notice."

Leibowitz could hardly contain himself. "Don't listen to him, Rabbi. *He's* the one who cheated. We agreed on a price of a hundred and fifty dollars for that perfectly fine chest but after he'd hauled it away I counted out the money and there was only a hundred and twenty."

"You, sir," said the rabbi, pointing to the buyer. "May I ask your name?"

"Borden."

"Well, Mr. Borden, before you agreed to buy this chest, did you check it all over, front and back?"

"No."

"Why's that?"

"Because this crook assured me it was sound and, like an idiot, I took his word for it."

The rabbi nodded. "Now, Leibowitz," he said sharply. "I know you're a good businessman. Why didn't you count Borden's money out before you let him take away the chest?"

"Why? Rabbi, even a businessman needs some trust. I took this thief for an honest man. We've done business before." He turned to Borden. "A dining room table, genuine mahogany, plus six chairs. Remember, Borden? I gave you a terrific price. You were beside yourself with joy. So, Rabbi, when he handed me a wad of cash and said it was a hundred and fifty I believed him. I know, I know. I was an imbecile to trust him."

The Rabbi looked from one to the other. "Would you be content to let me settle the matter, Leibowitz?"

"Certainly, Rabbi."

"Borden?"

"Pfft! Why not?"

"Good. In that case, the matter's clear. The transaction is fair. Borden, you keep Leibowitz's chest of drawers and Leibowitz you keep Borden's money. What this proves is how easily a person can be in the right and also in the wrong. Each of you has wronged the other and the two of you have already been punished for your sharp practices, punished by yourselves."

"How's that?" Borden demanded.

Leibowitz growled, "What do you mean *punished?*"

"You've both forfeited heavy fines."

"Fine?" asked Leibowitz.

"What fine?" said Borden.

"Think it through," the rabbi said with distaste.

"But, Rabbi, what's the fine?" insisted Leibowitz.

"Haven't you both already gone around telling everybody how you were cheated?"

"Well, naturally, Rabbi," said Leibowitz. "I owe it to my colleagues."

"It's my duty to warn other customers," said Borden.

"And those are your fines."

With that the rabbi walked out of the shop.

Schumsky on Sunday

Schumsky, a fifty-year-old insurance salesman, was unable to bear his wife's death. The couple had been childless. Though made of only two strings, their life was a Gordian knot. Now that it had been cut, he was a loose end. He became withdrawn and bitter. Friends shied away from him, but one made Schumsky promise to visit our rabbi. He came on a Sunday morning.

"I'm glad to see you, Schumsky," said the rabbi. "It's a fine day. As a matter of fact, I was just about to go for a walk. Care to join me?"

"If you like," Schumsky replied in the churlish tone he had adopted in the company of anybody who dared to appear happy.

All the way to the park the rabbi eulogized Schumsky's wife, a charitable woman, a frequent volunteer involved in all sorts of good works. He observed that she was intelligent yet not a gossip. "That's rare, you know," he said. "Yes, your wife was an excellent person in every way, and so generous. She cared for others so much that I can hardly imagine how much she cared for *you.*"

All this praise for his wife only made Schumsky feel worse. The rabbi's thoughtlessness astonished Schumsky. He held his tongue with difficulty and only out of respect.

When they arrived at the park the rabbi wound up his panegyric by saying, "I'm very sorry for you, Schumsky."

No one enjoys pity that is so personal; it is too close to contempt. This was too much for Schumsky who answered resentfully. "Most people," he said, "tell me they're sorry that my wife's passed away."

The rabbi ignored this and made for a stand of birches.

"There's something I've been trying to remember all morning. It's on the tip of my tongue. Tell me, Schumsky, do you happen to know the chemical formula for table salt?"

"Table salt?"

"Yes. Didn't you learn it in school?"

"Sodium chloride," Schumsky snapped.

"That's it! Thank you. Nothing's so irritating as when something's stuck on the tip of your tongue. By the way, have you ever made table salt?"

Thoughtlessness, pity, and now, irrelevance. "Of course I haven't made salt, Rabbi. Who makes salt?"

"And yet you know the formula. So then, I suppose knowing a formula really doesn't count for all that much, does it?"

Schumsky suddenly realized that the rabbi was speaking of those who had offered him their condolences in clichés and this made him even more irritated.

"People tell me you've become morose, Schumsky."

"That's what they're saying about me?"

"Only those who care for you would say so, you know; I mean those who want you to be part of their lives. Others, no doubt, wouldn't mind if you became a hermit out of grief."

Schumsky repeated this last phrase bitterly, though it also appealed to him. "A hermit out of grief."

"People do that, you know. They pull into themselves and wither away. It's a pity but, I think, still more, it's a shame."

"Why a shame above all?"

"Look at that child on the swing over there. You see her? Suppose *you* had a child, Schumsky, a lovely little girl like that. Would you stop feeding her and caring for her because you lost your wife? Would you refuse to play with the child because her mother died?"

Schumsky felt himself becoming furious. It was terrible of the rabbi to throw his childlessness in his face on top of his grief. There seemed no end to his callousness. "Of course not!" he replied heatedly. "The child would need me all the more."

"And why is that, Schumsky?"

"Obviously because she no longer had a mother. Why are you playing the fool?"

The rabbi ignored Schumsky's reproof. He stopped and put a finger to his chin. "I see," he said pensively. "Then you would care for the little girl all the more to make up for the care she no longer received from your wife?"

"What do you think?" cried the mourner.

"Well then, Schumsky, is it any different with the poor world? Isn't it shameful to deny it our care, no matter how little we can do for it, now that it has been deprived of your wife's?"

Schumsky on Tuesday

A few weeks later Schumsky came a second time to see our rabbi. It was on a Tuesday night, after dinner. This time he was in a different frame of mind. The rabbi greeted him warmly and invited him into his study.

"Rabbi, you were right. I mean that it's wrong to give up on the world. I'm making an effort to see my friends more. Also, I volunteered to tutor at the local elementary school, just as my wife used to do. I read books with the children."

"I'm glad to hear it."

"But I'm sleeping badly and I can't stop thinking. I can't accept that God would take Sarah away. Tell me, what's the secret of your faith? It must be a great comfort."

The rabbi raised his eyebrows. "Faith? I have no faith."

"What? No faith! But, Rabbi, what can you mean? After all you're a *rabbi*. Are you telling me you don't believe?"

"Believe what, Schumsky?"

"Well, in God, of course, in the judgment, in the Torah."

"Did I say I didn't believe?"

"But isn't faith believing? Isn't believing your—well, your business?"

"Tell me, Schumsky, you sell insurance."

"Yes?"

"In that case, faith is your business, not mine."

"I don't follow."

"And yet it's quite simple. Suppose everyone who bought a policy from you died a week later. What would become of your company?"

"But that's impossible."

"Why?"

"Excuse me, Rabbi. Apparently you don't understand the way insurance works. You see, we have these actuarial tables. These tell us how many out of a large group of people will die at fifty, at sixty, and so on. We know the probabilities."

"Pardon my ignorance, Schumsky. What does it mean 'to know the probabilities'?"

Schumsky made ready to talk shop but the rabbi forestalled him.

"Doesn't it mean to gamble on something you don't know for sure? Isn't that just what card players do?"

"I suppose. But our charts are infallible."

"Infallible? That means you haven't any doubts. In that case you really must have faith every time you write out a life insurance policy. In fact, Schumsky, your whole business depends on faith."

Schumsky was shocked. "Are you saying *you* have doubts?"

"About things I don't know for sure? Certainly. If I believed everything then there would be no need to study, to inquire. If faith were certainty then it would indeed be a comfort."

"But what about my wife's death? Why did God take her?"

"Schumsky, if I were to tell you I knew what I don't know and can't know, that there is some grand cosmic significance to your wife's death, that it is part of a benign plan, that I'm sure it was for the best and fulfilled some divine actuarial necessity—if I told you that, Schumsky, would you really be comforted?"

Brenda Goldman

Brenda Goldman was a precocious seven-year-old with a curiosity stoked by years of parental quizzing and meticulously programmed "learning experiences." The consequence was that she asked questions in the hope of putting adults on the spot rather than because she really wished to learn anything.

One Saturday morning after the Sabbath service, while her parents were talking to some friends, Brenda marched up to our rabbi.

"Rabbi, may I ask you something?" she said with cultivated sweetness, careful to say *may* and not *can*.

"Certainly, Brenda."

"I've been wondering where God lives. My dad says he doesn't live here, in the synagogue. He says that we just invite Him in. Mom says God lives in Heaven, but where's that?" The child pointed toward the ceiling. "Up there's just space. We learned that in school. So I thought you'd probably know. Where does God live?"

The rabbi directed Brenda to a pair of chairs in the corner and asked her to sit. Settling himself opposite her, he looked at her solemnly.

"Let's see. God's address. That's a difficult matter, Brenda."

The girl was elated. When adults began like that it always meant that they didn't know the answer. "Then you can't tell me?"

"You really want to know where God lives?"

"Yes, please," insisted Brenda, delighted by the rabbi's stalling.

"And you think I know?"

"You *must* know. I mean, you're the rabbi."

"I see. And where do *you* think God lives, Brenda?"

Another question! "I don't *know*," said Brenda petulantly, though the truth was she had always pictured a big mansion in the clouds, something like the giant's castle in *Jack and the Beanstalk*. "I already *said* I didn't know."

The rabbi looked at her calmly. "And what will you give me if I tell you where God lives?"

The conversation was not going at all the way Brenda intended. Still, this was a kind of bargaining with which she was familiar. She knew perfectly well what old people wanted from her.

"I'll give you a kiss."

"I see," said the rabbi slowly. "So, if I tell you where God lives you'll give me *one* kiss, right?"

"Yes," she said doubtfully.

"It's a tempting offer." He nodded, then brightened. "I'll tell you what! If you can tell me where God *doesn't* live, I'll give you *two* kisses!"

Helen Dimant

The rabbi had been surprised when his wife came to his study to tell him Helen Dimant had come to see him. "She's been humbled, that one. It scares her."

The rabbi went to his study, where Helen was waiting for him, sitting with her knees tight together, a clenched fist.

"Rabbi, I *can't* tell them. I *won't*. You have to promise me you won't either."

"I don't imagine it's because you're afraid of them, is it?"

"*Afraid* of them? Oh, they never get mad at me. I only *disappoint* them." She offered up a faint smile. "*You* know them. I

almost think they're capable of turning it into another achievement, another trophy for the mantel. Sometimes I think it
might not be so bad, disappointing them I mean."

"You're being spiteful. Don't."

Helen Dimant, for whom nothing had ever gone seriously
wrong before, was emotionally wobbly, not only spiteful but by
turns defiant, dismissive, and hysterical. The rabbi understood
that she resented her decision to bring her problem to him and
that she was challenging him to persuade her she hadn't made
a mistake. "I know," she said. "I don't even really have any idea
what I'm doing *here*," she said.

"Well then, what *are* you doing here?" he asked with an
insistence that was also gentle.

She made an exasperated, teenaged noise and suddenly
sprawled in the big armchair. "What *is* it with you? Do you
always answer a question with another question? Is it some
trick you like learned in rabbi school or what?"

"When you're ignorant you don't need lessons in asking
questions."

"Oh, *that's* profound! All right, what I want is for you to
tell me how to get out of this mess. I mean I *know* how to get
out of it but I need, well, I need to be *good*."

The rabbi rubbed his palms on the desk. "Why do you say
need, if you'll excuse another question. Don't you mean that
you *want* to be good?"

"Want, need—what's the difference?"

The rabbi picked up the glasses lying on his desk. "Last
month I bought these reading glasses. I needed them. I didn't
want them."

Helen rolled her eyes. "I'm not some stupid slut, you
know. I'm valedictorian!"

The rabbi let that desperate boast sit in the air for a moment
then folded his hands together. "There are these two leaves on a

tree. It's October but they're still green. As they watch, a third leaf tumbles to the ground. One of the leaves turns to the other and says, 'Look at that miserable leaf. All brown and wrinkled up. Ugh. That's never going to happen to *me*.'"

"Spare me the parable, Rabbi. It already *did* happen to me. You think I don't know *that*? What I want is some clear answers."

"Yes?"

"Okay. Why does God insist that people get married before they have sex?"

"Nature doesn't care how the world gets populated. I don't see that God does either."

"What?"

"We're told God made Adam and then Eve. So far as I can see he left it to them to work out the details."

"What about the Torah?"

"It has a lot of rules. Over six hundred of them."

"Well, I *violated* the rules. I got myself knocked-up."

"You want to evade that?"

"*Evade* it? Excuse me, but it's too late for that."

"Remember your Shakespeare? Hamlet and Lear and Othello are caught in their tragedies. No matter what they do, they're ensnared. Why should we suppose we aren't like them. . . even, if you'll excuse me, the stupid sluts?"

"So I'm supposed to just *accept* it?"

"I'm very sorry to tell you it makes no difference whether you accept it or not." The rabbi got to his feet. "Would you pardon me for just a minute?"

"You're *leaving*?"

"I'll be right back. Promise."

He closed the study door behind him and went to the kitchen. Before his wife could ask anything he said, "Quick. Have we got any oranges?"

She looked at him, puzzled. "Yes?"

"Good. Cut one up and give me the seeds. The pips. I'll be right back." Then he dashed out into the yard.

Moments later he was back in his study.

"Helen, can we agree to leave God out of it and just consider what's best for all the people involved?"

"A funny thing for a rabbi to say."

"Maybe I'm a funny rabbi. Just the people, then?"

"*All* of them?"

"Do you think the embryo inside you is a person?"

"That's what I argued against in forensics last month. I don't know if I really believe it."

The rabbi laid four pips on the desk. "Can you squeeze any juice from these orange seeds?"

"Of course not."

He laid an acorn beside the orange seeds.

"Can you sit in the shade of this acorn?"

The girl began to cry. "But the oak's *in* the acorn. I mean the acorn could *become* an oak."

"You're right, Helen. That it can become an oak is the most important thing about an acorn. We give up many futures every day, child. That's often tragic, but it's not unusual. It's human enough. What is *not* human, what is *not* forgivable, is that we shouldn't regret them.

Idol-Worship

To his distress, our rabbi was asked to participate in a university symposium. The Provost's invitation said he would be on a panel discussing a question of doctrine before an audience. It was to be the first in a series jointly sponsored by the Religious Studies and Philosophy departments. The rabbi would have liked to decline but his wife wouldn't hear of it.

"But, my dear, don't you understand? I'm supposed to discuss doctrine in front of an audience and at the university. Am I an expert that I should sit on such a panel?"

His wife considered him silently before delivering one of her crisp non-sequiturs. "And how many students did Akiba have?"

"Akiba ended badly," grumbled the rabbi.

She pointed a correcting finger at him. "Not badly. *Nobly.*"

The subject was idol-worship. The first expert, both a rabbi and an historian, read a prepared text. Erudite and comprehensive, he began with the Islamic tale of the child Abraham taking a hammer to the statues in his father Terah's idol shop, then proceeded to the disgrace of the Golden Calf, through the Hellenic conversions and the Maccabees' resistance, and wound up with sledge-wielding Protestants shattering the images of saints and martyrs.

A seminary scholar expounded next, for about twenty minutes. He began by concurring with the former speaker's implication that idol-worship is a form of polytheism. However, he wished to stress the broader significance of idol-worship, what he called "its figurative and limitless meaning." Money, he observed, could be an idol, or the state, heroes and even automobiles. Popularity was often an idol, indeed all the varieties of vanity. In sum, it was his view that the definitive gesture of idol-worship was the elevating of worldly goods above spiritual ones.

The third speaker was a professor from the philosophy department, a clever man who relished paradoxes. He acknowledged the contributions of his colleagues, albeit in a patronizing tone. With a donnish irony that evoked chuckles from his claque of knowing students, he said he wished only to append a few tiny insights of his own. This took more than half an hour.

One must, he said, begin by admitting that the prohibition against idol-worship is purely negative. We are told what not to worship: whatever can be touched or smelled or even understood. That is to say, the true God is unknowable; to the Hebrews even His name must never be spoken or written down. The very first commandment is the one against idolatry, not because it is the easiest to follow but precisely because it is the most difficult. All the other proscriptions—against stealing, murder, covetousness, adultery—these are merely the behaviors of people engaged in idol-worship. With a twinkling eye, the professor observed that the surest way to fulfill the first commandment might be to take care to worship nothing at all. And yet even atheists can be guilty of idol-worship. They often bow down before their own faithlessness and, still more, the reasoning that brought them to it. At last, with a smile at his fellow panelists, the professor speculated that one of the subtlest ways to err with respect to the commandment against idolatry would be to make an idol of the one true God Himself. Then he sat down, manifestly satisfied with his performance.

Applause and grumbles of displeasure rose from the audience. This was a mixed group. There were men with beards in black fedoras and the pallor of Talmudists, women in long dresses with covered heads, men in white caps, women in veils, students in blue jeans, academics with trimmed beards, priests in cassocks and habited nuns. Our rabbi recognized a few of us from his own congregation. As he looked over the crowd he realized that what unified them was not their faith, no common belief, intellectual curiosity or spiritual yearning. No, the one thing they all had in common was the certainty that they themselves were innocent of idol-worship.

After he was introduced our rabbi did not choose to stand at the podium as the others had done. He remained seated at the long table with the water carafes and the name cards.

"I'm very sorry," he began. "I have to apologize for not preparing as my colleagues have done and done so well. Hard as I tried, I couldn't think of anything to say. You see, I know hardly anything about idol-worship, except that it's not a good thing and, of course, what we've all learned tonight from these scholars. All I feel able to do is to ask a few questions. Perhaps if I put these to my fellow panelists, I may yet learn a little better what idol-worship is."

The rabbi looked down the table to the first speaker.

"Rabbi, didn't you say that idol-worship is forbidden because it's a kind of polytheism, or at least closely linked to it?"

"Yes."

"But what if someone worships only a *single* idol?"

The rabbi-historian smiled with amusement. "Historically speaking, that has never happened."

"Never? Excuse me, but I'm surprised you can be so sure. However, what I should like to know is whether it's *possible* to worship a single idol."

"I suppose. What of it?"

"Well then, wouldn't such an idol-worshiper be a mono-theist? Couldn't he even have his own version of the *Sh'ma*?"

There was a commotion in the audience.

"That's an outrageous proposition," said the first speaker with a politeness not meant to conceal his displeasure.

"Why?"

"Why!" interrupted the indignant second speaker. "Because the *Sh'ma* is the Jewish people's deepest acknowledgment of the one *true* God. An idolater is a pagan and to compare his superstition to the faith in the Most High is a great deal worse than odd—Rabbi."

"Pardon me. But to our hypothetical idol-worshiper pronouncing his idolatrous *Sh'ma*, wouldn't the god he worships be both one *and* true? Isn't that so?"

75

Here the urbane professor intervened. "This is really just a quibble, though," he allowed, "a not uninteresting one. The question presumably is whether idolatry lies in the *object* of worship or, so to speak, the *attitude* of the worshiper."

"Ah," said the rabbi, "thank you, Professor. That is well put. Would you give us the pleasure of hearing your answer to your own question?"

The professor leaned forward. "Certainly. It's simple enough. Obviously it can't, as you've implied, be the worshiper's *attitude*, by which I mean the intensity or sincerity of his belief, that makes him an idolater, but the *object* to which his faith is directed." Here he smiled slyly. "As I'm sure you'll recall, Rabbi, the priests of Ba'al could not bring down fire from heaven while Elijah could."

"I see. The proof's in the pudding. But why then did you suggest that one may fall into error by making the one true God into an idol Himself?"

The professor appeared confused for a moment. "I merely meant that one can imagine a case where the worshiper turns his faith into a superstition, such as when people pray to God to hit the lottery or that their team should win a football game."

The rabbi was silent for a few moments, giving everyone time to see how a clever man can be too clever.

"Rabbi," he said next, addressing the second speaker, "when does the Sabbath begin?"

"*Shabat*? What's that got to do with idol-worship?"

"Perhaps nothing. But please, when does it begin?"

"At sundown on Friday, as everyone knows."

"Yes, that we all know. But how do we know Friday is Friday? After all, calendars have often been corrected. One or two errors in almost six thousand years are hardly inconceivable."

"No, there have been no such errors or corrections. And if there were, it would be terrible."

"What would be so terrible?"

"Because if what you are perversely suggesting were true, then we have not been fulfilling the Law."

"Yes, that's possible, I suppose. But what does 'Friday' mean other than the day we all agree to call Friday—that is, the day on which *Shabat* begins? God lives in eternity. Do you suppose He really cares when we kindle the lights?"

"Have you forgotten that God participates in history?" declared the first speaker.

"A good point," said the rabbi. "But then how do we know *when* on Friday the Sabbath begins?"

The others were silent.

Our rabbi looked toward the ceiling of the hall. "I remember an old sage says somewhere that to discover when *Shabat* begins a Jew should borrow a length of white thread from his wife, take it outside, face west, and hold the thread stretched before his eyes. When he can no longer see it, that's when *Shabat* begins."

"Very amusing, Rabbi," laughed the professor. "But doesn't that depend on how good your Jew's eyesight is, not to mention the thickness of his wife's thread? We wouldn't all see the thread vanish at the same time."

"Why does that matter?"

The second speaker interrupted angrily. "Why does it *matter*? What if every Jew began to decide for himself when *Shabat* begins? It's no trivial matter. The Law must be fulfilled, carried out to the last letter."

At this our rabbi fell back in his seat. "Gentlemen, thank you. I'm in your debt. Now I know better what idol-worship is."

Inter Scoti Et Scuti

My shop, the finest in the village, stocks all sorts of goods, many exclusively available from me, so that it is no idle boast to say that everybody hereabouts is my customer, even my competitors. All the same, I am not so wealthy as to invite envy, and my family lives no differently from our neighbors. My success is precarious; I am never free of anxiety over the business. My wife worries even more than I do. Twice a day, and sometimes more, she totes up our assets and liabilities, fussing over them as if they were twins, one bad and the other good. Whenever I place an order she is in a state of tension until it arrives, and if it is late she becomes despondent and has to be soothed every half hour.

My wife and I have a standing agreement with a cousin of hers who moved to the capital eight years ago. This cousin was a restless youth and now he is a capricious man, not completely dependable. His whimsical character causes my wife no end of apprehension, since our business has come to depend on him. When, out of disgust with the situation here, out of boredom and dreams, he set out for the city, my wife made him a list of goods we wanted for our trade. We agreed on a commission of ten percent of the wholesale price of any of them he could procure and arrange to ship to us. Over my wife's objections, I also empowered him to use his initiative should he come across promising items not on the list. The agreement has proved profitable, overall, but is not without problems. Sometimes, perhaps out of absent-mindedness or the wish to have a joke at my expense, he will send us useless items, such as the two crates of rotten oranges that arrived last week, or the shipment of satin ball gowns I had from him seven months ago. Well, this is not so bad, I tell my wife. Life is probably hard for him in the city; he must miss his family and no doubt these little jokes comfort him and make him feel closer to us. One must make allowances, I tell her as she wrings her hands. Far more serious is the number of shipments that never reach us at all; for whether they arrive or not I have to pay up, including the cousin's ten percent. What becomes of these consignments is impossible to say. If I could hope to prevent these losses knowing might matter; however, there is no way to do so. They simply do not arrive and so must be written off. On these occasions my poor wife takes to her bed, cursing her cousin and breathing with difficulty. Some of these shipments may exist only on paper, as my wife contends, accusing the cousin of cheating us. Some may fall off the wagons that bounce along the rough mountain tracks that must be crossed to reach our village. It's probable that others are appropriated by freight agents who, underpaid as they are, believe they are entitled to pilfer and see nothing wrong with it. The greatest number of lost items, however, are stolen by bandits, at least if the carters are to be believed. These thieves are also my customers, at least on occasion, men of the Scoti and the Scuti.

These clans hate each other, and it is their whims and moods that control the weather of life in our village. I call them bandits and thieves because I am, after all, their victim, but perhaps these words are misleading. After all, bandits care about the things they steal whereas the men who hold up the wagons will frequently pass over valuable items—not only bulky ones like a piano, a bedstead, or a table, but even easily portable ones like linen and jewelry—for such trifles as rubber bands and pots of glue. In other words, the Scoti and Scuti steal for the thrill of stopping the wagons and frightening the drivers; they rob for the love of robbing, because it is their way of life and also because it undermines ours, which they despise. As for material goods, they do not want much, given their primitive mode of living and ignorance of money matters. Though my losses are substantial and, in fact, make it impossible for our business ever to be secure, these are as nothing beside what must go on up in the mountains where the Scoti and the Scuti carry on their interminable feud, stealing things of vital importance to them like horses, slaughtering each other over the smallest slight. Though I have never been able to discover the origin of the vendetta—when Scoti are asked they always snarl and curse the Scuti and vice versa—the bad blood between them is the chief fact of their lives. Their feud is the armature that gives their miserable lives what meaning they have and is never for a moment forgotten by them, cannot be forgotten just because it provides the content of their lives. We villagers would like nothing better than to be free of the Scoti and Scuti and their interminable feud; we do not take sides or care who is up and who down but, neutral though we are, it is our misfortune to be trapped between them.

Like a child stared on by half a dozen captious aunts and uncles, our village crouches in a valley under six mountains. Maybe it is because our ancestors abandoned them that we can't help feeling the everlasting peaks are vexed with us. Why did our forebears come down from the heights? It might have been the hope of an easier and more sophisticated life in a town, or the wish to live in stone houses and take up new work, or just the longing for the stability of flatness. I've given the question some thought and, in my opinion, it was the powerful yearning to escape the narrowness and bigotry of those mountain defiles and join the wider world beyond, a craving that we feel every bit as strongly today. And this is why, to us, the mountains are not beautiful, are not noble peaks, but so many reproaches and the high doors of a prison. We also dislike the mountains because they are where the Scoti and Scuti dwell. To them we are no better than apostates and weaklings. They take malicious pleasure in seeing how their mountains keep us from getting more than a few hours of full sunlight even in high summer. On the other hand, if the mountain folk were ever to be candid with themselves—though honest reflection is something of which they are incapable—they might acknowledge the benefits they derive from us and give us our due. We are their marketplace, their recreation spa, purveyors of those few luxuries they can no longer do without. Above all, we are the buffer that prevents an all-out war between them, the spring that absorbs their aggression, the valve through which they blow off excess steam. Moreover, they find our young women irresistible and why should this be if not because the girls were reared in the village and not in the mountains? You can see the almost indecent hunger on their young men's faces whenever one of our girls walks by. They are excited by our girls' beauty but what really awes them is the girls' freedom to walk alone in public, to walk with one another and not with a man, liberties which the Scoti and Scuti find titillating and which, with a hardly concealed lasciviousness, they long to crush. Scoti and Scuti women are hardly ever seen in the village. It is not permitted.

The two highest pinnacles are covered with snow year-round but the others are brown. Tough, stunted trees do grow on the slopes but there is not enough water to sustain real forests. So the Scoti and Scuti use their herds' dung for fuel and consequently they stink of it. The run-off in our valley is sufficient, with the little sun we get, for one crop of vegetables each year. Our greens are prized by the mountain people whose diet consists almost exclusively of meat and cheese, also a disgusting porridge made from goats' blood mixed with wild barley from their high meadows. No doubt the austerity and harshness of life up there encourages their vendetta. All their songs are about their feuds; all celebrate theft, rape, and revenge. Fed on these verses it is little wonder that the young men come into town spoiling for a fight and rejoice when they find one. Few of these brawls are with us, however. This is not just because we are careful to avoid giving offense either to Scoti or Scuti but because their contempt makes us, in their eyes, unworthy even of beating. These young men live outside themselves, in the eyes of others, and so honor is everything to them and there is little to be had in smashing a villager's nose. The Scoti prefer, of course, to fight with the Scuti, and the Scuti are quick to go after the Scoti; but, failing that, the young men of both clans will choose to fight with one another before coming after us. Toward us their aggression takes the form of grabbing whatever they want, intimidating our young men, ogling and beguiling our daughters. It is terrible to be laughed at but what is worse is how well we have learned to bear it.

Though there are few assaults on us these days, we are under perpetual strain, always in expectation of an attack; for there was a time not long ago when the Scoti and Scuti both attempted to annex the village. This was not because either clan really wanted to rule over us—even they know they are not up to such responsibility—but to prevent the other from doing so. Both succeeded for brief periods but were quickly undermined by the other clan whose subversion strengthened our dogged efforts to regain our autonomy. Our sullen refusal to cooperate coupled with the opposing clan's guerrilla tactics soon made the conquerors withdraw. In any case, neither group is able to bear village life for long. They ache to return to their mountains and, in their way, the Scoti and Scuti fear us, a notion which they would ridicule. Perhaps it would be more precise to say they are afraid of our influence on them, that we will soften them and make them like us. This fear also played a role in their so quickly giving up their grip on us. Both found that they preferred an independent village to one under their enemy's thumb and so a kind of balance developed. This balance is in a way good for us, but it is likewise bad. Since neither Scoti nor Scuti have been able to defeat the other—and there is a serious question as to whether they would even desire to do so, despite their noisy and bloodthirsty oaths—interfering with us can serve as a surrogate for open warfare and its unreckonable cost. We are always there to provide a quick, if insignificant, victory, should one be needed. To be sure, there are economic benefits in controlling us; if there were not the Scoti clan would not have labored so hard to free us from the Scuti, nor the Scoti from the Scuti. Though it has been two years since either clan has made an attempt to move in on us we are never certain when conditions may change. The consequence is that the equilibrium in which we live is as precarious as a tightrope walker's.

Though we never had to suffer the rule of either Scoti or Scuti for more than a few months this does not mean we are free. On the contrary, what passes for our freedom is almost worse than being occupied. An occupation is at least a certainty and one can make one's accommodations, while the expectation of an attack that may or may not come fore-stalls planning and saps our hope. We have often thought we were again under attack when it was only a raid by a band of teenagers satisfied with a little vandalism. And yet each stone shattering a window could be the precursor of another all-out offensive. A policy of resistance, of armed self-defense, which might seem the best as well as the most honorable course in our circumstances, was only attempted once, under a mayor who had not been raised among us but had himself run away from the mountains as a boy. His policy was a catastrophe, for we could not match the ferocity or the skill of the mountain dwellers with their horses and marksmanship, their hardihood and their ruthlessness. The toughest among us was soft beside them, even the bellicose mayor whose strategy we had reluc-tantly adopted, more out of shame than from any hope of suc-cess. So it seemed to us fitting when he was the first to be killed. Since then we have made a law against any naturalized citizen becoming mayor. We are merchants and artisans, glaziers and potters; we are not warriors and don't wish to be. Honor does not suit us. In fact, those of our young men who are drawn to the life of war usually slip away to join their distant relatives in the mountains and return as strangers, the most zealous of the bullies. But few of our sons have chosen this path. We have lost far more of our daughters than sons to the Scoti and the Scuti.

In the early days, before we had torn ourselves free from our roots among the mountain clans, a few village girls were married off in hopes of maintaining family ties and good rela-tions with both the Scoti and Scuti. At least that is the official story. Though we never speak of such things, it is acknowledged that it was the girls who wished it. Nothing has changed in this regard. Every year some girl will fall in love with a brawny, foul-smelling herdsman who struts through our streets and disturbs our peace. These girls believe themselves unhappy in our narrow lanes and what they foolishly imagine to be the constraints of town life, with being too much indoors and under the eyes of their families. They complain that they cannot bear the prospect of becoming the wife of some shopkeeper or a smith. And so they go away and are married up there and are never seen again. These marriages cause us much sorrow. Not only do they deny parents the joy of being near their daughter and watching their grandchildren grow up but, collectively, they bind us to the Scoti and the Scuti and depress our population so that it has never grown to the point where we can dream of overcoming them by weight of numbers. As for the girls, it may be true that our lanes are narrow, that we get too little sunlight, even that our customs are strict; yet a girl's life here is expansive and unfettered compared to what it is up there. We warn them that the Scoti and Scuti enforce rules of exacting rigor, especially on women. Have you asked yourself, we say, why you never see their women in town? Or why, if one does manage to sneak down here, she looks furtively left and right and gazes on our houses with envy? Haven't you observed how their men cow them, the violence with which they throw their elbows and shoulders around? But such warnings are of little use. Young people always delude themselves just because they are young, especially those taken by the urge to go up into the mountains. They imagine freedom lies on the heights. They know that they are related either to the Scoti or the Scuti and so think of life up there as a return to authenticity. They even find the clans' endless vendetta romantic. These girls are so confused that they endow those brutes with every kind of virtue, including tenderness. Who knows all they imagine? As for the strictures the Scoti and Scuti impose on females, these they underestimate or, if they do grasp a little of what it means to live up there, they see it as an antidote to the selfishness and aimlessness of adolescence. It is difficult to dissuade a young person who believes she is acting in the cause of virtue. It is usually the lonely ones, the dreamers, and also the most scrupulous who succumb to these illusions. The young cannot distinguish between feelings of loneliness and those of real individuality. And even if they are individuals in the full sense the best thing they can think of to do with their intense awareness of self—a sense that is always strongest at that age—is to throw it away by binding themselves to the Scoti or Scuti.

It may seem surprising that the laws of both clans are identical. In fact, to us the Scoti and the Scuti long ago became indistinguishable. The men wear the same wide trousers, tie the same bandanas around their throats, favor the same short beards, fringed jackets and white caps. They all speak the same dialect and are driven by the same passions—boundless self-regard as well as hatred of one another and disdain for us. Once again, we are ourselves, albeit in a vestigial sense, Scoti and Scuti. And since we villagers are descendants of the two feuding clans it has taken all the tact and eloquence of generations to overcome the temptation to fight among ourselves. We have not always succeeded. How could we with the constant provocations from the Scoti and the Scuti working in the shadows against our peace, plotting, spreading rumors, doing all they can to fracture our community and drive not one wedge but dozens of them deeper and deeper until, so to speak, we could be fragmented and even lose our identity as villagers; for what is our village but the place which has overcome the parochial allegiances and rancor of tribes in favor of a wider vision, one that yearns to become cosmopolitan? It would be surprising indeed if, under the perpetual strain of living between these two colossal, mutually repellent magnets, intermittently bullied and set upon by rowdy adolescents and their bloody-minded fathers, losing our wayward daughters and vain sons who dream vaguely of heroism on high—it would be surprising indeed if our village had escaped all civil conflict. In fact, hardly a month goes by without some incident—a window broken, a doorway defaced, a brawl among schoolboys, insults exchanged by angry drinkers. But these minor scuffles we have learned to endure and to suppress. The memory of what happened in our grandfathers' time has not yet faded so completely that even the most partisan among us would again risk the massacres of that terrible year when the village came close to tearing itself to shreds, when everything we had built up almost unraveled like bad knitting, when those who imagined they were Scoti fought with those who supposed they were Scuti. Out of that time came new laws and a resolve never again to fall back into the barbarism of our forebears. In fact, a kind of pride took hold in us, not that of the mountain folk with their daggers and grudges, but the modest pride of civilization, which is always born of revulsion. Still, even with all this, the surest anchor of our village's neutrality is simply our inability to tell Scoti from Scuti.

The mountain clans despise us for denying that we and they are the same people while at the same time declaring in every way that they are glad not to be like us—domesticated animals. It offends them that we should want to look beyond our valley and not be obsessed with their vendetta. At the very bottom of their contempt is the conviction that we have sold off our identity for elevated twaddle.

So the Scoti and Scuti scorn what the best of us hold dearest. "Gains usually show up before losses. Isn't that so, shopkeeper? You villagers cower before us just the way you're doing now. You tremble and bow," roared a leonine old Scoti or Scuti to me while appropriating a few items from my shop. "This is despicable enough but it only hides something worse, that you're actually proud of yourselves and believe you've become citizens of something called the world. Well, the truth is that all you've done is to stop being members of your clan. You think this is all to the good, but it isn't. It's like choosing nothing over something. You'll find that out soon enough. It's a lesson we'll keep teaching you until it cuts through all that nonsense in your heads. You'll see." The old dog shook his fist in my face, smiling in a way that made me shiver and my wife cry out. Then he marched to the door and slammed it behind him.

Our situation is not completely hopeless. On the contrary, in fact. According to a letter I've had from the cousin, in the capital they are talking about building a new highway into our region, perhaps even a railroad, in which case our village is bound to flourish. We will spread out; we will grow larger and larger until the Scoti and the Scuti will be no more to us than so many fleas. Instead of our young people impetuously running off to join them it will be their young who steal away to find a richer life with us. Even if this rumor of the new highway should prove false there is still the hope that the Scoti and Scuti will forget all about us and finally fall on one another with all the murderousness they have held in check and so annihilate each other.

In the meanwhile, even if we cannot flourish, we can endure. We can sit by our windows dreaming of better times when the mountains, whose stillness is now a constantly looming threat in the corner of our eyes, deepening the darkness of our dusks, immovable ghosts of a past we have relinquished, will have proper houses at their bases, tilled terraces on their flanks, and peaks that will no longer glare down on us but stretch upwards towards a heaven that is empty but clean.

Standards of American Measurement

She noticed that the air in the hotel bar was chilled and still. It was quiet too, but then it wasn't yet three o'clock in the afternoon. Subdued lighting gave the place the feel of permanent dusk. Abigail thought momentarily of Sleeping Beauty's enchanted castle, the scullions, chambermaids, guards, the royal couple, all suspended in time, waiting for happy hour. There were no briars but also no windows.

In a corner booth three fortyish men in ties and jackets spoke in low voices. She recognized two of them from the convention. They could have been negotiating a deal or perhaps it was a job interview, somebody who wanted to jump ship or was being inveigled into doing so. In another corner two young women were listening attentively to an older one. Abigail guessed she was telling jokes, the bitter kind at which nobody is supposed to laugh out loud. They were all dressed in sweaters under dark blazers. Abigail didn't recognize any of them.

Other than the bored bartender and the even more bored cocktail waitress, no one else was in the place. Abigail walked up to the bar, sat on a stool. The bartender's hairline was receding; the track light reflected off his forehead.

"What can I get for you?" he asked. He didn't smile at her, nor did he frown.

"Tonic. Lime twist."

"Coming right up."

Ari had promised himself he'd get up and leave the third time the speaker used the word *valorize* but stayed put until the fifth. Feeling guilty about his rudeness, he thought of hiding in his room, perhaps reading something to clear his head and palate; but, craving pretzels and something fizzy, he chose the conventional refuge, a haven where nothing was likely to be *foregrounded* or *problematized* for at least a couple more hours.

He could hardly help spotting Abigail right away, no more than he could help thinking of a cello when he did. He too saw the groups in the corner booths, *conspiring*, he thought, as in breathing together rather than planning to blow anything up. More escapees, he figured.

Ari was at the hotel to deliver a paper on Joseph Conrad's *The Rover* at the regional Modern Language Association Conference. His chairman had suggested he "get out more," hinting that "a few presentations wouldn't hurt" when his contract came up. So he had cobbled together a proposal that was accepted. He'd written the paper in two days the week before. Though it valorized nothing, it did praise valor.

There was another conference at the hotel, or rather a convention, something about indoor air-conditioning. He'd seen the two notices side-by-side in the lobby welcoming the forces of scholarship and sales. Whimsically, he imagined giving a presentation to the other crowd. It would be about how global warming was a godsend to business. He'd do an upbeat PowerPoint correlating rising temperatures with the projected sales of indoor air-conditioning units, how more units would mean more electricity made from burning more fossil fuels which would release more carbon dioxide leading to still higher temperatures and so demand for more air-conditioning units. "The apocalypse is a business opportunity," he'd have explained. "Planetary incineration's the ultimate positive feedback loop. It's an ill wind, etc."

Abigail sipped her tonic and wondered what might go on at a Modern Language conference. "Well," she mused, "nobody's going to be speaking Latin or Hittite." She had witnessed a member of the hotel staff rolling his eyes as he derisively referred to the scholars as "the brown shoes." Academics aren't big tippers, apparently.

Soon enough Edith, George, and Mr. Calimonte would be there. Well, maybe not George. In the meantime, it was a relief simply not to have to see any more x and y axes, bar graphs, bullet points.

Ari chose a stool two down from Abigail.

The bartender came over, raised his head then his eyebrows.

"Virgin Mary," said Ari.

Abigail turned toward him

Ari shrugged.

Abigail pointed at her glass. "Virgin G and T."

"So, not much vodka going today."

"Oh, just wait."

"You hiding out too?"

"Hiding out? No. Just not *there*."

He nodded. "What was the last straw?"

She sipped at her tonic, looked at him a little wickedly. "Sales figures for eastern Nebraska."

"I'm guessing flat?"

She laughed. "You?"

"Oh, for me it was—wait, I don't want to get this wrong." He took a folded program from the side pocket of his tweed jacket, opened it and read: "*Men Without Women Without Men colon the Hermeneutics of Bakhtinian Polyphonic Unfinalizability in Barnes, Baldwin, Hurston, and Hemingway.*"

"Oh, the alliteration."

"The colon's more essential."

"Essential?"

"It's how you make a title for an academic paper. First you come up with a misleadingly alluring phrase, then the colon, then what it's really about."

"Irritable colon. Irritating, I mean."

"I myself have gone post-colonial. No colons, ever. I want to start a trend."

"So do you choose just the deceptively fascinating phrase or the boring honest one?"

He raised his hand and fluttered it in the universal *com si, com sa* gesture. "It depends."

"On?"

"How good a misleading phrase I can come up with."

"What was it? The Hermeneutics of—?"

"Bakhtinian Polyphonic Unfinalizability. It would be devastating in German."

"It sounds sort of German, actually."

Ari cocked his head, she nodded, and he moved to the stool next to hers.

"There was this famous mathematician, von Neumann," he said.

"German, I'm guessing."

"Surprisingly enough, born in Hungary."

"The Germans got around. So, von Neumann."

"He came up with the *microcentury*."

"Microcentury? Is that short or long? It sounds both."

"Good question. Can be either, I suppose. It's von Neumann's measurement for the maximum length of a lecture."

"Which is?"

"Precisely fifty-two minutes and thirty-four seconds."

"Not bad. Not even all that German."

"Or Hungarian, I suppose. Anyway, von Neumann became an American. We Americans have our own ways of measuring things."

"Miles not kilometers, you mean? That sort of thing?"

"If we possessed a more law-abiding nature we'd use kilometers."

"That's true. Every year in school we had to study the metric system. Every September the science teachers would say we'd be on next year."

"See? Americans are good at ignoring stuff like that. Directives."

"Tea in Boston Harbor? The Whiskey Rebellion?"

"Right."

"Beverage directives especially."

The bartender came over, pointed to their glasses, raised his eyebrows. They both shook their heads.

"Once upon a simpler time," said Ari, "in some area codes, lunches were measured out in martinis."

"Three, I think."

"Bad old days. Like Sherlock Holmes' three-pipe problems."

"That's English."

"True."

"So what's *really* American?"

"American Standards of Measurement. Well, let's see. The aircraft carrier. That's for big, powerful things."

"Not very exact."

"Okay. The football field. Our national standard measure of distance. Long as three football fields. Wide as three football fields."

"The Brits would say pitch."

"Probably. Okay then, Rhode Island."

"Rhode Island"

"Sure. Means big when referring to icebergs, small when referring to countries."

"Like Andorra?"

"Or San Marino."

"Give us another."

"Root canal."

"Root canal? How's that work?"

"Standard measure for level of pain. You know, as in sitting through reports on sales in eastern Nebraska."

"*Worse* than root canal. Right."

"Exactly."

"I've got one."

"Shoot."

"Bottles of Tabasco sauce."

"A measure of—?"

"Marriages. How many bottles of Tabasco sauce between the wedding and the divorce. Average is seven. Did you know the Cajuns used to give a bottle as a wedding present? It's kosher, too."

"You don't say."

"I'm from Baton Rouge, so I know."

"Red Stick."

"Better in French, don't you think?"

"I suppose the French have their proper measurements, too. But I can't think of one."

"Expensive as Chateau Lafite-Rothschild? Fattening as pâté de foie gras?"

He was impressed. "I'm Ari," he said and held out his hand.

Later, when the others crowded in, Abigail introduced Ari to her colleagues as a regional manager from Armonk, New York, and he introduced her to his as an associate professor from Notre Dame, expert on Joseph Conrad and Nora Ephron.

The following morning, she read out his paper on Conrad and gave the most astonishing answers to the panel's questions, while he delivered an extemporaneous talk he called *Carbon Dioxide, Our Best Friend*. It lasted just over fifty-two minutes.

That night Abigail said the day had been a real Rhode Island and Ari presented her with a sumptuously wrapped bottle of Tabasco sauce.

At last check, they were on their fifth bottle.

Confession of
an Adolescent Arsonist

The trouble began when Uncle William took an old chest of drawers on the *Antiques Roadshow*. A smartly-dressed woman from New York City ran her fingers over it greedily, smiling like a well-stoked pothead.

"This is truly magnificent, sir. A treasure. The finest example I've ever seen of Rhode Island block-front. Any idea of the age of the piece? No? Well it was made around 1780, at the time of the American Revolution. Do you know anything about John Goddard? No? Well, John Goddard, of Newport, is considered the first American craftsman to build block-front furniture. Notice how the contour of the piece's front is made by three blocks: the middle one concave, the outer two convex. . ."

She then grandly pegged its value at around $18,000—"at auction." They always say "at auction." I think it's to cover their tails. I mean, the expert didn't say *she'd* give Uncle William eighteen grand for it, dovetails, scrollwork and all. Anything can happen at an auction where fools can bid as well as connoisseurs. Anyway, that whole show exists to exhibit the astonished faces of your neighbors, to hear stuff like "You're joking" and "Oh, My God, and we've been letting the children climb all over it." Sure, once in a while they'll throw in a dud. "I'm sorry to say it's not Meissen but a souvenir of the 1939 World's Fair at Flushing Meadows, New York." They need the contrast; moreover, it's entertaining to humiliate some avaricious idiot who's expecting his putative porcelain to pay for a year's medical coverage and a yacht.

When I say the trouble began what I really mean is the feud, the vendetta. According to my mother, William "just *took* that chest" after Nana had to give up the old Victorian and move to Assisted Living. "He had his pick," she snarled, "his *pick*." That Uncle William picked that chest hadn't seemed to bother her before *Antiques Roadshow*, though. In fact, I remember she once referred to it as "that hideous huge dark thing with the bulge." Her own taste ran to the clean, dull lines of what she called "Danish modern." She always stressed the "Danish" part, I think, as if Denmark were so up-to-date it had just been invented. "I need *light*," she'd say passionately, like a Manichean or a sunflower.

It wasn't as if Uncle William put the thing up for auction and pocketed $18,000. No, he held on to the chest. He actually liked it. He was proud of it and thought it an heirloom. He wanted to keep it in the family. It was also something he had to remind him of his mother. I pointed all this out to Mom but it was as if I'd lit a two-inch fuse to a bundle of dynamite; she went off that fast. "And what do *I* have? The jewelry that that wife of his didn't want."

"That's not true," I said reasonably. "You chose first and, anyway, we've got lots of Nana's things. Dishes and silverware and those compote things. And what's with calling Aunt Janice 'that wife of his'?"

"Don't be so fresh," Mother barked. "Oh, the *mouth* you've got on you—and taking *his* side. . ."

At this point my older sister Beth, who, being preoccupied with her college applications, paid less attention to all this than I did, stuck in her oar. "But it's true, Mom."

"*Et tu?* Oh, how sharper than a serpent's tooth," Mother quoted. She tended to come out with Shakespeare when she was worked up because she'd been in the Drama Club at Bryn Mawr. When we were younger and more obedient, she used to make us read Shakespeare all together. Beth and I hated it—and I'm still pretty immune to bardolatry—but Father went along, if he couldn't come up with a ready excuse. He took directions and corrections to his diction with cheerful equanimity. Beth and I used to think he was cowed but then we realized it was just that his life was elsewhere: tennis, golf, business. It was easier for him to go along, within unstated limits. So, in the matter of "the Goddard Chest," as Mother took to calling it, Dad punted. He wouldn't discuss it. When she got wound up he'd just leave the room or turn on the TV or tactically fall asleep.

"Well," said Beth when we discussed his avoidance behavior, "it's always been his method, hasn't it?"

"Not sure. Actually, his usual method's just to agree," I observed.

"True. But this is different. She's *obsessed*. How much raving you figure he's had to listen to that we haven't?"

"Eww. Lucky thing we've got all this homework."

"And college applications."

We giggled.

"And Facebook," I added.

"And texting." Beth made her Mother face. "What do you read, my Lord? Icons, icons, icons."

"OMG. LOL."

"Seriously, this thing with Uncle William seems to have driven her right up to the edge."

"It's sibling rivalry," I said authoritatively, hot from a two-week unit on psychology. "It's obvious. I mean the chest's a symbol. That Uncle William has it means Nana loved him more."

"Or that he loved *her* more," Beth added subtly.

I shrugged. "Or. . . or maybe it's just the eighteen thousand bucks. And the getting on TV."

"She can be petty."

"But she's ours."

"And Dad's."

"Dad's not here much."

"And next year I'll be away at college."

"Yikes! Don't remind me."

Beth took my hand as if to say, "Let's never be like them." We'd always been close. "A pair of confederates," Mother called us. Seeing the way she and her brother were behaving made us want to fortify our alliance.

Beth was seventeen and, though I was only fifteen, she let me vet her boyfriends. I didn't have a boyfriend yet, if you don't count Freddy DeMaria, who had a crush on me and rode his bike up and down our street every day for two weeks but was too shy to say anything and gave up when he caught sight of Beth and me giggling behind the living room window. After that, it was like I had the plague.

For my sister and me the worst consequence of the feud was that we didn't see our cousins, Seth and Brian. Though they lived forty minutes away and went to a private school it was rare that two weeks went by without a family cookout at either their place or ours. Seth was a year older than Beth and they liked each other a great deal. Their names rhymed. As for Brian, he and I were born two days apart on the same floor of the same hospital. The boys could act like jerks, of course, but that was seldom and even then probably more hormones than character. We loved them like brothers, which Beth remarked on when we hadn't seen or heard anything from them in three weeks.

"You don't think they're mad at us, do you? Don't they miss us?" I wondered.

Beth grinned. "I guess they'd have called if Seth didn't have a new girlfriend who, by the way, is sweet and pretty and named Sylvie. Then Brian's pretty much all about lacrosse these days, isn't he?"

"Preppies," I said the way I'd say it to Brian when I wanted to tease him. He'd snap back, "Townie," and give me a light punch on the arm.

So we called them up.

Seth apologized "We've been wanting to call. We're as exasperated by this crap as you are."

"It's so incredibly *stupid*," Beth said.

I took the phone. "Our dad's kind of checked out. What's your mom have to say?"

There was a pause. "It may be a little harder at this end."

"Meaning?"

"Well, your mother did sort of start it so Dad feels it's up to her to end it, nothing he can do. Mom told him just to send her the damned chest."

"Really? She said *that*? You *heard* her?"

"Yep. We were all eating dinner together. But Dad said that would only make things worse."

When I told Beth what Seth said she took the phone back. "He's probably right. Mom would only say he was showing off how much richer he is than we are. You never heard the way she went on when you guys transferred to Whitemarsh."

"I guess it goes back a long way."

"Long way, yeah. That's what we think, too. Pre-*us*."

I grabbed the phone. "So. . . so what do we *do*? I mean, we've made our speeches already."

"Well, we do have a kind of wild idea, but I really need to think it through."

"What is it?"

"Look. Gotta run. I'll call you in a couple of days, okay? I promise At night. Say, ten-thirty."

Beth and I filled each other in on what we'd missed then stared glumly at each other, cross-legged on her bed.

"Not altogether satisfactory," was her laconic verdict.

Things grew worse, Mother was so possessed by resentment that Uncle William's "treachery" became almost her sole topic of conversation. Actually, there were no conversations, only screeds. She summoned the ghosts of slights long past, toys broken, taunts, insults and injuries. You'd have thought her childhood was one long tale of abuse, her adolescence an ordeal of scorn and mockery. "I always admired that chest," she whined at last, adding a still more fatal revision of history: "And that's why Mother wanted *me* to have it, not *him*."

Father took to coming home later; he invented more weekend errands, more games with his cronies. Beth and I gave up arguing with or even trying to propitiate Mother in favor of avoiding her.

Brian and Seth called back and said things were getting nearly as bad at their end. Uncle William, who used to be so easy-going, had turned peevish and irritable. He raised his voice to Aunt Janice because she insisted he make it up with his sister. When the boys seconded her the result was that he just became more defensive, resentful, and isolated. He said that he what he expected from them was support, not mediation.

"And," Brian added, "he polishes that damned chest every Sunday. The house stinks of lemon oil all the time."

Seth really did have a plan but one which, in retrospect, didn't make a lot of sense. At the time, though, it seemed brilliant and audacious—the one way to cut the knot, lance the boil. Perhaps it appealed to me because I so seldom transgressed and it was a way of playing at illegality, a clever, safe adventure. Anyway, I took my cue from Beth and she went for it right away.

The plan was to steal the famous chest—to abduct it, rather—and keep it hidden until the adults came to their senses. The logic of the thing was that if the source of the feud was this hunk of wood, then if we removed it everything would go back to normal. Later, we could think about restoring the chest and everybody would have a good laugh. Seth said he had this friend with a pickup who knew of a perfect place, an abandoned shed. He'd already offered him a hundred bucks.

Beth explained all this and put her hand over the phone. "I'm going to insist on going along," she whispered.

"Me too," I answered with joyous recklessness.

Seth and Brian weren't keen. They had good arguments against including us: the risk, the space we'd take up in the truck, the additional excuse-making, the more complicated timing. But Beth said that our participation was, in fact, vital because, after all, this was *family* business. She was adamant, hitting her knee with her fist as she argued.

The boys gave in, eventually, and Seth promised to phone back the following night with details. He did but first he dropped something a tad thermonuclear.

I couldn't hear his voice but Beth said later it sounded kind of choked, funny. "Look," he said. "I don't know how to break this except to say it straight out. Your father and our mother—they're having an affair."

What I did hear was Beth. "*What!*"

"What is it?"

She waved me off and went on saying "What!"

"What *is* it?" I repeated, feeling suddenly scared and curling up at the foot of her bed.

She hissed at me out of the side of her mouth. "Seth says they're having an affair."

"*Who* is?"

"Dad and Aunt Janice."

"*What?*"

"And you know this how?" she demanded of Seth.

"You're father's been gone a lot, hasn't he?"

"That doesn't prove anything. He's just hiding from Mom. So are *we*."

"Well, our mom's been gone a lot, too. Said it was a new yoga class. We trailed her. They use this motel out on Route 45."

"You *saw* them?"

"Well, we didn't peek through any *key*holes. But we saw their cars; we saw her get out; we saw them kiss each other and the way they did it."

"Jesus."

"*What?*" I yelled.

"Shh. Later," Beth snapped at me.

Seth then explained the plan and made it sound more urgent than ever though we really ought to have realized it was pointless.

Uncle William and Aunt Janice were going to a dinner party on Saturday night. It was easy for us to convince our parents we had a double date and would meet up with the boys at an imaginary, highly chaperoned, school dance. Dad thought that was cute; Mom didn't seem to be paying attention.

Seth's friend Josh had a tattoo of a Chinese dragon on his left arm. I picked up right away on the way he looked at Beth and the way Beth looked back. It was a case of irresistible bad boy/good girl magnetism. Brian and Seth noticed nothing; they were focused on burgling their own home, of course.

Beth and I squeezed into the cab, with Beth next to Josh. Our cousins rode in the bed with the chest which the three boys wrangled neatly though the garage. Josh took it slow, wary of cops and liking Beth right up beside him like that. We drove out of town on Route 45, passing three motels, turned off the highway at Rosedale then headed into the country. The shed was about twenty yards from the dirt road Josh drove us up. There was one of those weathered, tumble-down barns that always make me feel sad. Seth and Brian had brought along a chain, a tarp, and a padlock. Beth and I ran along beside them as they hefted the big old thing into the shed. They'd rolled up their sleeves and that's when I spotted the Chinese dragon. Josh smoked, too. I saw the pack of Marlboros in his shirt pocket.

Brian and I wanted to sit in the bed on the way back. We were feeling pretty wild.

"You think they'll get divorced?" he shouted over the noise of the wind.

"I don't know."

He moved closer to me. "If your dad married my mom, what would that make us?"

I considered this puzzle. "I'd say it was a wash."

"Oh yeah. I guess." He punched my arm gently. "God, this is *fun*, isn't it?"

Beth began going out with Josh. Well, not "going out" exactly; that sounds conventional. Sneaking out's more like it. With Dad so busy with golf and tennis and Aunt Janice and

Mom drilling further into her apparently inexhaustible gusher of bitterness, there wasn't anybody to disapprove except me.

"You've got him wrong," said Beth, eyes all a-glow.

"It's you who've got him wrong," I retorted and reminded her of the jerks I'd pegged right. I said Josh was worse than all of them put together.

An infatuated seventeen-year-old is going to listen to the wisdom of her little sister? Right.

One Saturday night she didn't come home until Sunday. Mom didn't notice and Dad was away for the weekend on a "business trip."

Meanwhile the boys told us Uncle William had begun to crack. When they got back from the dinner party he called the police at once. The officers were more suspicious than sympathetic: no locks broken, nothing else taken, a insurance policy recently taken out on Goddard's block-front masterpiece. Brian phoned me and said his father was practically beside himself; he felt guilty for not protecting the thing better.

"Maybe we should, you know, give it back?" I suggested.

"That would make everything worse," he said morosely.

"Things are pretty bad as they are," I allowed.

He perked up. "Tell you a secret?"

"Shoot."

"We're going to do it again."

"What?"

"Another house. Seth's friend Angela's. She's mad at her mother and wants some jewelry taken."

"Are you crazy?"

"It'll be easy."

"Josh too?"

"No. No Josh this time. You don't need a pickup to boost a few bracelets and necklaces."

And things went on like this for about a month.

Then at around ten one night I heard Beth crying and went into her room.

"What's the matter"

Her face was all boated and teary. She was clutching her old stuffed lamb.

"My life's a catastrophe. Grades all gone to hell. Josh says he's joining the Marines."

"The Marines? Why?"

"Look. I'm. . . pregnant. All right? Don't tell!"

I dropped on to her bed. "Jesus, Beth."

She looked forlorn. "I tore up my college applications."

"You what?"

"My life's over, what's the point?"

"Don't say that."

She looked away from me, at the far wall. "We were sitting on this bench in the park when I told him and he stood up and told me what he was going to do and then he just walked away—straight to the recruiting office, I suppose."

She started to wail, but quietly, so Mother wouldn't hear her, though Mother wouldn't have heard because it turned out she was downstairs listening to Dad tell her he wanted a divorce.

Uncle William and Aunt Janice separated. Dad moved into a garden apartment and Mom hired a lawyer—"a real barracuda," she called him. She even found some Shakespeare to quote at us for the occasion: ". . . as the long divorce of steel falls on me, make of your prayers one sweet sacrifice, and lift my soul to heaven." It's so obscure she must have looked it up. "The operant word, girls," she said furiously, "is *steel*."

Josh went to Parris Island and then overseas. Beth had a secret abortion—paid for by Seth and Brian with some of the money they'd gotten for all the stuff they were stealing. Then they got caught. Unfortunately, Seth had just turned eighteen, so he went to prison. The judge gave Brian two years parole on the grounds of being so young and under the influence of his brother.

As for the Goddard chest, it was turned to ash when I went back to the abandoned farm and burned down the shed.

Sickness and Health

1.

Many affairs of this life are fueled by money but one doesn't think about it unless the gas runs out. So, all beginnings being to some degree arbitrary, I will begin with the money made by the Heller Machine Tool Manufacturing Company of Zittau. The worthy founder and sole proprietor of this firm died an early death which was reasonably ascribed to overwork. That Konrad Heller's efforts exceeded what was necessary was proved when the firm not only survived without him but expanded. He had to be on the floor overseeing every detail of the operation from the ordering of lubricants to maintenance schedules; he would recalculate all his bookkeeper's sums, review weekly the personnel records of each of his employees and he wrote personally to every customer once a month. The business he nurtured and its profits passed directly to his widow, Roswitha Heller, one of the most remarkable women I've ever known. Frau Heller hired a first-rate manager down from Dessau and a Czech Deputy of Operations from Ostrava. For a year she kept her hand on things until she felt assured the ship was in good order. After instructing the German and Czech to keep a close eye on one another and send her monthly reports, she moved her household from Zittau to Karlsbad. Her only child, Hilda, soon married the eldest son of a banking family from Brno who came en-masse to take the waters and went away with Hilda, with her mother's resigned blessing.

Frau Heller, a sensitive woman, intelligent and active by nature, had her own ideas and advanced tastes, especially in the arts. Her interests extended even to the unsavory theories of Dr. Freud, two of whose public lectures she traveled to Vienna to attend. At a reception I once overheard her say tartly to a small-minded millionaire, "Jews don't frighten me."

In Karlsbad, Frau Heller rapidly became well connected. She was a gracious hostess who fed people well and so they called on her. She liked this, and invited more of them. She cultivated artists, writers, musicians, architects, and designers, helping some with money, others with introductions. Hilda, as she well knew, took after her father, had little interest in conversation, and none in the arts. She was, in fact, a happy Philistine the height of whose ambition was to be a proper wife and mother, an aim which her stolid husband and his dull family firmly seconded.

When Frau Heller learned that her nephew, the fourth of her brother's children and the only son, had revealed a precocious musical talent, she more or less took him over. Neither her brother nor his wife put obstacles in her way. While the railroad company had given Johannes Austecker the pompous title of Deputy Chairman for Moravian and Silesian Freight Operations, his salary was considerably less impressive; moreover, the females in his house were of the costly variety and the boy was sickly. Roswitha offered to see to her nephew's education and his other needs and the offer was accepted with a decent if perfunctory show of hesitation. Thus, at the age of nine, the fate of Werner Austecker passed into the hands of his aunt.

2.

Though it was only September, the day on which I made the short train ride from Prague to meet Roswitha Heller might have been plucked from late November, dull gray with a cold, steady rain soaking the countryside. I watched the drops race one another across the window of my compartment. I was alone and the whole train was nearly empty because Karlsbad's high season was over and real life reasserted itself, rainy and chill. I had been taken for a brief stay at Karlsbad when I was a child; perhaps that is why I thought of the place as exempt from the commonplace, like an amusement park. It seemed odd to me that anybody actually resided there, in a regular house.

Frau Heller's villa was charming, even in the foul weather. Though large, it was not imposing; though elegant, it was not ornate. The gardens, even in that unpleasant weather, were gorgeous. A young maid opened the door for me. From her accent I could tell that the girl was from somewhere near Pilsen. "You're expected, sir," she said, and showed me straight into a drawing room. Frau Heller greeted me politely. "Best not take my hand," she said considerately. "I've caught a head cold." The girl from Pilsen brought in a platter of small sandwiches of wafer-thin ham and radish cheese, then a pot of excellent tea. "It's English," Frau Heller explained, when I complimented it. "It goes down well with a cold. I'll give you some to take back with you." She was a handsome woman still, even with her raw red nose and rheumy eyes.

"Herr Rybar," she began as soon as I had set down my cup, "you wrote that you had something to tell me that touches my nephew. Since you are one of the first violins in the Orchestra, I presume it has to do with the premiere of his symphony."

I thought it best to pretend to be surprised. "You know about my position?"

She smiled. "Oh, not only that. I also know that, before you changed it to Miklos Rybar, your name was Klaus Fischer."

This really did surprise me. "Your sources are excellent," I said tremulously, feeling a little ashamed.

I told her what Prazak was up to and, as she asked, offered my speculations on his motives. She listened carefully and with too much dignity to make any personal comments about the conductor.

"And what measures do you propose?"

So I told her that as well. Why else had I come?

3.

Tomsa Prazak's wife Helene happened to be with three of her friends at the Café Magus when the young pianist who had recently been hired to entertain the patrons astonished everybody by performing three pieces by a Negro-American named Joplin. They are called "rags," from "rag time," a sort of syncopation. Hints of this rhythm can be found in Beethoven, yet what Joplin wrote is entirely different, wonderfully jolly. The pianist was Werner Austecker and the pieces were "The Maple Leaf," "The Entertainer," and "The Gladiolus." I've heard them; you can hardly help leaping up to dance. Helene Prazak was enchanted by the music and charmed by the good-looking young pianist, who followed the Joplin with Schubert's *Impromptus*. She had no idea that his name was known to her husband, still less that Tomsa would be so displeased to hear it, or that this displeasure would be exacerbated when she extolled the American dance music.

Tomsa Prazak was a fierce nationalist of the old school, steeped in Beethoven and Brahms, in Haydn and Mozart, in Schumann and Mendelssohn, whose work he knew intimately and conducted splendidly, but he hated the German language. His heroes were Garibaldi, Washington, Hus; his gods were Smetana and Dvorak, both of whom he knew and several of whose works he premiered. Hohenzollerns and Hapsburgs he loathed and said so, albeit in private. Though it would be an overstatement to call him a reactionary, he did dislike most of the new trends in music, whether, as he once put it in my hearing, they "spewed up from the South or oozed down from the North"—that is, whether they were German or Austrian. Wagner he called a tyrant and a bore; his fulminations on Mahler were very nearly comic. In a political sense, however, he welcomed the modernism that disgusted him; he believed it was hollowing out the Empire for whose collapse I believe he prayed every day before breakfast. The programs he chose were, of course, conservative—he would say "undecadent"—and by 1910 this had become a sore issue with his orchestra manager and board, also with the younger subscribers. It had been years since the orchestra had given a first performance of anything.

With age, Prazak's once commendable nationalism had turned rancid. From embodying the humane and life-affirming spirit of Czech music, he turned to simply hating Germans and Jews, calling the former "interlopers" and the latter "parasites." Of course, many of the most talented and advanced thinkers and artists in the Czech lands were precisely these German-speakers. "They are sick, sick or mad," Prazak would mutter whenever he heard them spoken of with approval.

Little as there was of it, Prazak had heard an example Austecker's music. After the affair of Joplin at the Magus, his wife insisted he go with her to the Ballet for the premiere of

Apollo and Daphne, a neo-classical gem in this humble fiddler's opinion. By rights, the music ought to have pleased Prazak, being such a tuneful and stringent antidote to Wagnerism; it even incorporated folk melodies. Yet he was quoted in the Prague press as saying: "To give him his due, the young fellow has talent, but his work is so frivolous it might just as well be French."

Austecker bore a German surname, hailed from the German-speaking north, and, last and worst, he was a protégé of the formidable Roswitha Heller who incarnated all Prazak so detested: a rich and progressive Germanophone. And now her precious nephew plays Negro music at the Magus, in front of Czech women, in front of his own wife! It was enough to make the old conductor apoplectic.

Let me be fair. Prazak was by no means a bad man. He hated groups, certainly, and said ugly things about them; but put an unhappy or needy member of one of those groups before him, and he would be solicitude itself. He also had some endearing eccentricities. For example, he cut his own hair (very badly) and rebuked any instrumentalist who made a slip during rehearsals—one of the first violins, for instance—by gently cajoling and calling him by his given name.

4.

-Now, come over here, Werner. There, that's good.

-What is it, Aunt?

- I've arranged an audition for you at the Conservatory in the capital. It will take place in two weeks. Just think—the Conservatory!

-Thank you, Aunt Roswitha.

-You understand, there's no guarantee you'll be accepted.

-Naturally.

-And I'm afraid the Committee can be expected to be especially hard on a boy with a name like Austecker.

-And why is that, endlessly generous Auntie?

-That'll do. You know perfectly well why.

-Yes, Aunt. Perfectly.

-Well then, I have a suggestion.

-How delightful.

-You *are* a rascal, Werner.

-Austecker, not Rascalnikov.

-Enough, you *enfant terrible*. Here's what I wish you to do. I want you to compose something for the audition.

-Won't there be required pieces?

-Oh, most likely, but it doesn't matter. I'm sure you can perform whatever pieces they want and also the new composition.

-Which has yet to exist. Well, what's my assignment? What am I to compose in two weeks?

-One week. You'll need a week for practice.

-Why not? A week, then.

-I've consulted a friend and he thought something to flatter the Committee wouldn't hurt.

-Flatter the Committee?

-That is to say, Prague.

-Oh, I'm to flatter the entire metropolis?

-He advised that you choose a theme from *Don Giovanni*. The Czechs still think of it as written expressly for them.

-*La ci darem la mano*? It's been done and done, Aunt. But still, I very much like the idea of writing some Mozart variations. What do you suppose your good friend would say to themes from K. 504?

-Stop teasing your old auntie. K. 504?

-K. 504 is Mozart's thirty-eighth symphony, called *The Prague*. First performed 19 January, 1787, conducted by the

Maestro himself. He and Prague were crazy about each other back in 1787. Peddlers in the streets whistled tunes from *Figaro*, fiddlers scraped them out in taverns; and that's why Mozart wrote for them this great and odd three-movement symphony. But there's a particular reason I'd like to try some variations on it.

-And what's that, you precocious monster?

-Well, Aunt, you see, Mozart thought along the same lines as your friend; I mean he wanted to cater to his audience. He inserted a theme from *Figaro* into the finale, *Aprile, presto aprile*, and, of course, he marked the whole movement *Presto*. Charming, no?

-*Oui, c'est charmant.* And?

-And so the crowd went wild, so wild that they compelled Mozart to stay and improvise at the piano for another hour— twice the length of the symphony, by the way.

-I see. You *are* clever.

-Clever perhaps, but sickly certainly. *Sollers Sed Infirmus* could be my motto.

-Nonsense. You are *not* sickly.

-My adorable, never-to-be-adequately-thanked Aunt, you don't really believe I'll see thirty, do you?

-Please don't talk that way, Werner.

-Very well. I'll go and write some variations instead. To the Bechstein with me.

I'm no Thucydides; still, I too may permit myself to invent what might have been, or ought to have been, said on a significant occasion. I do know that Austecker was granted an audition at the Conservatory at the age of fifteen, that he played a set of original variations and more than won over the professors in their pince-nez, trimmed beards, and stiff Czech collars.

"I thought of Mendelssohn," said one afterwards.

"Mendelssohn! A German—and a Jew to boot," retorted his colleague, thinking himself droll.

"Mendelssohn was a Lutheran!" came the indignant reply.

At the Conservatory, Austecker flourished; his brilliance was recognized, and yet he was not well liked by most of his peers and instructors. His ability set him apart, as did an intimidating penchant for sarcasm. Still, he made a few close friends and a larger number of admirers.

For a few years after leaving his lessons, Austecker lit up Prague's musical firmament. So as to miss nothing of his career, to be close to and protect him, to give him a place to live and work, Roswitha Heller leased a spacious apartment on Zborovska. In addition to *Apollo and Daphne* and popular recitals that included his *Novelleten* and *Ballades*, there were his *Bohemian Dances*—an homage both to Smetana's *Czech Dances* and Dvorak's *Slavonic*—with four astringent polkas, plus that lovely and piteous Polish mazurka, and the final, sardonic waltz which some took to be a sly comment on Vienna. It was a period of activity that was, in more than one sense, febrile. Early in 1909 Austecker began coughing up blood; the diagnosis was quickly made and, at Roswitha's insistence, twice confirmed.

-You see, Aunt?

-You're going to the Tatras. No arguments.

-Skiing?

-The Villa Dr. Sontich. It's in Novy Smokovec and I'm assured that it has an excellent reputation.

-For cures?

-Don't be flippant, Werner. They practice the climatic cure; there are sun-beds. You'll have good clean air, plain, wholesome food, and, above all, rest. Plenty of rest.

5.

The Villa Dr. Sontich was established in 1876 by a Czech physician of that name—one wonders, though, whether behind Sontich a Sonntag may be hiding. Two decades later the place had expanded to two dozen buildings in all, including twelve summer houses. One of these small lodges was specially winterized and fitted out with a spinet at the expense of Frau Heller. Here her nephew contemplated peaks and abysses, death and nature; and, if this confrontation did not alter him, it certainly transformed and deepened his music.

It was in the Tatra mountains in 1909 that Austecker composed the mighty symphony—Mahlerian in scope, Brucknerian in length—which he titled *Krank und Gesund.* "Far above the busy parts of the earth," he wrote to his aunt with an uncharacteristic absence of irony, "my senses are sharper and, in general, I've become more acutely conscious. I can see the voles moving in the high grass, hear pebbles tumbling from the ridges. I am able to make out every pore on little Fraulein Hausner's pretty face. Yesterday, I was sure I could distinguish one falling snowflake from another. Precious, no?"

The symphony is complex and inventive; Austecker yanks at the form as a child might taffy. It is in five huge movements and six different keys, major and minor—and often ambiguously either, both, or neither, as if to show that life is a jumble, that in dying there is living and vice versa. The orchestration requires automobile horns, cow bells, an electric motor, bird calls, twice the usual complement of double basses and four saxophones. There is a sequence in rag time. The *Andante* so slow and ravishing that one feels one is dying as one listens to it. The finale is joyful; audiences, having been through so much, eagerly assent to its happiness with palpable relief.

The demands this piece places on musicians are unrelenting, and not just on their skill, I can say first-hand, but on their souls as well. As for the conductor, well, he must obviously be in top form and indefatigable; but also he must understand Austecker, feel in sympathy with a genius dying young and so becoming old.

His aunt's announcement that she would be visiting him in the Tatras did not surprise Werner, nor the eagerness he felt to see her. But he was uncertain whether to tell her about the work he had been doing, hard and exhausting work. He had fibbed when he wrote her that he was doing no work whatsoever, only breathing deeply, eating heartily, reclining on his sun-bed, and, once in a while, amusing himself and his fellow patients with the spinet. He had also lied to her about getting better and rightly presumed that the doctors would do likewise.

Roswitha Heller pulled into the Villa like a freight train loaded with stern love.

-What have you been writing?

-Writing?

-I'm not yet the old fool I'll doubtless become, Werner.

-Very well, then. It's big. Enormous, actually. An elephant. A whale.

-You bad boy.

-Yes, that's just what I am, Aunt.

-And what is this Behemoth?

-A symphony. Can't imagine where I got the nerve, but then everybody up here gets light-headed.

-I know where you got the nerve.

-Shall I show it to you, the score? I'd play some but it really needs an orchestra. *Two* orchestras would be better.

-It's finished?

-It will be. Before I am, that is.

Roswitha resolved that her dying nephew's *chef d'oeuvre* would get the premiere it merited, that he deserved. He would hear it precisely as he imagined it, cow bells, electric motor, double basses and all. She would do whatever was necessary; she excelled at arranging things and spending money.

First she approached our orchestra manager, who was eager to please. Then she invited the two members of the board whom she knew best to tea at the Grand Hotel. It all turned out to be amazingly easy.

-A happy coincidence.

-Just what we've been looking for.

-Ah, but will Tomsa Prazak do it? Is he even up to it?

That was indeed a question. But the matter was placed before the conductor by the full Board in pretty stark terms: he could go on being a venerated conductor or he could be merely venerable. The orchestra needed a premiere; everyone was clamoring for something new. Frau Heller had undertaken to cover the cost of the extra musicians; she would even pay for advertising.

"It will be quite an event," said the Chairman of the Board from his wide English leather chair at the head of the table. He looked over at the Manager and grinned. "They may even raise their eyebrows in Paris. What do you say to that, Dusek?"

"A scandal wouldn't be an entirely bad thing," allowed the Manager.

The old conductor saw how things stood, so he also stood, nodded at the Board, ignored the Manager, and walked out of the office growling under his breath, "And how does one conduct an electric motor?"

6.

And so, we return to my visit to Frau Heller's villa in Karlsbad.

Werner Austecker was still high in the Tatras, worrying his aunt and pretending to obey his doctors, but would descend to our busy world for the premiere of *Krank und Gesund*, for which our orchestra was supposed to be preparing. I say "supposed" because Maestro Tomsa Prazak was not preparing us; in fact, just the opposite. For one thing, he canceled three rehearsals in a row, pleading illness. Worse still, he introduced major changes into the score, all of them to the bad. He speeded up the *Andante*, redesignated *piano* passages *forte* and vice versa; he altered rhythms and dynamics. Worst of all, he rewrote whole passages, substituting vulgar tunes in some and simply making a hash out of others. We sent the Concertmaster to question him on our behalf. Prazak was short with him, shamelessly insisting these were all last-minute emendations by the composer.

When informed of what was afoot, the Manager made light of it. All he wanted was the premiere of something new— and to him new did not mean original or daring, let alone sublime, only unfamiliar and strange. Dusek had the soul of an accountant and loved Strauss waltzes. "What do you want *me* to do about it?" he said in the best Pilate-manner.

So I wrote to Frau Heller who invited me to Karlsbad. She had left the apartment in Prague and returned there as soon as her nephew departed for the Tatras. I expect she was glad to get away from the hostile nationalists of Prague who sneered at her name and accent.

"And what measures do you propose?"

"There's the alternative of getting another conductor, of course," I said just so that she would have the opportunity to reply as she did.

"No. I don't want another conductor. No last-minute substitutes. Tomsa Prazak may be a bigot but his absence would diminish the importance of the premiere. What's more, he would then be free to ridicule my nephew, the symphony, and whoever replaced him at the podium."

"Just so," I said. "My idea is to let Prazak go on as he is doing."

"Undermining my nephew, you mean?"

"Precisely. However, with a little financial help from you, I believe we can defeat him. By 'we' I mean my colleagues who are as little pleased with Prazak's conduct as I am. Czechs and Germans alike."

"Go on, Rybar...or is it Fischer today?"

"We secretly rent a hall. We secretly rehearse. The Concertmaster can take charge, and certainly would for a small fee. The same for my colleagues, I'm sure. We could even manage without any conductor at all—that waving really is overrated. We have the original score copied, learn our parts thoroughly, and, on the night, we simply pay no attention to the old man. We ignore him. He could be conducting *The Moldau*."

Frau Heller regarded me almost with alarm, but only for a moment. Then she broke into a smile. "*Sehr gut*," she said decisively. "Can I trust you to handle the arrangements with your colleagues?"

"Yes."

"And the money as well?"

"If you like, Madam, but I think it would be best to arrange things through a reliable bank, one of those that are known for their discretion."

"A Jewish one?"

"Yes, that would be ideal."

7.

The look on Maestro Prazak's face the first time we musicians waved farewell to his conducting was worth the price of a ticket, though, unfortunately, it was the one thing the audience couldn't see. Even before the end of the opening movement he had gone from confusion to perplexity to fury. Acceptance, if that is what it was, at last arrived, fittingly, during the long-breathed Andante, where our bows moved at about half the velocity of his arms.

Werner Austecker was seated in the third row, off to the left, between his splendid aunt and a pretty girl, possibly Fraulein Hausner. Fresh from the mountains, he looked deceptively robust, with his suntanned face and bright eyes. Even his thinness suggested youthful elegance, not the withering away it really signified. Three times I saw his body convulse as he pressed a handkerchief to his mouth. After that, I stopped looking his way.

Prazak's wife Helene was in her usual box. I enjoyed looking up to see rapture on her face and pride in her husband's new progressivism.

Though I had been a member barely a decade, I doubt the Orchestra ever delivered a more remarkable performance than it did that night. Our secret night rehearsals, held in the gymnasium of the Makovica Academy, were long and full of contention. We felt the lack of the strong hand and iron will to which Prazak had accustomed us. The Concertmaster was a fine fellow but he hadn't the authority to keep us quiet and in line. Gradually, though, we adjusted to this new democracy and, in my opinion, benefited from it, hashing out together an interpretation of the composer's intentions, re-imagining what he heard up there in the high Tatras.

When the performance ended, we were exhausted and exhilarated, while Prazak appeared almost ghostly. But I should
give the old man his due; he played his part. He never stopped
waving his baton and, after the final crushing cadence, turned
to face the audience. As for them, the crowd remained silent
for a full half-minute. Imagine the awful weight of the silence
of a thousand overdressed, influential people, the suspense of
it. Then, as if at a sign from Roswitha Heller, the applause
began to roll forth, then cheers, the rising din breaking like a
thunderstorm over Novy Smokovec.

What then? I was summoned to a last tête-à-tête in
Karlsbad during which Frau Heller pressed on me her grati-
tude and a munificent check.

Her nephew lived to see 1911, but only just. He worked
until the end, producing the settings of Chinese poems for
baritone and orchestra he called *Hsi-Wei's Skull* and the frequently performed *Suite for Two Pianos,* a piece that always
makes me think of a pair of cavorting lion cubs, full of the joy
of their new lives. Austecker died at twenty-six.

As for Tomsa Prazak, his waning and parochial career re-
vived when he received the two unprecedented invitations, first
from Vienna and then Berlin. They wanted him to conduct
Austecker's *Krank und Gesund.*

Crazy About Her

Only after appropriating a chair from the adjacent table and shoving it between two of theirs did I ask with an insouciant grin, "May I join you?"

Of course I chose to set the chair directly across from her. She looked wonderful after two years, especially if you subtracted the shock and horror from her face. There she was, all grown up with earrings and a Tribeca haircut. I suppose I was shocked too just from seeing her only four feet away. My hand trembled with the old magnetism, and there was the familiar weakness behind my knees. I coolly watched the horror leach below her features and tried to appraise my emotional state. I felt a number of things and one of them was intimidated. It wasn't just the blouse and the black business-suit. Her beauty had always cowed me a little—now, it seemed, just a little more. I wanted to cry all over her but I sat on my feelings; I shored up my tottering self-possession. She was happy here among her crowd, I thought, but so far as I could see not intimately attached to any of them. I had looked hard before I leapt, searching for signs while I crouched in the restaurant's shadows, waiting to make my move, wondering if I'd really do it.

They all gaped at me, five swans interrupted by a warthog. "Oh," I explained breezily, inching my chair forward, establishing at once my territory and *bona fides*, "Phil didn't tell you I'd be joining you?"

She frowned down at her plate as if at a chessboard on which I'd just made a stupid move.

I turned my gaze on one after the another, spread my elbows, and screwed up my face as if just noticing something. "Where *is* Phil?"

Two of the men had sandy hair. "Oh, Phil," piped up one of them, making a dismissive gesture with his left hand. He held a wine glass in the other. The beer and wine bottles on the table made a crowded little skyline.

"Phil?" he said.

"Yep. Phil. I mean he *said* he'd meet me here."

"I thought Phil turned us down," said the man sitting to her left. He had dark hair and a ridiculous brown mustache that looked as if it had been grown expressly for the occasion. He rubbed at it.

"Phil?" he mumbled dully. "Lucky bastard."

"Phil's not here," said the other woman. She had short hair, an extremely low neckline, and regarded me with suspicion. "Why would Phil be here when he said he wouldn't? Why would he tell you to meet him here?"

"Oh, you know Phil," I said airily. "Of course you do. He works—worked—with you. He said you'd all be celebrating. That the right word? *Le mot juste?*"

"We don't all know Phil," said the second sandy-haired plutocrat. I could picture him playing lacrosse a few years back. He was seated on my right, elbow-to-elbow. He looked down his nose at me and his nose was as short and straight as the barrel of a .38.

"*You* know Phil," I said to her, endeavoring not to sound menacing, more or less.

Nobody asked me to leave. The ghost of Phil hovered over the alcoholic cityscape, vouching for my presence. The mustache passed me a wine bottle and an empty water glass. I looked around at the five of them, the Yuppie unemployed. They didn't appear to mind losing their jobs. They looked like they expected new and better ones.

Mammon takes care of his own.

I was locked up for eleven days during my senior year. During this time I thought about Phil once or twice. It made a change. Mostly, of course, my thoughts dwelt on her and what I so desperately needed to explain to her for which exclusive preoccupation, for a devotion everybody deemed to have made me dangerous, I was locked up. Eleven days isn't all that long but at the time I had no way of knowing it wouldn't be for the rest of my life. Release came with the proviso of a restraining order which I thought ludicrous and instantly plotted to violate. I was certain that if only I could explain everything would be fine, would in fact be glorious. But I didn't violate the order. Why not? Because, after all, I wasn't mad. Instead of committing a crime, I completed my senior thesis and even graduated with, so to speak, honors.

But, as I say, I did think about Phil a couple of times in the lockup. Phil knew us both. Phil was well disposed. It was Phil who had introduced us, a deliberate act which carries some responsibility.

Like most people at the end of their second decade on the planet I was accustomed to think of myself as normal. Abnormality could be defined by the degree to which ways of thinking, saying, doing, feeling, tastes and opinions departed from my own. I had the conviction of being the point of the compass, the Golden Mean. But this illusion, arrogant in its self-assertion yet humble in its avowal of mediocrity, was impossible to hold on to in a locked ward with deranged neighbors, bad food, suspicious doctors, and orderlies who looked like sanitized bouncers. So, Phil displaced me and became my new emblem of the normal, the stolid commonplace, for being what Flaubert called *dans le vrai*. Phil knew what he was after: a business degree, a remunerative job, a plasma TV, championships for the Mets, Islanders, and Jets. It was fine with him if the nation tried to be better than it was but he was sure that none was better even as it was. Social justice did not consume him. His thought went no deeper than required. His hair was not too long or too short, his wardrobe and tastes in reading conventional. He made friends, not just contacts, laughed readily and in a way that made you think the world couldn't really be going to hell. Though on the fringe of my own irregular circle, the coterie of a loner, Phil knew both me and her, yet he didn't know much. Phil was a walking, talking *via media*, solid as oak. Phil was the kind of guy who would listen to you whine and then, if you asked, lend you twenty bucks.

I hadn't thought about Phil for two years. I knew that after graduation he went to Wall Street. It was when I read about the spectacular overnight collapse of the firm that had taken her on right out of school that it occurred to me good old clubbable Phil worked there too. An old synapse, I suppose, undecayed. Google confirmed my hunch. Phil worked in a different division from her—the "good" one that was snapped up like Ishmael while the rest of the place sank like the *Pequod* with almost all hands.

I sent Phil an email. He replied to me at once. He was courteous, said he was glad to hear from me, hoped I was doing well; he managed to be distant and friendly at once. I wrote back, pressed him about his place of employment, dropped her name, asked about her division and its fate. He knew all about it and it must have been irresistible to tell me. "They're mostly taking the debacle pretty well," he wrote. "In fact, some of them are having a sort of Last Supper party this weekend. I'm pretty sure your old squeeze is one of them. A friend of mine asked me to join but I turned him down, of course; under the circumstances it'd be pretty awkward." He even gave me the time and the name of the restaurant, did dear old normal Phil.

The first poem I wrote for her was called "The Lover Triumphs Though the Poet Fails," which title is a little poem in itself though it now reads like I was angling for a compliment. It never occurred to me that my ardent little tribute in verse might alarm her. On the contrary, I imagined she would admire it and warm to me. I was naïve; I was romantic; I was, above all, twenty. Now I'm three and twenty and know that poetry's no proof of love's reliability or a lover's sincerity, rather of the poet's vanity. And the better the poem the more suspect it is. Probably she sees it that way but I don't know for sure. You can't be a romantic unless you find women mysterious.

Here's the demi-sonnet I wrote to her two days after we met in the Food Court where Phil introduced us. She was wearing shorts and a tank-top and I presumed a good deal:

I miss you with my stomach and my nose.
Your body is no metaphor to me.
Your hair smells as it smells. I disdain those
vainglorious tropes that would betray your
rare torso, the uniqueness of your toes.

I miss you with my ears and with my nails.
The lover triumphs, though the poem fails.

The poem fails, the poet fails, and the lover failed worst of all. And it was his fault, his folly. Mine, that is.

"And what do you do?"

It was my impression that the short-haired woman cared for me even less than the Hitler Youths. Perhaps she knew exactly who I was; maybe she'd been told the whole awful tale. They couldn't have talked shop all the time; besides, I suspect women like to share biographies with each other, mostly, I think, their histories with men. "Here's what they did to *me*. . ." I suppose exchanging confidences about the intermittent truces reminds them of their alliance in the perpetual war.

If she had told what would it have sounded like? A passing anecdote, a tale of gothic trauma? Well, probably not a diaphanous lyric of regret. Had I been reduced to a little glob of rue, like getting a C on a freshman paper?

And what do you do? That *And* was certainly hostile. *What* held a least half a pound of contempt while the double *do* made it sound as if whatever I did I might as well not have. I would have liked to reply to one ill-willed query with another: "Why are you so proud of your boobs?" But I had to be charming, had to beguile the blond, the stacked, the mustachioed. *A soft answer turneth away wrath*, I reminded myself. *Sufficient unto the day is the evil thereof.*

And what do you do? W. H. Auden wrote that, after answering that question with "I'm a poet," he resolved thereafter to say "medieval historian."

I smiled. "I'm a medieval historian."

Her eyebrows leapt up; her face shot forward; her hair remained short. Auden had pretty much guaranteed that "medieval historian" would put an end to any further discussion, said it had won him hours of undisturbed quiet in railway compartments. I wasn't so lucky.

"Medieval historian, eh? Well, I think the Middle Ages were just a—well, just one big *mistake*? Don't you?"

I chuckled, the agreeable lad, the clawless academic. "Excellent," I burbled with effervescent donnish appreciation. "You've summed them up admirably."

"What about the cathedrals?" chimed in the mustache, defending nine centuries. "And the *fairy* tales?"

"And what about the *universities*?" added the Aryan to my left.

Was there really going to be a debate? Would I have to participate or even mediate?

Through all this she said nothing. She stayed mute, *tacit in ecclesia*. Her face wasn't defiant, wasn't angry; it was as blank as fresh vellum in a scriptorium. I could write on it whatever I wanted.

"So, tell us something about the Middle Ages," challenged the drunken, suspicious woman, the sidekick. *Papieren*, demanded the faces of the Aryans.

"Well, let's see," I said. "Do you know how the universities got started?"

"Everybody spoke Latin," observed the mustache.

"No women allowed," said short-hair.

"True, true. But here's how it all began. For a blessed time in the twelfth century, in Toledo, in Moorish Spain, Christian, Jewish, and Muslim scholars gathered for what came to be called '*disputatios*.' These men exchanged ideas and manuscripts instead of blows and pogroms. Their excitement must have been boundless. Such delight to find one another, to live the life of the mind, free from religion. Aristotle's *Politics* and *Organon*. Plato and Homer, Pliny and Plutarch. Pure joy! Then the Fundamentalists rode into town and wagged their scimitars. So the infidels fled, bearing away all the books they could. They ran to Italy where they tried to continue the fun. In Bologna the foreign students organized a union to negotiate with their landladies. The word for union in those days was '*universitas*.' And that was the first university, Bologna's exotic boarders. The second one popped up down the road in Padua where the teachers organized to bargain with their students, who hired and fired them. They invented the degree so that they'd have the power to withhold it, I suppose. The *licentia docenti*, the license to teach. So these early universities, like the early Church, were gaggles of people, not bunches of buildings. As you say, they all spoke Latin so when they ran into trouble they could just move along and set up in another town—Paris, Oxford, Prague, Wittenberg. And the towns saw that it was good and welcomed them, good for business, good for prestige. And so the universities spread abroad like dandelions or cancer."

"Really?" said the mustache deep in his cups.

"*Gaudeamus igitur*," I said, raising my cup, raising it to her.

What the doctor ought to have said:

"Obsession with her is obsession with yourself. What you call love for her is loving yourself. This city in which you think you live alongside her is a city of one, not even two, let alone thousands. Thoughtlessness and lack of imagination are antithetical to love, not its natural consequences, imbecile. Your tantrums are infantile; your threats are tyrannical, so much pounding on a podium. You look at the world through a prism that distorts everything; and, since it's made of crystal, you think it isn't there. You don't believe me, do you? Privileged and pampered is what you are. Soiled and spoiled. Egotistical and conceited. You don't want to learn anything; above all, you don't want to be *taught*. You prefer a name to cling to, an exculpatory phrase, some get-out-of-jail word. You're a medieval realist when by now reality should have taught you some hard-headed nominalism. I mean that you make objects out of words, and call it poetry, worse yet. You're sitting there now thinking about how all this will someday spice up your precious biography, as if madness were just a sexy handmaiden to the grand queen of your fame. Listen up: love's the digging, kid, not the potato. It's a verb you've turned into a noun. You think if you can just clutch this potato you'll prove you know how to plant and sow and reap. You're not just full of yourself; you're full of shit which, like a two-year-old, you smear on the wall for people to admire. You think sickness made you do what you did whereas the truth is exactly the opposite. You say you need to explain yourself to her, that your words have the power to restore what your words exploded. I need. *I* need. Do you even hear yourself?"

What the doctor actually said:

Borderline personality disorder with suicidal ideation.

All right, I thought. John Berryman did some suicidal ideating while leaning over the Washington Avenue Bridge. Hart Crane indulged in it leaning over the Gulf of Mexico. Delmore Schwartz must have practiced it often while squirreled away in the Hotel Marlon. And didn't they all live on borderlines?

The men had ordered after-dinner drinks, brandies, and these they sipped. As I watched them all, my mind stepped outside the restaurant for a moment for a smoke. I imagined Manhattan lit as dimly as eternity; I thought of it marching on like a maimed man who has yet to notice his wound. Flattened markets, defunct firms, exploded scams, bled-dry accounts of desperate debtors, hopeless creditors—all the detritus of avarice discreetly covered by a warm nighttime rain streaming up from Uncle Remus' Southland. In lofts and apartment blocks, penthouses and suburbs, the scared parents hunkered down with their fear, whiskey and pills, every one both a protagonist and a critic.

Wouldn't she even acknowledge me? Didn't the others notice her silence?

Madness is thinking too much on one thing, sweeping away everything else right to the horizon. It's being lost in some process and oblivious of its consequences. Madness is a grossly mistaken exegesis of the world's crabbed text. It's inching a bit too far out on a limb or forgetting you're in a cell called madness. Madness can seem relative to the sane and absolute to the mad, or vice versa. The poet's madness is to believe that much madness is divinest sense.

Our four-month romance came to an end, I thought, when I ended it, I thought. I was jealous. I blew up at her. My words carried axes and assault rifles. My anger turned into a hurricane that sucked power from the humid ocean of my madness. I smashed a chair into a wall and called her terrible names, the very worst I could think of. Indignant, self-righteous, blind, I stomped out, sick at heart, certain that the original sin had been committed against me. It was late. The campus was suffused in an infernal infra-red glow that only I could see. She had covered her face with her hands, like a boxer in the corner protecting herself, then she'd pulled her knees up, clasping her legs with her arms, making herself as small a target as possible.

I only stuck it out that last month because I was afraid. I was afraid you'd hurt me or yourself. I didn't know what to do. Leave me alone. Her last email.

One tortured night a week later I saw my colossal error. Bereft, but certain I could retrieve what I'd thrown away, I raced to her room. It was three a.m., which Fitzgerald says it always is in the dark night of the soul. The door was locked. "Go away," said her frightened roommate.

I beat at the door, raved like a senile king on a heath, importuned, supplicated, abased myself heroically, shot words like battering rams from my almost-frothing mouth. I threatened.

"Go away or I'll call the police," yelled the terrified roommate, a nice Midwesterner majoring in physical therapy, a person who looked at you like an open-faced sandwich.

I persisted in shouting my incoherent epic, my philippic, my jeremiad none of which was intelligible, except for the rage.

Then the police came. Then the hospital, the doctors, the restraints, the therapeutic conversations, at last the restraining order.

I wanted to become a Buddhist overnight. I read Watts and Suzuki. I yearned for calm, *satori*. That too was vanity, of course. For me yang never would fit into yin and life could not go on without desire and suffering. For me, they *were* life. I knew my poems would never please anyone alive, only, perhaps, misfits yet to be born.

They let me out. I finished my dreary senior thesis, got my degree, didn't see her, which was indescribably hard. Two hundred yards is very far, even if years of midnight reading haven't made you myopic.

Then, filled with my defeat, I went home, moved into the basement, got used to the looks my parents exchanged. When I screamed in the night I imagined them shutting their eyes and putting their hands over their ears. Their only child was screaming with trills and flourishes and they didn't know what to make of it or how to cope. I got a job at a hotel—front desk—and quit after two days. I got another in an insurance office and was fired after three weeks which was better because I could collect unemployment. In the afternoons I played ferocious playground basketball. I read the wretched prose of *The Self-Blocking Self* fourteen times and for a while I even mouthed its muddy jargon. I, who worshipped Yeats. I watched the rich passing in their land yachts and honed a peasant's resentment, conjuring up apocalyptic snapshots of collapse and slaughter. But every night I dreamed of her. I childishly nicknamed her Ms. Dow Jones.

I went back to writing poems, one after another. Even as I scribbled I knew this was the basest kind of self-expression, mere vomiting, Pollack poems, dripped all over the page. Fame is the spur. I bought stamps and envelopes and sent them out to journals. One poem was actually published. But I took no satisfaction in it because it was the only one I hadn't written as myself. I composed it by pretending to be an old man who had negotiated his terms with life, so beaten down that he could put the contract into resigned meter and sentimental rhyme. It too was about her, of course; but just this once my device was to include her as an absence. I wanted it to appear to be about brushing teeth, the evening news, lunch. I wanted to shade in everything that wasn't her, by indirect communication filling in the doughnut around the hole. I called it, misleadingly, "One Consolation."

As we grow older so the world grows
ever more complex, more forgetful too,

135

as if wisdom and ignorance joined hands,
pressed cheeks, and staggered through a clumsy dance
to time's quick jigs and long sarabandes.
Life's banal days and undistinguished nights
must not be despised since they're all we can
return to from our odysseys, our flights
through the remote latitudes of our dreams.
Though quotidian tunes weary my ears
with routine rhythms punctuating years,
such music may be sweeter than it seems.

I'd gotten down to just the single first-person pronoun.
That's one consolation.

"For God's sake, he's not a medieval historian," she said suddenly, exasperated.

I went stiff and stared across at her, furious with love. At last, at least she'd said something, albeit she hadn't said it to me.

"Tell me," I said softly, "I was the reason you switched your major from English to management, right?"

I'm not sure she heard me but she threw up one arm and looked away.

The others were making confused noises, the way people do when everything changes unexpectedly, when the train that seemed to be moving turns out to be still. Somebody knocked over a wine bottle.

"So what *is* he?"

She didn't move. No doubt she was pondering many possible answers, none of which was likely to do me credit. Then she chose. "He's a poet," she said.

"A *what*? A *poet*?"

One of the blonds gave out with a trust-fund guffaw.

"Go away," she mouthed at me, dry-eyed, not for the first time.

The others addressed her, not me. I'd become an object.

"Come on, what is this jerk *really*? A stalker?"

"We could take him out in the alley for you."

"The alley, hell. We could beat the crap out of him right here."

"A *poet*? Jesus Christ."

The mustache looked over at me. "Give us a poem, then. Recite one of your poems or we'll kick your ass right here."

I half-stood. "I'm sorry," I said to her, all my painstakingly studied eloquence gone. "I'm *sorry*."

"Come on, a poem, a poem *or else*. There once was a man from Peru."

I pushed the chair back and rose to my full height. I looked down on these oligarchs demanding their post-prandial hexameters. "You want a poem? Fine. I'll give you one for the planet I'm ashamed to share with you. I wrote it expressly for you, anyway."

One of them clinked his wineglass with a knife. "Go on, then."

She preferred looking at the table to looking at me.

"What the hell's it called? What's the title, Shakespeare?" People were turning in their chairs. The maitre d' took a few steps our way. My hands shook but my voice came out firm, too loud.

"It's called 'Post-Industrial Screed Number 1473.'"

General laughter.

"Wow," said short-hair. "Number 1473!"

They scoffed, all the temporarily unberthed who had despoiled others of their jobs, houses, made bitter their old age.

My delivery began slowly then accelerated, gathering momentum like a fugue, a roller-coaster about to jump the tracks. What I didn't remember I made up on the spot.

> Out there in California the hour's
> earlier and so is the weather; or
> rather, the sun moves west, the wind east; that
> is, the winds move, the earth moves, but the sun
> doesn't budge at all; I mean, the sun does
> move but not the way we used to think and
> go on thinking because Copernicus
> contradicted not just Aristotle,
> Ptolemy, and His Holiness but common sense
> which is why he published posthumously
> showing both prudence and humility. Not very
> many like Copernicus, are there; that is
> to say, who go over easy on the ego
> not sunny side up as on the West Coast
> of the Disneyfied imagination
> or in Greenwich made of greenbacks,
> landscaping and ersatz aristocracy
> where it's me and you (admiring me) by
> the pool, at the party, at the fund-raiser . . .

By now hands were grabbing at me; I could hear the grunts in my ear but not the words, being too intent on my own.

> . . . padding off to bed with a lonely spouse,
> an aromatic starlet, a nice firm hunk,
> effervescent comedienne, threesomes and

foursomes and power lunches, paparazzi,
papaya bean curd salads, distanced from
the latest race riot, expiring addict,
raped runaway all these being the salt of
the bland yet fecund earth. Do you hear
America singing the body electric? The
same low down number on ten million
stereos, Nebraska, Alabama, Illinois,
Rhode Island, the last being our standard
of smallness except when some portentous
iceberg slides off Antarctica (same
song, different sun, variable winds). The
brains of the outfit puts his feet up
in his corner office hatching conspiracy
theories which is the conspiracy whilst
far below the put-up feet and busy brains
the parking garage fills with SUV and
Mercedes Benz, for you are not just what you
gobble up but what you drive what you buy no
less than what you sell, even if it's your
own pate on the block, branded like beef on
the hoof, like those handfed Japanese steers
massaged thrice daily by virgin geishas
right down the road from the Lexus factory
to whom being slaughtered seems a fair
enough price. Furthermore, going further
and always wanting more, discreet Cape Cods
steroided to MacMansions with four-car garages
plus one truck, deep freezes like family crypts,

Rhode-Island sized TVs, inert treadmills,
mammoth ranges, centrally air-conditioned
to a temperate turn where white microwaves
silently pulse and the dubiously processed
floodlit food rotates like the earth while the
sun stands still yet rushes to not even
Mikolaj Kopernik himself knows where.

I was dragged away long before I finished. Her hands covered her face. Her shoulders rose and fell.

The earth is the center only of itself. Same for me.

When they twisted me through the tables, the falling chairs, the trays, I was still reciting, at least in my head. "I'm sorry," I screamed back from the heavy doors. And then there was a shove and my borderline personality tumbled onto the wet pavement of the broken city.

Terminus ad Quem

Three weeks ago I graduated from the University of Pennsylvania Law School. A month before that I learned that I had secured one of the most sought-after and worst-paying of placements, a berth in the United States Department of Justice. I've found a small apartment not quite in Georgetown and here I am waiting to take up my post as a public servant, scouting out the grocery stores and pizzerias. My girlfriend—quondam girlfriend? ex-girlfriend?—graduated with me, side-by-side so to speak, and now Monica Goodman is in Oregon, answering the call of environment law. In fact, she's already enmeshed in her first case, part of the team, something to do with salmon, erosion, fertilizers. "It's unbelievably complicated," she bragged to me breathlessly, "and already in its third year."

My parents separated when I was eleven, divorced when I was twelve. It was a fairly bad time, in all the customary ways. But my older sister Denise was a brick—she still is, too—and took me on her back, showed me how to behave, how to take it, how not to be consumed or self-centered. Mother was a brick too, only a slightly more crumbly one. Like a good Roman Senator, she did everything she could to maintain the status-quo, as if, after the one big change, any small ones might prove lethal. So it was the females who pulled me through. As for my father, he behaved well, comparatively: he stayed in all our lives albeit in a peripheral capacity and if you were wearing blinders you might miss him; he was never mean about money, custody, or vacations. We were his first marriage. The second lasted a quarter as long, the third about half as long as that, neither eventuating in any offspring ("to contest the will," Denise joked in a rare, endearing moment of wickedness). After the third wife, a horsewoman, he gave up, apparently. Now he lives alone in a vast four-bedroom argosy on the Upper East Side, hard by the museums whose curators would salivate at the stuff on his walls.

As such parochial celebrity goes my father is famous in the profession which is now mine as well. I have, of course, thought a good deal about this and I'm convinced it really isn't a case of wanting to put my little feet where his big ones have trod, much less to launch a postponed Oedipal contest. I'd have become a lawyer even if my father were an anesthesiologist or a fireman. It almost goes without saying that I'm the only one who believes this.

There are plenty of smart lawyers, even a surplus of them. But my father is also honest, well connected, and wise, the kind of counselor with lots of bottom on whom powerful people in difficulties like not just to call but to depend. I happen to know he could have had a seat on a high bench three times over if he'd given the nod. Of course he never mentioned this to me. It would be bragging but also letting me too far inside. Dad's a nice, imposing door that's seldom even ajar.

I'm close to my mother and Denise—something on which Monica once commented ambiguously—but my relations with my father resemble those between, say, France and Korea or Argentina and Finland. We have no history of serious conflict, no common borders—we've never discussed the Law—our interactions are infrequent, polite, and there's good will on both sides, or at least not a bad one. Would forested, frigid Finland discuss its internal affairs with hot-blooded, steak-chomping Argentina? Still, I've read that Finns adore the tango. You never know when an affinity may leap up and grab you or when a stuck door may suddenly fly open.

My father traveled down to Philly for my graduation; he even sat with his first wife, his daughter and son-in-law, one more person who believed I was becoming a lawyer because he was one. He also assumed I'd applied to the Justice Department because of the sort of work he'd done when he was starting out, and still does, I suppose, though in loftier and less official zones. He said as much when he phoned to let me know he'd be there. "I can't tell you how it makes me feel. It's really a nice surprise." Nice surprise? Did he mean that I'd bowled him over or that what surprised him was how my choice made him feel? Good? Proud? Either way he sounded so gratified that I dispensed with the usual disclaimer. Why not? He'd been generous in his fashion, so could I.

He wanted to take me out for a big dinner, just the two of us, and spent an extra night in town to do so, waiting for the others to leave. I wouldn't be off for another three days and I knew the food would be free and fabulous so I said, "Wonderful" and he said, "Bookbinders—the original one, not that new one. It's still here?" That he thought I'd know was amusing.

Bookbinders, the olde original near the Delaware, dark wood, thick carpets, businessmen, tourists, a huge menu and a thick wine list. To go through the latter my father put on a pair of those half-spectacles which made him look owlish, a soupcon of Ben Franklin. He ordered not one but *two* bottles of something which turned out to be white, French, and lip-smacking good. *Larmes de Tristesse*, said the fancy label, put in the bottle in the chateau, it assured the anxious. There was a line drawing of the castle and I made a joke about the weeping oenologists of Burgundy, tossed in the oubliette by a jealous Duke. This was Argentina tangoing, trying to get a rise out of Finland.

We both had snapper soup. He ordered a boiled lobster; I asked for scallops.

After that we drank and ate and not much was said.

Then, suddenly, "You don't think I got a call from Justice, do you—because I *didn't*. And I didn't call *them* either. Just wanted you to know."

I shrugged. "I didn't tell you I'd applied. They don't know I'm your son."

"Right," he said, cracking open a claw. He was working hard in his lobster bib, smeared with lemon butter, which made him look like a big, dignified baby.

More eating. Then, "Where's your girlfriend?"

"Monica?"

He'd met her once, when we'd gone for a weekend in New York. He took us in a cab to a steakhouse in Brooklyn and presented us with tickets to *La Bohème*.

"Yeah. Monica."

"Packing for Oregon." I checked my watch. "Nope. On her way."

"Oregon?"

I explained while my father polished off his bottle of wine and poured himself a glass from mine.

When I'd finished the short tale of Monica following her vocation rather than me, delivered without a trace of resentment or male chauvinism, he asked, "So, it's over between you?"

"I think we both accepted that it was temporary—you know, until graduation. It might have gone differently, I suppose, but it didn't."

I don't think I'd ever heard my father sigh before and it was memorable, the loud, sincere exhalation of a pachyderm.

Did he ever say "I love you" to me? Did he ever just grab and hug me? Not that I can recall. I think paternal love was for him a kind of stipulation between the parties, agreed on at the outset and requiring no subsequent mention. While it may have been the root, impetus, and *primum mobile* of all that followed, it tended to disappear under the horizon, like Aristotle's God. You know it's there but a little proof wouldn't hurt. My father's sigh was something; still, I found the preposition elusive: had he sighed *at* me, *to* me, *with* me, *for* me—despite me?

I asked him straight out, "Why the big sigh?"

He curled his lip in a buttery smile, as if about to tell a dirty joke, then his face grew serious; it clouded over.

"What is it?" I said with real concern, putting down my wineglass.

"Later," he promised. "With the coffee."

And so I had to wait for the clearing away, the ordering and serving of dessert, then the coffee. I liked that when I asked for chocolate mousse he said, "Me too," like a child.

He stared down at the surface tension on his coffee and not at me, his hands toying delicately with a spoon as though it were a key he'd remembered but had forgotten the lock.

Lawyers of his caliber speak only when they're prepared to do so. I knew better than to prompt him.

"They have a phrase down south, *the same as no difference at all*. Well, when I was your age—or the same as no difference at all—just out of law school like you, I went to work down there, in the South. You know that. Funny thing, I hear it called the Civil Rights Era and sometimes it sounds pompous and sometimes rueful and sometimes all wrong and sometimes just right. . . .We were a band of youngsters, exactly what the

government wanted—idealistic wise-asses, acid to the segrega-
tionists' base, brand-new knives just hankering to get at something that badly needed stabbing. But you know the kind of
work we did, probably even how dangerous it was."

That work was legendary, so the implied question was
rhetorical and I waited in the Bookbinder hush.

"It was a hothouse atmosphere. Maybe you can imagine.
There were three young women among us. We felt protective
of them, worried over them, even though they were all reading
Betty Friedan. Couples formed. You know. Danger, intensity,
the common cause, the absence of air-conditioning, youth—it
was inevitable."

"You—?"

His look silenced me. This was to be a monologue, a lecture, momentous and unprecedented, delivered by a father to
a son he supposed was like himself—or at least the same as no
difference at all.

"We were lawyers in love with the Law; justice was in our
titles and our blood." He indicated his empty wineglass. "We
were a little inebriated with it but not so naïve that we didn't
know we were . . . ." He looked up at me almost defiantly.
"She was beautiful, just a beautiful person. And a firebrand.
Burning, brilliant. But, as I say, we were lawyers and we knew
we were on an adventure, a crusade, that it was all real enough
but at the same time not real at all, not real the way our lives
would eventually be. Afterwards. So everything was provisional, we thought. And that's why we made the contract, she
and I. We would be lovers until it was over, until we left the
South. That way there'd be no recriminations, no hurt feelings,
no confusion. We thought it would free us and it did. We were
as passionate as we could be and maybe it was because we knew
it was temporary so there was no point in holding anything

back, in *pacing ourselves*. I wanted to be with her every minute. I'd find opportunities to brush by her, smell her hair . . . . It was like that," he said slowly and so sadly I guessed at the unstated corollary: *and it was never like that again.*

He fetched up another elephantine groan. "And when it was finally over, when we were pulling up stakes, I waited for her to say something about our agreement, our commitment not to make a commitment, the contract we'd signed before hopping into bed. But she was obviously detaching herself and, though I waited and even hoped, I followed suit, couldn't bring myself even to mention it. Why? I was too in love to risk it. I know that doesn't sound sensible, but that's how it was. I didn't want to spoil things and have her throw the contract in my face and, well, maybe I thought too that this *wasn't* real life and didn't have the balls to put it to the test."

I sat still, in case there was going to be more.

He looked at me sheepishly, one more unprecedented expression. "Any questions?"

"A few," I said.

"Okay. Shoot."

"Did this have anything to do with the three marriages?"

He gulped some water. "Probably," he allowed and I could see it was hard for him.

"Did you ever see her again?"

"Once."

Now that he'd gotten it all out, his gasp of romanticism, he'd turned monosyllabic.

"And?"

"We met a dozen years ago." He looked around. "A place like this."

I calculated. He had just left my mother twelve years ago. "And so?"

"Married. Happily, I think. Two daughters. Stopped practicing after the second was born." He couldn't even bear to incarnate her as a pronoun.

I pushed. "And?"

"And she told me the terrible thing I wanted to hear and didn't want to hear. That she'd been waiting for *me* to say something. That's all."

"So you kept—what?—trying?"

"Not any more," said my father in his brusque court voice, and called for the check.

Maybe my father never became a judge because he didn't trust his own judgment. He had reason not to. I don't doubt he told me about his mistake because, in the way of parents—perhaps especially distant ones—he thought I was repeating it, just as it pleased him to believe I'd become a Justice Department lawyer because that's how he'd started out. I have to ask myself if he was entirely wrong, if it is in some measure true that I'm trying to please or outstrip him, and I'm just refusing to admit it. I have also to block my resentment of him, my exasperation with his presumption—an arrogant one, to me—that his past explains my present, predicts my future. Undeniably, though, Finland has tangoed for Argentina, given it a glimpse into its deep lakes and fjords, and as a consequence their relations may grow warmer, more intimate.

So here I sit, near Georgetown, future about to begin, past just ended, and I'm nearly certain that no, this story isn't about me, not in the least, not at all about my romance or my unhappiness or why I'm alone.

Pornstar/Daredevil

She's walking briskly through an airport, pulling a wheeled suitcase. It's green. She's got on tight jeans and a tight turtleneck under a short leather jacket. Her blond hair's down. She's bouncy; that is, her hair bounces as she walks and so do her breasts. She nears a gaggle of college boys—four of them, jocks dressed for Spring Break in t-shirts and cut-offs. Mentally and morally, they're already in Cancun. "Jesus," one of them exclaims, grabbing the arms of the two on either side of him. "What the . . ?" They all look where he's looking. At her. "Damn," says one. "Is it? No shit?" "Swear it is." "Fuck. *Severine*." "Yep, in the fucking flesh." "Come on." "Quick, dog. Move it." They toss their backpacks over their shoulders and rush toward her. The backpacks make them look like schoolboys, but also soldiers. They surround her, blocking her way. She looks from one to the other, more irked than scared, annoyed rather than intimidated.

"Remember your Aristotle? It's improbable."
"No, it's not. It could happen. In fact, it establishes—"
"Let's see. You told me she'd only done porn for a year and it's now—what did you say?—five, *six* years later? How are four post-adolescents in an airport going to recognize her, especially if she's got clothes on?"

"They *might*, if she's a particular favorite of theirs and hasn't changed much, which she hasn't because she only did it for a year and so didn't turn too hard or burnt-out. And the pictures and films are still on the Web, remember. This is the woman they've studied night after night, the face and body that filled their filthy dreams."

"Oh, go on."

They hassle her. Individually, they might not behave like such jerks, but there are four of them and they're on Spring Break and so they're all over her—celebrity-worship and sexual harassment all mixed up. They can't believe their eyes, their luck. They all remember the way she moaned and the positions she got into. Only eighteen, barely legal, just the right mix of innocent and depraved. This really is the girl of their dreams, their private sexual mascot, the whore who performs on demand for everybody with broadband. Millions have masturbated staring pop-eyed at that torso, those boobs, and, now that they see her, can actually *touch* her if they dare, the thought of the million onanists who *aren't* them makes them angry; it feels like a betrayal of their having fallen in love with her, in the crudest sense, and they turn into these pipsqueak Othellos.

Get the idea? Things like this would have happened to her before. She denies, affects surprise, looks everything but terrified and this is just what convinces the boys that she's really *their* Severine. They press closer; one grabs his crotch. We can take it just so far. But she has to be at least a *little* scared, I think. You agree? These jocks are big boys and even if it's a public place, she's bound to feel threatened. Who knows what they might do? She'd tell them to leave her alone, that she's trying to make a connecting flight. The tension rises. The bouncy music turns to the minor, comes in stabs. . . . And *that's* when *he* shows up and, well, *rescues* her. Yes?

According to Robert's wife Ceci, the reason she wasn't jealous was that Robert and Imogen had met, been to bed, lived together for three months, and decided to keep their collaboration professional—all before he met and married her. Ceci actually explained this to Imogen the first time they met, about a year earlier.

"I feel we should get this straight right away. The way I see it, any sexual tension between you and Robert went poof two years ago. He's been entirely open. He told me the two of you gave it a shot as lovers but it didn't work out. So the way I see it I've got nothing to worry about—at least from *you*. No reason we can't be friends, is there?"

Ceci's little speech made Imogen feel discarded, relegated, small. In fact, Robert had suggested the break-up and she'd agreed and then he'd married Ceci, the divorcée real estate agent who sold him the bungalow he decided he had to have, with alarming, even suspicious dispatch. Imogen mocked herself for suspecting Robert had married on the rebound or that Ceci seized a chance while showing the master bedroom to a vulnerable man. She wasn't sure about being friends with Ceci, not after that opening speech. What Ceci said was correct, but that didn't mean it was true. Imogen wasn't sure whether it was *she* who was jealous. Had she and Robert really put all that "tension" behind them? She would have said so herself—but when Ceci said it she wasn't so sure. Anyway, Ceci had once talked to her about shoes and a famous client who'd gone into rehab.

Imogen and Robert had been partners for over five years. They'd hooked up back in film school, did a project together, found themselves to be complementary: Robert was a factory of soaring ideas, sometimes brilliant, but just as often ridiculous or incongruous; Imogen was more down-to-earth but also a deeper thinker. She'd find what his better ideas were about, tease out their potential, analyze the characters he invented.

For more than a year they couldn't sell anything. They lived together in a cramped fourth-floor apartment and bought cheap cheese, bruised fruit and eggplant at the local food bank. Then came their first success, a comedy called *Just Desserts.* "Maybe if we weren't so hungry for fancy, empty calories we'd never have written all that breezy dialogue," Robert had joked. Five thousand dollars from their first paycheck went to the food bank.

The rescue won't be corny, Robert insisted. He's sitting in the waiting area with a newspaper in front of his face but sees everything that's going on. Was he also watching her bounce across the terminal? It's ambiguous; it's not unlikely, but it's not clear. He sees the frat boys leap toward her, stop her, move in like a pack of beagles. He frowns. He sighs. It's an old-fashioned kind of sigh-and-frown combo, the pre-action routine of a strong but thoughtful hero—Wayne or Cooper. I've thought up a name for him, tentatively. Teunis Wagenhall.

What?

Wagehals is German for daredevil and a guy name of Teunis drove the cab I took from the airport last week. I like it's outlandishness. I had the idea in the airport and so . . . Well, anyway, he's not a *big* guy, Teunis; he's lithe and wiry and rather well dressed as things go at airports: gray slacks, say, an open shirt, a decent sport coat, a pair of those good English shoes. He looks Continental because, though he's from Oklahoma, he now lives in Zürich.

Zürich? Switzerland?

Yup, *that* Zürich. Be patient. I'll get to it. Anyway, he walks up to the group with this sort of aristocratic self-assurance and touches one of the boys on the shoulder, as if cutting in at the prom. "Pardon me," he says with the kind of politeness that's a little menacing then turns to the woman. "I thought I must have missed you, sweetheart." She looks back, momentarily perplexed, wondering about frying pans and fires.

The most belligerent of the boys is on the point of protesting, as if this were a bar and not an airport, but the one next to him squints at the stranger and says, "Hey, you're Teunis Wagenhall! Damn, this is too much." In no time the four college men regress to ten-year-old hero-worshipers. *Teunis, Teunis, omph, oomph!* they begin to chant, as if at a drinking contest. "That time you . . . I saw you when . . . Hey, man, can I get an autograph . . . ?"

As this is going on, the woman begins to back away, not bouncy now but slow and furtive, as if uncertain whether to make a run for it. One of the boys turns, looks sheepish. "Come on, guys. We're holding them up. Let's go," he says, and offers an almost courtly obeisance to them both. He's thinking it's going to make a great story. Jesus, Teunis Wagenhall and Severine, as improbably magical a coupling as DiMaggio and Monroe.

"So," Imogen said, "*that's* your big opening scene?"

Robert looked at her sideways, defensively. "It *establishes* a lot."

"You're not going to insist on *Teunis Wagenhall*, I hope. As for her, her real name's not *Severine*, is it?"

"Of course not. Severine's her *porn* name. Obviously."

"You on a European kick or something? How come Severine? Uh-oh, don't tell me *you've* got a favorite pornstar with that name? You've ordered—you should stop looking at the menu."

He laughed. "Menus can be looked at after you order. And there's always dessert—*just* desserts—and the list of fabulous ports and cognacs. Anyway, you've got to give a lot of thought to names because they're little stories. I like Severine. There was this obscure French singer by that name. We can work it all out later, with the backstory. She was eighteen, remember, a college freshman. Would she have chosen her own name? A good question. I mean, you know pornstars all have these *noms-de-guerre*, aliases. Presumably it's the pornographers who assign them. Brutally sexy names are popular but cheesy. Cherry, Angel. Last names with double X's or stuff like Towers or Melons."

"You know way too much about this."

"As I see it she'd insist on picking her *own* name. She's a girl with a will, a *smart* girl. A pornstar with a 150 IQ is more interesting than one without. She can explain about the name to Teunis later, something like: 'I figured French is sexy, so I thought I'd go for something Gallic.' Then she could mention the singer and say, 'It sounded cute and young but what I liked is that it has *severe* in it. Severine . . . dignified, exotic, and kind of innocent all at once.'"

"That you talking, or her?"

"Of course her *real* name will be something white-bread common or maybe unpronounceable—maybe Polish?"

"You're asking me?"

Imogen laid down Charlotte Brontë's *Shirley*, sat up in bed, and tried to imagine the inner life of a pornstar, an ex-pornstar, an ersatz Severine who did it for tuition, so she could read books like *Shirley*, and got out the minute she could afford to.

One year as Severine followed by eight of respectability; but on computer screens across the globe she's always there, always eighteen, naked and performing sex acts.

Imogen conjured up some awful parents, a backward Bible-belt town, groping men smelling of whiskey, a precocious mind and body. Clichés. And yet she went along with Robert's ridiculous idea, knowing he'd pick up her reluctance. She'd even suggested flashbacks.

"You know I hate flashbacks," he'd said.

"Me too, but the exposition's going to be hell without a *few*. We could make them short and punchy."

He raised an eyebrow and grinned, thinking he'd hooked her. "Punchy, eh? Like?"

Imogen remembered her impromptu examples with some shame. "Like Severine doing a three-way in the apse of an Episcopal church, like Teunis—or whatever we call him—jumping his motorcycle over the entire Mormon Snabberwackle Choir."

Where did that religious stuff come from?

"But," Robert had said with a pout, "it's all going to depend on the snappy dialogue. Remember? According to *The Hollywood Reporter* snappy dialogue's what we *do*; it's our specialty, our *forte*."

"Forte, schmorte. You believe the *Reporter*?"

"Only when they say nice things about us."

Robert wasn't wrong about the interesting being a border category. To be interesting Severine and Teunis really would need to have very good minds, given that their lives are dominated by their bodies—their *public* lives. Imogen saw the pair as physical celebrities who aren't pleased about it. Celebrity culture is a shame culture. Celebrities are like barbarians, like Greek heroes, and live through the opinions of others. But Severine and Teunis are modern people of sensibility and so they also live in a private guilt culture. They're vertical beings trapped in a horizontal world of beer-besotted spectacle-fans, horny adolescents, frustrated bald men, secretive lesbians full of unmentionable yearning. They'd hate this. In her case, the reason's obvious. But if he hates his notoriety then why does he do it? The old standby maybe? A father problem?

Severine's mind outstrips her body, so to speak. She'd want normality, but how could she have such a thing? With men, that is. Having been a pornstar, having done what she did.

All the men she met would either know or they'd find out.

"I only did it for tuition. Only for one year."

So lame. The men might nod but they'd think to themselves she must have enjoyed it, think they could never compete with those studs with penises like truck pistons, that . . . no, not men, but *one* man, the husband of her failed marriage. He'd have thought he could get past it but then he couldn't. She'd try to reassure him but her attempts only provoke him, and if she does anything *unusual* in bed all he'd think of is where she learned such sluttishness; if she tries being passive and submissive then he'd be sure he was boring her. She could see that; see how the flesh of his love would be picked clean by the crows of sexual anxiety. The marriage fails. She's single. Better yet, she's celibate.

Robert said he sees Teunis as unhappily married too. He makes his home in Zürich because he moved there for the sake of his Swiss wife. But his wife's a cold careerist banker; it's her way of coping with his weird career. She ignores what he does and thinks only about her job. For her, sex isn't much different from breakfast or a yoga session. She fell in love with the dashing daredevil but that love was superseded by the Swiss passion for money, tending it, counting it, making deals with it. Teunis' hygienic wife wouldn't want a baby whereas Severine might long for children, for sex to be redeemed by being consequential.

Imogen thought about Robert's childishness—and Ceci's childlessness.

"I'm going to die alone," she said aloud as she flipped off the light.

"It's the family business. You see, his father did it and his father before him. Teunis' granddad died falling off the wing of a biplane performing an Immelmann."

"What's an Immelmann?"

"A thing that a guy named Immelmann used to do."

She shook her head in disapproval, sorrow. "Too recondite."

"Doesn't matter. Okay, the grandpa died in a crash pulling a sign with an exhibitionist's proposal of marriage: THELMA, WILL YOU MARRY ME? *That* better?"

"I don't know. If *I* were Thelma I'd take it as a rotten omen."

"Anyway, the point is that Teunis himself never felt daredevilry to be his *calling*, not exactly. I mean, he's not by nature a man of action, at all. In school he loved the sciences, mathematics, especially physics. As a boy he'd lose himself in the infinitesimal world of quanta or in picturing the formation of the heavy elements in the immense heat of the big bang. Yet he was forced faithfully to attend all his father's stunts—as soon as he was old enough, he had to help out. Though he saw the mob's adulation for what it was, the glamour got to him, the amour-propre of going fast, wearing interesting clothes, being looked at, admired. Teunis was an only child, the last of the Wagenhalls. His father, a cagey man, never once insisted that he had to follow in his footsteps, said that otherwise his heart would be broken—instead of the usual ribs and femurs."

"Stop being snappy. Okay, you see Teunis as a reluctant daredevil, an intellectual amusing himself by defying death, a physicist who ends up doing physical stunts. That it?"

"Wait. The clever father knows his son. He also knows his wife and lets her oppose the idea unopposed, so to speak, never raising an objection to her objections, letting her plead that the boy should do anything but jump from airplanes or leap over things. The old fellow knew his son was not only exceptionally bright but also, like many boys who are good in school, terribly anxious not to be taken for a mama's boy. In Teunis' family, after all, when a boy becomes a man he does stunts; no need to mention the fact. He knew that every time his wife railed, cajoled, implored, or guilt-tripped Teunis she inched closer to losing her case. The father adroitly involved Teunis in the *science* of his stunts, let him work out the many calculations of the innumerable variables. This, he knew, the boy wouldn't be able to resist."

Imogen wondered whether Robert too had worried about being taken for a mama's boy but knew better than to ask about it.

"Teunis' maiden stunt was colossal, well beyond anything his forbears had attempted. The announcement made news across the world, as he intended it should. Impatient but calculating, Teunis reckoned that only something that looked convincingly suicidal could suck up the kind of press oxygen he wanted for his debut. Awful to think of an eighteen-year-old novice attempting such a feat. And he was secretive about it, didn't even tell his father until just before the public announcement."

"Did you figure out the big stunt, too?"

"You bet. What the boy'd planned out was to jump a motorcycle from the top of one World Trade Tower to the other."

"Whoa! That's going to offend people, you know. It offends *me*."

"No, no. Trust me. It's *daring*. Great for the trailer. Remember, he's a daredevil."

"But are *we*?"

Robert gave her a Yiddish shrug. "You want maybe he should strap a rocket on his back and zoom across Lake Superior?"

Imogen sighed. "Oh, go on, then."

"Good. Look, the kid does all the computations and concludes that it depends on wind speed and direction—that he'd simply have to do it at just the right moment. 'For God's sake, start smaller!' his father thunders, but he can't dissuade him. His mother takes to bursting into tears and wearing black clothes.

"The press is all over the father, of course, who, being a real professional, calmly promises that his son will succeed and that then, as a matter of course, he will himself retire, suavely alluding to Leopold and Wolfgang Mozart, to Picasso *père et fils*. Though he speaks with smooth confidence, privately he's completely terrified. In the end, awed by his son's almost nonchalant self-assurance, he gives in and pulls the strings to get permission."

"And the boy succeeds, of course."

"Would we have a movie if he didn't? He pulls that first stunt off with cool detachment, not even raising his fist when he lands, the way his father and grandfather would have done, playing to the crowd. In fact, Teunis's thing is *never* to become excited, *never* to play to the crowd. His style is *anti*-showmanship. For him every stunt's just a physics problem and he wants people to know it. He's a post-modern daredevil, you see. His dispassion only increases the applause and hikes the amount of money he collects."

"How's he make *money*?"

"Oh, people put up cash—he has sponsors, endorsements. There are TV rights. He's stingy with interviews but when he gives one his shell is never penetrated. He happily explains his *methods*, the math and all that, but he comes across as incapable of fear and shows no interest whatsoever in his public. The guy's made of ice. That's how I see him. Bottled up, aloof."

"Like . . . Severine?"

Imogen, alone in bed again, thought about how the two of them would spend their first night together. According to Robert it would be at the airport hotel. They'd tell each other everything, of course. Two bottles of champagne popping together, total self-revelation, sincere but with the dialogue appropriately snappy.

She has an idea. Teunis takes a rolled-up canvas out of his suitcase.

"What's that?" Severine asks, sitting on the bed, still in the jeans and turtle-neck.

He unrolls the canvas. It's empty. "My first experiment in surrealism," he says mock-pompously.

"Explain!" she demands with a chuckle. It's plain that she's enjoying herself.

He holds it up under his chin. "I call it *Self-Portrait a Century Ago*."

Do our lives begin as blank slates, empty canvases? Is that the idea? And *then* we mess them up like Jackson Pollack?

Teunis' view of the physical comprehends both the practical and the abstract; still, it's bound to be different for a girl who gets breasts at eleven and by thirteen is being hit on by college boys and uncles. She'd see at once that her body's a source of power, then a moment later that it's also the opposite.

Imogen flashes momentarily on a scene of Severine on a set, klieg-lit motel room: "Love the camera!" yells the hack director. "Come on, sweetass. *Moan!*" Little wonder if she'd never had a real orgasm.

Imogen imagines the couple falling asleep chastely after their night of talk and hilarity and sudden joy and then, just before dawn, waking together and making love like a couple that's been contentedly married for a couple of decades. Severine will wonder at all the marks on his body; he will marvel at the preternatural perfection of hers. Both would have complicated feelings about their bodies—bodies that have to be housed, fed, bathed, clothed, medicated and in the end betray you, their ineluctable bodies scrutinized by others. Maybe they'd laugh together over their bodies, curling together, desire too gratified for either to want whole-heartedly to be pure mind.

Toward morning Imogen had an improper dream about Robert and woke furious with her wicked, ungovernable unconscious.

"It's just the mystery of love and it starts when they have coffee together after the rescue. They start talking to each other as neither's ever done before. He's on his way to a stunt out west. Arizona? Utah? Something to do with the Grand Canyon or Monument Valley? She's on her way to visit an old friend, the woman who got her into porn years earlier. Now the friend's married and living on a ranch with a doting husband who, incidentally, *doesn't* know about her past. He's not a computer-user, at least not a porn-addict. A couple towheaded kids. She misses her plane and he misses his. So . . . they go on talking and talking—"

"We have to *write* all this talk remember. We have to make it *snappy*."

"Don't be so negative. We hear music; there's a montage. They spend the day together, leave the airport. We *see* them talking while they're *walking*, in a cab, visiting a gallery, shopping, *whatever*—but *always* talking like they'd been starved for it. He takes her to a fancy restaurant for dinner and then, it's so late, they decide on the airport hotel."

"So they can go *on* talking?"

"Right. It'll be tricky to show that sex isn't on their minds while it's so much on ours."

"Why *shouldn't* sex be on their minds?"

"What you said about the morning fuck. So what happens in the morning comes more as a relief than a climax. Isn't that your idea?"

"Bingo. And it's got to be just *wonderful* to them. When they wake we should feel *he's* found an interest in life and *she's* gotten her virginity back. It's not sex, it's rebirth. But what's all this talking supposed to be *about*?"

"Well, their lives first."

"And not about sex? Like, *you* know."

"No. Like what?"

"Like he says, 'You did it for the money but the men you've met didn't believe that, did they?' And she's so glad to be understood, she says, 'But that's it exactly. Men are funny about sex; they *impose* so much on it. My husband couldn't forgive me for making him believe himself inadequate. Secretly he'd look me up on those horrible web sites. He thought I didn't know.'"

"*Heautontimoroumenos*," said Robert. " A self-torturer. As usual, the Greeks had a word for it."

"Classics!"

"Only a minor, remember. Film major, just like you, kid."

Imogen hummed at this. "And he says—Teunis, I mean, or whatever we're going to call him—*he* says, defending himself,

'Men aren't all alike, though you must have good reasons for thinking so.'"

"And she'd snap back, 'Don't tell me what I *have to* and think.'"

"Sharply."

"Very sharply. It's their first spat; it shows how independent she is."

"'I couldn't convince my husband that my orgasms weren't all faked.'"

Robert jerked his head. "Huh?"

"A good line, don't you think? Remember it."

Robert looked a bit unnerved. Oops, had she inadvertently gone and hit a nerve?

Imogen reclines on her living room couch, book propped on thighs, paging idly through her favorite writer of non-biodegradable lingo until she comes on lines for a motto worthy to be inscribed below her tiny coat of arms: pens stillatitious on field inky:

> *Mirth is the Mail of Anguish—*
> *In which it Cautious Arm,*
> *Lest anybody spy the blood*
> *And "you're hurt" exclaim!*

She bridles a little at the cliché: smart girls—unhappy, lonely girls, at least, which is most of them—forging themselves a neat carapace of jokes.

She lays Emily aside and focuses on Teunis and Severine, whom she thinks of as waiting for her to pay some attention to them. She pictures them fantasizing a future as *exes: ex-porn-star, ex-daredevil, ex-wife, ex-husband, ex* being an efficient and mighty prefix—signifying a kind of demotion and deliverance, rather backward-looking. To Severine and Teunis, though, it is purely liberating, just the way to the freedom to limit their freedom, to become a new Sartre and de Beauvoir, shedding bad faith, defining themselves anew by their choices. That's romantic comedy for you, she mused, existentialism for a date flick.

Her mind was fully engaged now, at last. She'd begun to care about Robert's pornstar and daredevil. All their successful collaborations had had to wait upon this moment when his imaginative half-stories wormed their way into Imogen's mind where his flat characters took deep breaths and rounded out. For him, it was mostly about what happened; for her what counted was whom it happened to. He was propelled by the anomalous (pornstar/daredevil); for her it was just the opposite—it was the normal, albeit with a twist of lemon. When they'd found their middle-ground, then they'd join hands, so to speak, and square-dance their couples to a happy ending— when the cameras switch off, before real life gets a chance to assert itself.

Her intuition about Severine and Teunis was that these two odd people—interesting ducks, full of potential—have been half-killed by repetition: her year of sex acts, his seasons of death-defying feats. They both want their respective exploits to be external to them and so have had to be careful to remain untouched by them. For them, detachment is equally style and defense. They had faith that their essence could be preserved no matter what they got up to in lit-up bedrooms or on thundering Harleys. Imogen's insight is that they have in common the identical error, that being can remain impregnable to doing and that, even if the prisons of their peculiar notoriety have made their inner lives more vital to them, both have been hazardously isolated. Imogen all-too-readily identifies with that kind of disconnection; for her, romantic comedy is always about such people—interesting people with an unused capacity for love—and how they are pulled back into life. For her, the triumph of life is the only happy ending.

"Remember, the fantasies of fifteen-year-olds," she once quipped sententiously to Robert, "are the ones that really matter." She'd loved the way he had laughed when she said that—laughed with her—and wondered whether Ceci would care to be laughed with in such a way. Ceci didn't fear her, not even a little. This was because Imogen too was an *ex*, not the kind who takes off but the kind who's been fired.

Fascination is an alloy of attraction and repulsion, she philosophized. Severine and Teunis fascinate others because they did what these others didn't but would have liked to do so that they have relieved others of having to take these risks. Nevertheless, they weren't monsters because, though their acts of obscenity and recklessness were outside normal human behavior, they are nonetheless *completely human*. No, not monsters. What was lacking to them was only normality yet that is quite a lot.

"By marrying I think I was trying to set up a completely conventional private life," Teunis confesses.

"Me too," says Severine. "But your attempt seems to have worked."

"Not really. Just lasted longer. Your husband was too obsessed with your past."

She catches his thought. "And your wife is uninterested in your present?"

"Utterly."

She smoothes her hair, her long, very attractive hair. "Do you love dogs?"

"Yes."

She wonders: would it be too hackneyed if he bought her a puppy? Would a man give one to *me*? How would I feel if Robert, for instance, made me a present of a puppy? She thought about it. She tried out *loved?* then thought, *nope, burdened.*

Mid-morning at their office, a single large room in a downtown tower that they generally avoided using. Outside the smudged window the California sky was the color of dried mud. Inside, the air was stale. Imogen came in bearing two coffees and a blue folder.

Robert reached for the coffee. "Thanks, I need it. What've you got? More of your Freudian notes?"

"No, wiseass. Some dialogue. Rough, of course. Give a listen?"

"Mmm," he growled, drinking up. "Snappy?"

She sat down and began to read.

TEUNIS: In school I was good at math, chemistry. I just have that kind of brain. But physics is what I loved most. I dreamed of becoming a scientist. A researcher, a theorist, not an engineer.

SEVERINE: Is that because you love purity? Or is it complexity?

TEUNIS: Maybe both. It's a mistake to think that purity is always simple or that complexity's invariably corrupt. But yes, pure science *is* what I wanted to do. There's a hierarchy. *Der Ruhm über das Geld, Einstein über Edison.* But as it turned out, what I do is the lowest, most pointless form of applied physics—it's not bravery, not even athletics. It's nothing but premeditation. This speed, that angle, this far.

SEVERINE: Why do you keep doing it? Do you need to keep risking more?

TEUNIS: No. I don't know.

SEVERINE: My excuse was money.

TEUNIS: Okay, then. I do it for the money too.

SEVERINE: Now I make money selling advertising space. Did I tell you?

Robert stopped her. "This isn't what I'd call snappy," he said. "*Und lieber Himmel*, no German, for crying out loud."

"You were the one who said he lives in Zürich, but you're right. No point doing porn, stunts, *or* screenplays except that the money's good," said Imogen sardonically.

Robert, seated at the desk, looked down, pushed a pencil around pensively. "Remember that thing you said about her orgasms? That her husband wouldn't believe she didn't fake them?"

"What about it?"

"What do you think? *Did* she?"

Imogen considered how to answer this. Robert often talked about their characters as if they were real people, but what were they really talking about? "Not with her *husband*, no."

"And she *told* him that?"

"Sure. A hundred times."

He poured another dose of caffeine into his scowl, picked up the pencil and pointed it at her. "In my opinion it'd be better if she *did* fake them." Unless she was very much in error about one or the other, his tone was twice as bitter as the coffee.

Robert insisted they leave early, barely forty minutes into the movie.

"But it's the premiere," Imogen whispered in protest. "All these big bigshots."

"What do I care? If they're dumb enough to stick it out, so much the worse for them."

"All right, all right, but keep your voice down. Please."

Out on the sidewalk Robert took a deep breath, squared his shoulders, and swore. "That actress, the one with the boobs who played Helen?"

"Gwen?"

"I wouldn't want *her* for Severine."

"No? Who *would* you want?"

"I want Bardot—the post-sexual Bardot of forty years ago. Remember the opening of Godard's *Mépris*? 'Do you like my feet, my thighs? Is my ass cute?'"

"You think Severine's insecure?"

"Insecure? *Bardot*? The *mépris* was all hers, and Godard's."

"*Mépris* . . . That mean contempt or mistake?"

"If it's female it means mistake; if male, it's contempt. Very clever of the French. A lot of male mistakes lead to female contempt."

Imogen was silent for a minute, letting the bitterness of this French sagacity buzz around them like a wasp. "Well," she said to change the subject, "the stunts were pretty awful."

"Horrendous."

"I mean, all that computer-generated crap. Phony as Gwen's chest. We wouldn't want anything like *that* for Teunis."

"Nope. Give me Keaton any day."

"Diane?"

"Her—or Buster."

They laughed and headed to the parking lot to find his used Volvo. Ceci had the pre-owned Lexus.

"She's working late," he'd explained over the phone, "showing a beach house or going to a beach party or something. Siegel sent me two tickets. Whaddya say? Please?" He didn't want to go alone and, anyway, Siegel would rather she saw his latest masterpiece than Ceci. "She doesn't really care about movies that don't have Tom or Brad or Russell in them."

"That's kind of nasty," Imogen said, pleased to have to defend Ceci.

"Just the truth, kid."

"But she told me she loves Truffaut films. *And* late Bergman."

"Pretentious fibbing."

"I'm sure you're exaggerating."

"I'll pick you up?"

As soon as they pulled out of the parking lot he began to play his plot game again. "Okay, listen to this. The next morning, after the airport motel, Teunis flies off to jump the Grand Canyon or skydive onto a two-foot mesa or something while Severine goes to see her friend, the one who'd gotten her into porn and is now married to a Fundamentalist rancher. He doesn't know about his wife's porn years, of course."

"And the tow-headed kids?"

"They don't know *either*. Anyway, Teunis is distracted; he's lost his detachment, you see, can't stop thinking about her. This makes doing the stunt dangerous. Meanwhile, back at the ranch, Severine's friend invites another couple over for a barbecue and the guy *recognizes* her—Severine, I mean. Before leaving, he pulls the husband aside and tells him. The Fundamentalist confronts his wife in the bedroom, forces the truth out of her. He goes wild. He goes for a *gun*. The friend rushes out of the bedroom, grabs Severine and the women jump out the window and into a pickup. They're fleeing for their lives, careening across the range in panties and tanktops. The husband goes for his Jeep and tears after them, full of rage and tears, a *crime passionel* on wheels, biblical retribution on his shattered mind, Jezebel on his lips. Severine's behind the wheel of the pickup so she naturally heads for the Grand Canyon or Monument Valley or wherever the hell Teunis is. All-night driving at top speed. Car chase. Then they all wind up together. There's a fight, a precipice—"

"Cut!" Imogen howled, laughing. "It isn't some derivative *thriller*. It's not about the *plot*. We do romantic comedy, remember? Anyway, it's too *Thelma and Louise*. Two women and a precipice. I mean."

He was determined to kid her. "No. Try picturing it. Teunis's stunt, the enraged hubby, the terrified, scantily-clad women, the excited mob . . . ?"

"Oh, shut up."

He pulled up in front of her building. "Okay, you do better."

"Oh, I will," she said, and started to get out of the car.

Robert leaned over and grabbed her arm. "Wait a minute."

"What?" she snapped.

He yanked her across the seat and gave her a kiss—on the cheek. "Sleep on it," he said ambiguously.

Imogen was exhilarated, stimulated by the rotten movie, Ceci's bad taste, the ridiculous conversation in the Volvo, Robert's challenge and surprising peck on the cheek, but above all by the cup of coffee she improvidently drank when she ought to have been sauntering off to what her father called the Feather Ball.

To settle her nerves, she sat at the little desk she never used, cleared away the debris, and laid down a legal pad. It was like she was taking dictation from a boss with a full bladder; she could hardly keep up.

Severine does visit her friend at the ranch and the husband does find out, just as Robert said. But instead of turning into an enraged feminist plot device the man just falls apart. He may be a Christian but not in the worst sense. His wife comforts him. Mary Magdalene stuff. It's touching, sad, and edifying all at once. Severine discreetly calls a cab but, being on a ranch, has to wait a long time for it. She looks in on the tow-heads, remembering a line from her old professor: *If they see she's got a mother's soul the audience will forgive her anything.* With time to kill, Severine sits on the porch and looks at the moon, a lonesome cowgirl not at home on the range. The cab finally comes and she decides to head for the airport, see if she can get to Teunis and his stunt, which she'd earlier told him she couldn't bear to watch.

As Robert said, the daredevil's distracted by thoughts of Severine. That night he takes out his laptop, unable to resist checking the porn sites. Not a good idea.

He's going to skydive and land on top of a mesa. His assistant is checking the meters and tells him the wind isn't right but he climbs into the plane anyway. Big crowd. Cameras.

Severine parks the rented car and joins the crowd staring up at the plane from which Teunis is about to jump. She's just in time or, could be, a wee bit too late.

Imogen paused for breath and thought, "If this weren't a romantic comedy I'd freeze it right there—Severine looking up *from* and Teunis looking down *on* America's gloriously indifferent wide open spaces.

She was up surprisingly early, still excited. She phoned Robert and told him to meet her at the office. Then she put on a pair fishnet stockings she found in a box of Halloween costumes, an old miniskirt, her tightest top; she laid on the rouge and eyeliner, let down her hair and gave it a good hundred strokes. After she'd put on some pink lipstick she found at the bottom of a drawer she appraised herself in the bathroom mirror, the way she might have done as a ten-year-old at a makeup party.

"*Severine, c'est moi,*" she giggled.

"Jesus! What the—"

She twirled around girlishly for him and put her finger to her salmon-colored lips. "Shh," she said. Then she pulled the chair right up to his, pulled out her notes, and read.

"Not bad," he said in the grudging fashion in which he conveyed all physical or artistic compliments.

"But there's still one problem," said Imogen, crossing her legs.

"And what's that?"

"We've got to get rid of the wife."

Robert's eyes were on the fishnets and his mouth formed an ironic smile as he said the two words that made Imogen's vertebrae quiver, from cervical all the way down to lumbar.

"*Whose* wife?"

Harbor Islands

1.

The unemployment insurance was going to run dry at the end of the week. My room in Washburn's tinderbox of a three-decker had to be paid for every seven days, in cash, a weekly reminder of just what the two of us were worth. I'd found the room in Washburn's after I had to give up the studio apartment where I'd moved after losing the condo. My economic and residential slide was about to end where all slides do.

The condo had five rooms, not counting the state-of-the-art bathroom, plus a view of the western end of a park. The spanking new building was now as empty as a Detroit factory. I hadn't worried a bit about covering the mortgage, the furniture, the car payments. Wasn't I on my way? "You've found your niche," my dying mother had said when I landed the job, entry-level but with prospects. The word *niche* wasn't exactly pleasing to my ear; it made me feel both trapped and diminished. But I shrugged off this sign of the narrowness of my mother's expectations because she was so ill and, I could see, relieved. My future had become yet another thing of which she could let go, like television and the reading group. It comforted her that her only child had found a little nest in which he could snuggle for the long haul, secure amidst the world's whirlwinds. So my success, I felt, was bringing her closer to the end she wanted. In fact, she died only three weeks after I landed that once-promising ex-job of mine.

What with the cheap calories, inadequate toilette, worn-out wardrobe, and the effects of nearly two years of anxiety and rejection searching for any sort of work, my appearance could not be called prepossessing. Even if I should be lucky enough to be granted an interview somewhere, I wouldn't look to a personnel officer like much in the way of human capital. And, to boot, it was November.

One morning at ten I decided to head to the convenience store for a loaf of bread and pint of milk. Winter was in the air, a winter when I'd be on the streets. The wind blowing in from the ocean stung, as if there were little tacks in it. A young man with an exiguous beard and dressed in a green parka that must been made before he was born was stationed at the corner handing out flyers. Most people shifted aside and nobody looked at him.

Unemployment changes your attitude toward flyers handed out on street corners—also voting, traffic lights, police officers, children, dogs, patriotism, advertisements, cell phones, college students, sports utility vehicles, and the weather. With respect to flyers, all you see is the twenty bucks the poor hander-out stands to make and you wonder how long before he tosses the things away and finds a place to get warm or drunk or high. As I drew near him, the scruffy young fellow looked me up and down in an almost offensive way. In fact, I was about to point this out to him when he thrust a flyer at my hand and said the last thing I expected. "Here, take it.

Pretty sure it's meant for you." It goes without saying that the unemployed, especially the long-term jobless types like me, are the very people flyers aren't meant for; and, since we don't care to be reminded of this, we don't take them. I laughed. "Meant for me, eh?" Still, I took the paper and read it as I continued down the sidewalk.

He wasn't wrong. In block letters that reminded me of old wanted posters, it read:

Seeking Employment?

Interviews Today

9:30 a.m. to 5:30 p.m.

The Longman Center

421 Cod Street

The Hesiod Corporation

Longman Center is cavernous, rented out for car and boat shows, high-tech exhibitions, and political conventions. I had been in it once, back in my salad days—when salad was a side-dish. My company sent a bunch of us junior executives to hear a famous business guru explain why commerce is really Buddhism by another name.

It was just short of noon when I arrived at the Center. The place wasn't merely filled; it was teeming like steerage in a coffin ship, if the coffin ship happened to be the size of an aircraft carrier.

A mob milled at the entrance— unorganized, noisy, passively resentful or nervously hostile. Once inside, however, we desperados were greeted by young, well-coiffed people in red sports coats with the logo of Hesiod Corporation stitched over their hearts. We were funneled into queues as if we were a new army there to be shorn, to be issued uniforms, canteens, helmets and rifles. I shuffled along between an uncomplaining and patient obese woman whose legs I feared might buckle and a thin, hyperactive fellow with a mustard-colored mustache. He pestered me with questions. "So, what kind of jobs are they offering? What are they looking for? Shit, I forgot to bring my résumé—you got yours? Hesiod, aren't they into energy or is it finance and insurance? You know where their home office is?"

There were long tables set end-to-end with chairs on either side. Those used by the Hesiod personnel were padded. The interviews lasted no more than two minutes after which most of the applicants departed with shoulders slumping, mouths muttering, eyes tearing.

It made me sad that the obese woman had trouble fitting on the hard plastic chair. I was afraid it might break beneath her; it made me feel a little indignant. Before I could see what happened to her though, I was myself motioned to an identical chair well down the line.

A fortyish woman sat before me, looking down at papers and wielding her pen like a scimitar. Her lank hair was brutally cut a few inches below her ears as if by a guillotine and her long nose made me think of an organ pipe. She steadied her pen and quickly demanded my name, age, and state of health. She still hadn't looked at me.

"Sex male," she said and ticked off a box. "Final year of education or name of degree?"

I told her.

"What was your last job and when did it end?"

I told her that as well. Why not?

She moved on to the next box needing a check. "What sort of books do you like to read?"

"I prefer ones written in or, better yet, translated into, English."

This provoked a look at me, quite a dour one.

"Very well." She pointed to the screened-off area. "Go there. They'll tell you what to do next."

I didn't trouble to thank her. Anyway, she was already readying her forms for the next candidate.

At either side of the opening in the screened-in area stood a stripling and a maiden in their red Hesiod jackets. They looked about fifteen, smooth-faced, eager, apple-cheeked. Each held a stack of paper and a box of pens. They welcomed us one at a time. I got the maiden. There was red in her hair. She handed me a sheet of paper printed front and back and a ballpoint.

"It's just a little test. Nothing major," she said encouragingly and pointed at the paper. "You write your name there and answer all the questions as best you can. Then return the test and the pen to the person at the front. All there is to it."

It was like elementary school, neat rows of small chairs with desk arms, but I felt the opposite of nostalgia.

I took a seat and looked at the paper, front and back. I remember there were twenty questions in all. I can't recollect all of them but I wrote some down that night when I returned home from dispatching a meat-loaf dinner at the Omega Diner. I scribbled the questions on the back of the flyer, which I found folded up in my jacket.

    1. Business is to wealth as
        a. oranges are to orange juice
        b. war is to devastation
        c. solitude is to inspiration
        d. tuberculosis is to poetic talent

2. Frenchman is to foreigner as
   a. crayfish is to spider
   b. the Sombrero Galaxy is to the Milky Way
   c. women are to girls
   d. Rottweiler is to canine

3. Despair is to loneliness as
   a. sadness is to depression
   b. happiness is to joy
   c. boredom is to ennui
   d. libido is to lust

4. (Circle your answer or answers.) Would you tell a lie to protect
   a. a family member
   b. a co-worker
   c. your employer
   d. a stranger?

5. Which is the worst for you:
   a. dark chocolate
   b. tobacco
   c. margarine
   d. cognac?

6. Answer Yes or No.) Do you see others as abnormal in so far as they are unlike you?

7. Napoleon Bonaparte was a war-loving tyrant of over-weening ambition but also a talented, hard-working leader who spread the ideals of the French Revolution, established salutary legal reforms, and inspired both high art and high fashion. What is your opinion of Napoleon I?

8. Do you ever talk to yourself? If so, how many times a week do you do it out loud?

9. Where is Indiana University of Pennsylvania located?

10. Why is December 10 a significant date?

11. What was Buffalo Bill's real name?

12. What is your favorite variety of tree?

13. What is the difference between obedience and submission?

14. Do you think employees owe more, less, or the same level of loyalty to their employers as employers owe their employees?

I imagined Hesiod's extravagantly-paid staff of social scientists devising this quiz, all devoted to the metrics of human response and enemies of disruptive individuality, people for whom every exception proves some rule. What did I think of Napoleon Bonaparte? The real question I needed to answer was the one Mustard Mustache had asked, *What are they looking for?*

I did the best I could, handed in the test and the ballpoint to another Hesiod adolescent. He motioned me to the back where there was yet another screen; the whole rear of the hall was a labyrinth. On the other side of the screen was a waiting room with upholstered chairs and three small tables. Here I sat for half-an-hour with others who had made it through the sieve. Reading material had been considerately placed on the tables, a heap of pamphlets and newsletters: *A Brief History of*

The Hesiod Corporation, The Hesiod Chronicle: Works and Days, Hesiod's Holdings and Partnerships, Sustainability Programs at Hesiod, Annual Report of The Hesiod Corporation, Philanthropy at Hesiod, Holidays at Hesiod. I learned that the Corporation was big, had many enterprises, made a lot of money, operated everywhere under the sun, threw extravagant office parties, cherished the environment and that, wherever they set their feet, fostered community development, labor harmony, and furthered the cause of cultural understanding and peace on earth. Amen.

From time to time a youthful Hesiod employee emerged from behind yet another screen, called a name, and told those who responded either that they would not be detained further or invited them to step through.

I was invited into the sanctum sanctorum. Behind a gray table sat a tall, manifestly unhappy, balding man. He was a dead ringer for the foreman of the construction crew on which I'd worked the summer of my senior year, a man who monitored me for the least slip so that he could growl "College kid!" and make the other men laugh.

"We require a few particulars. Date of birth, approximate height, weight, and" here he added a phrase redolent of battlefields and Appalachia, "next-of-kin."

I answered and he filled in his form then looked up at me.

"We may have a job for you," he said. "Know anything about boats?"

"Sure," I lied.

In a voice as unexpressive and metallic as the table at which he sat, he said, "Good," then made an official note of my fib.

2.

The job paid all of a hundred and fifty dollars a week but came with a three-room apartment, plus modular bath, in the old

Carter warehouse. This Victorian red-brick edifice stood across a cobbled alley from the dock where I was to tie up my refurbished lobster boat, the *Caroline V*. Mr. Harkness, a supervisor who did very little supervising, told me I was welcome to help myself from the ample stocks of food in the warehouse, which was supplied with an industrial sized freezer, though he warned to expect random audits. Room and board, it was all in the contract. Unless I failed in my duties, or the Hesiod Corporation changed its enormous mind, I was guaranteed two years' employment, including membership in the company's medical and dental program, with an option to re-up should the project proceed.

It would be a lonely job, Harkness said, and physically taxing, so Hesiod gave me both a physical and a psychological. I was to do all the loading and off-loading myself. A dolly would, of course, be provided and the boat furnished with block-and-tackle. Oddly, I was given no test of my fitness to captain a boat, my knowledge of maritime law, harbor currents, channels, or sandbars. All such matters were covered in a 372-page print-out, spiral-bound so as to lie flat. The *Caroline V* had her own radio but, according to Harkness, most of my communications were to be carried out by cell phone. When I asked, timidly, about licensing and insurance, he said airily, "Oh, the Company will take care of all that."

I was to see to the boat and guard the warehouse, but my chief duty would be delivering supplies to sixteen of the twenty-one islands that were spread over the harbor, the ones that were large enough to have names. On each of these bits of land another newly hired Hesiod employee would be living. The company had thrown up a small, winterized house on each island and installed a small dock, all identical. My first responsibility would be to drop these people off at their posts, then bring them provisions according to a rotation schedule. Supplies would be delivered to the warehouse, also on a regular schedule, as detailed in another spiral-bound print-out. Harkness handed me a map of the harbor, told me at which dock I was to fill up the *Caroline V* with diesel fuel and that charges would go directly to Hesiod, then took his leave.

Apart from my ignorance about operating the boat, how to keep the thing from sinking, running aground, smashing the docks and what to do in foul weather, it was pretty much straightforward.

The first thing I did after Harkness' departure was to head for a waterfront bar and look about for the person I needed. I found him in Captain Martin, retired tugboat skipper, a man who combined the bitterness of a deposed emperor with the joy of a six-year-old. He was more than willing to take me and the *Caroline V* for a spin around the harbor. He leaped at the opportunity to get behind the wheel and, like some of my professors, he could deliver a fine lecture even with a few drinks in him. As for me, I was just as eager to play the apt pupil; so Captain Martin and I got on very well. I studied my printouts and tried a few solos around the islands the week before four islanders—my first passengers—were to show up.

What Hesiod was up to was never told to me. Of course not. Harkness was so evasive that I could see he didn't know either. My first speculation was a romantic one, that I was part of some sort of secret psychological research ("The Crusoe Experiment" I dubbed it). Next, I thought the new islanders would be assigned to gather meteorological data and information on currents. But this was as absurd as the Crusoe idea. One night, a couple of weeks after all my charges were installed on their tiny domains, I stopped by the bar where I'd found Captain Martin, who could be relied on to be there whenever I stopped by. "Take a look at this," he said, leaning across the table with a groan and tapping his forefinger on a newspaper headline. According to the article, the Hesiod Corporation had tried to purchase the islands outright, but the State refused, offering the company a six-year renewable lease instead. It was obviously a political compromise of some sort, said the reporter. As she knew no more about Hesiod's intentions than I did, she also speculated. Hesiod could be looking at a sewage disposal system, checking out the potential of tidal energy; they might be planning a wind farm, shellfish aquaculture, even a harbor theme park. It's possible that Hesiod's bosses themselves, while they wanted the islands, didn't know precisely what they wanted with them. Maybe one division of the concern had plans that some other division hadn't approved or was trying to undermine. Meanwhile, in the legislature Hesiod had its allies and enemies and the Senate minority leader was foremost among the latter. According to the reporter, unable to block the deal entirely, he insisted as a condition of the lease that the islands be occupied year-round, a ridiculous and expensive proviso which he hoped would scotch the deal but didn't.

3.

April rain poured down that Monday like a judgment. The first islanders staggered up the cobblestones with their luggage, straggling in one at a time. The two women looked sad, the men even sadder, and all of them were drenched. They would have walked a long way from the subway. I felt like a host to a bunch of refugees and tried to make them comfortable. I set out crates to sit on while they dried out.

"Two years," sighed Mrs. Jasinski, a fiftyish widow who looked to me as if she could stand up to a good deal more than a spring shower.

"Three for me," said Mrs. Jackson, whom I recognized as the obese woman from the Longman Center. She hadn't lost any weight.

Pete Voricelli looked about twenty-five, near my own age, a carpenter who had lost his first and only job a year earlier. "My older brother's," he said, pointing to an old Navy duffle bag at his feet.

Mr. Glatthorn, less forthcoming than the others, allowed that it was a pity about the rain and wanted to know when we'd be leaving.

"The supplies are already on the boat," I said cheerfully, attempting to sound encouraging and competent. "How about we have a cup of coffee first?" I was in no hurry; I was hoping the sky might clear up.

So we had a chat. It turned out we'd all been hired that day at the Longman Center. We laughed about the test and compared our answers to the questions we could remember.

"I chose the elm," Mrs. Jackson said. "They took the last one down the year my Ralph passed."

"Osier," said Pete. "Always liked the sound. Osier."

"Beech," said I. "No, copper beech."

"Spruce. Blue spruce."

"Well, we won't be seeing many trees from now on. Hey, what was all that about Napoleon anyway?"

"And how about that business with loyalty? What was *that?*"

We figured out the only thing we had in common, apart from desperation, was the lack of a family. "Must have been that next-of-kin question," said Mrs. Jasinski, nodding her head.

"And the willingness," Mrs. Jackson added. She impressed me, did Mrs. Jackson, as an earth mother, a wise woman. She reminded me of the earliest piece of art we'd been shown in my Art History class, the tiny and colossal Venus of Willendorf. "When you're alone you never think you can be *more* alone," she observed, "and then you find, well, yes you can." A month later, in a speech like the messenger's in a Greek tragedy, she told me why she no longer had a family.

Their luggage didn't amount to much. Mrs. Jackson had two small suitcases, old-fashioned ones of stiff cardboard. Glatthorn had a big green contraption with a single wheel.

I went aboard and started up the engine, then came back for their bags and stowed them under a tarpaulin while everybody huddled just inside the entrance to the warehouse. Visibility was poor, and I was filled with dread.

Pete dashed across the cobbles and jumped on board. "I'll cast us off," he offered cheerfully, like a little boy who's made a satisfactory leap of faith.

The other three needed help to climb the two thick planks that served as a gangway. Glatthorn had a bad back; Mrs. Jasinski was frightened of falling in the water. Mrs. Jackson went last. She had a bad hip that gave her gait a seafarer's roll. The planks bent under her as she gamely took my hand. "We go down, we go together," she said with an affable grin.

I could see by the way they eased up in the cabin that they trusted me. The water was gray and choppy, the island docks unlighted. The day before I had made a run past their four islands, but that was in bright sunlight and calm water.

Pete sensed our short trip wasn't going to be an easy one. "I'll take lookout in the bow," he whispered to me. "Good man," I said gratefully, and he brightened right up, like a watered violet that had been dying of thirst.

I had to double back a couple of times. The harbor was a slate-colored waste with specks of filthy yellow foam. It felt like the voyage—what with my errors and the unloading and getting each of them settled—took the whole day. Yet I was back in the warehouse apartment by two. I opened my last pale ale and fried some eggs and bacon. Then I fell asleep and when I woke moonlight was glinting off the bottle I'd left by the window.

With fine weather, the next couple of days went more smoothly. The islanders arrived on time; I had the boat ready. They were mostly quiet, resigned, steeled for their two years. They all looked hungry. I expect they opened the cartons of provisions I deposited in their cottages before I was back on board. The *Caroline V* and I were getting accustomed to one another. As my fear of sinking her waned my confidence grew and I began to feel real affection for the old girl.

On Thursday, three of the last four arrived together, as appointed, at nine a.m. This lot were almost cheerful, determined to make the best of things, bucking each other up, cordially kidding around. George Gissell told us jokes while we waited for the last to arrive. This was a young woman, who loped down the cobblestones in a pair of red high-tops, two athletic bags hanging from her broad shoulders, apologizing all the way. She had close-cropped hair and was the tallest woman I'd ever seen, so tall I hardly noticed how pretty she was or how miserable.

It was to be expected over time that the islanders and I should get to know one another. After all, I was the only human being they saw and, in a sense, we were colleagues. Most wanted to tell me about themselves, some resisted doing so. I never asked, or had to. I discovered that Joe Geritas was a veteran who couldn't stand civilians, though he made a half-hearted exception for me. Susannah Rothman ran toward me at the dock one morning, almost hysterical, threw her arms around my neck, and confessed that she'd survived a fire that killed her husband and son. This must have been cathartic because, after that, she was mostly fine. I was always bringing books and paper to Paul Rheinach, who told me he'd spent fifteen years eking out a living as an adjunct professor at half-a-dozen schools. He said he was a "member of the proletariat of the spirit," admitted he had a Ph.D. but asked me never to call him "doctor." Pale, thin Jamie O'Brien was raised in a Franciscan orphanage and fancied himself a Christian hermit of the old school. He ate only cereal, lettuce, macaroni and cheese and looked it. One day he blessed the *Caroline V.* Mr. Simentera, an immigrant, lost his job when the fisheries died. He admitted that he'd grown morose but insisted that he had never been violent—in fact, he insisted on this point so vehemently and so often that I doubted it. His wife and children went back to Cape Verde with his father-in-law, who warned him not to even think of following them.

Sooner or later I heard everybody's story. Curiously, only two of the islanders ever asked about mine: Mrs. Jackson, who said I could call her "Ma," and the tall woman, Cicely Weston, though, in her case, it took the best part of six months before she did so.

Most of the islanders were obsessed with food. Their tastes, like their strolls, narrowed. For example, Mr. Glatthorn ate little beyond soups and bread. When I managed to bring him a soup bone or a fresh baguette, he almost leaped with joy. George Gissell became a vegetarian and took all the parsnips I could spare. Keith Saunders, an aging rich kid at thirty, banished by his family for what he called "good and sufficient reason," kept trying to reproduce the Italian sausage with onions and green peppers his father had bought him at the ballpark when he was seven. "I think the trick is steaming the rolls and cooking the onions and peppers so slowly that they taste exactly the same." Keith lasted only three months, by the way, but wasn't the only one of the islanders who quit. He was replaced by Mr. Simentera, the ex-fisherman, who wouldn't touch seafood of any kind. What he loved was beef and vegetables and a thick, old-country chicken soup called *canja*. Mrs. Jasinski had brought her grandmother's 1936 edition of *The Joy of Cooking* but only used three recipes: sole Veronique, stuffed chicken breasts, and beef goulash, for which I found her a tin of sweet Hungarian paprika.

Cicely Weston, on the other hand, never spoke of food at all; she just took whatever I gave her, even when I began to include a variety of delicacies, like duckling, aubergines, artichokes, herring in wine sauce, and, most consequentially, a double chocolate cake I presented to her one blustery November afternoon.

"Why the cake?" she asked.

Cicely favored sweatpants, fleeces, and loose sweaters. On her island she let her hair grow out like Rapunzel's. Thick and straight and chestnut, her hair called attention to the femininity her wardrobe denied. I doubt she was aware of this but I certainly was. I avoided standing too close to Cicely. She stood well over six feet, and I suppose even a man more sure of himself than I've ever been might be intimidated. She wasn't unfriendly; I would say she was brusquely polite.

I told her that I was fond of double-chocolate cake and thought she might be too. "It's just the golden rule as applied to dessert," I said.

It was a lame joke but it made her smile.

"I must be your last stop. I always *am*, aren't I?"

I admitted that she was. In fact, I had arranged things that way but couldn't have said exactly why.

Cicely crossed her arms, looked down at me. When she tilted her head her hair fell over half her face, like a movie star's.

"Well, why don't you come up to the house and have a slice. It's cold. I'll give you a cup of coffee for the ride back."

It was late, and the days were, as they say, drawing in. I ought to have refused; I should have been steering the *Caroline V* to her berth.

On one wall Cicely had hung a framed photograph of a flat green field with a romantically decaying barn in the middle of it. This was the chief distinguishing feature of her abode. All the houses were identically furnished by Hesiod: a sharp-edged table, chairs of light wood, a love-seat and matching easy chair that would have looked at home in a bail-bondsman's office. The dimensions of these cottages were not extravagant; Cicely had to stoop to pass through the doorway and, had she wanted, could have painted the ceiling without the aid of a step ladder.

She poured the coffee, sat down opposite me at the table. From the way she kept brushing the hair away from her face I could tell she was still not used to its length. She cut the cake, placing big slices on plates for us both. She forked a small piece of the cake into her mouth.

"Mmmm."

"Glad you like it."

"Oh yes. Nice of the Company to give us all a treat."

I didn't like to tell her that the treat was on me; that all of them—aubergines, herring, etc.—were. On the other hand, neither did I wish to lie to her. So I decided to change the subject with a question she was bound to answer.

"Where are you from?"

"Oh, I'm just an Oklahoma farm girl." She was quick to denigrate herself, I noticed.

I pointed to the photograph of the field and the falling-down barn.

"Not *our* place, but still a little reminder of home."

"Happy childhood?"

"Oh, you know. Yellow school bus to limestone school in the morning, chores and homework in the afternoons, trips to town and the occasional rodeo on weekends. I had a normal childhood, I guess, which means I lived the healthy, unconscious life of a little animal."

"Sounds nice. So, when did you become conscious?"

She smiled. "In sixth grade I shot up eight inches and the other kids backed off. I felt gross, out of proportion, you know, just plain clumsy. I can't say when it was for you but in Oklahoma sixth grade was the start of the whole boy-girl thing."

"And the excruciating self-consciousness that goes with it."

She nodded once, like a cowboy. "*Isola*, that's Italian for island. I felt isolated, so this isn't. . ." Her words were swallowed up inside her coffee mug, one of the thick white ones supplied by Hesiod.

"I remember sixth grade," I said.

"Of course you do."

"It was like a European court that had just found out about love and sonnets."

"Yep. And on that emotional hothouse I looked down from outside."

"Boys are insecure," I offered.

She rolled her eyes. "Tell me about it," she said, meaning there was no need to tell her about it. "By eighth grade I had two inches on my father. He did what he could. Set up a basketball backboard for me, one of those things with a base you fill up with water. Lemons to lemonade, I guess he figured. I gave up on my classmates and went in for hoops. I also discovered books—you know, *real* ones, the kind they don't assign in middle school. An orange ball for the body and long stories for the soul."

"For me it was *Crime and Punishment*."

"I liked that one too, but in those days it was the novels by Victorian ladies I loved. They bore me out like friends. Well, of course they did; they were written by misfits."

"One of my old teachers said it's the books we read between fifteen and twenty-five that count."

"In that case, I got an early start."

"Was it escapism, all that reading?"

"You bet. But maybe I'm like your old teacher. I think it matters whether the books are good ones, even if you're reading them in a bad way. Don't you?"

It was growing dark. "Go on," I said because I knew she wanted to and because I liked her accent.

"Well, let's see. Around the time I began on Elizabeth Cleghorn Gaskell, the high-school coach found out about me. Boys wouldn't come anywhere near, but I was just the apple of Coach Harmon's eye. He was an old physics teacher, about to retire, but he put it off until I graduated and we'd won two state titles."

"Congratulations."

"Shucks," she said with a twang, "'tweren't nothin'." She made a wry smile.

"So, what next? Recruiters?"

"My suitors, yes. Oh yes. Plenty of 'em. I picked the school with the English department that offered the most Brit Lit courses. I fell in love with Thomas Hardy my first year. Senior year I wrote a thesis on the *other* novels of Mary Shelley and we made it to the Final Four, though not the *truly* final two, let alone the *definitively* final one. Still."

"Yes, still. And then what?"

"Oh, I've had a busy post-graduate life. I played in Italy for a year. For Lucca. Lovely place. The Italian men were aggressive, up to a point. They gave me a nickname."

"A nickname?"

"All the girls got one. Mine was *La Mandriana Gigantesca* which means the enormous cowgirl. Then I got hurt. Came home. Did a stint as a hostess in a steak house owned by a pal of Coach Harmon's. You can imagine how *that* went."

"Not well, I take it?"

"Not for long either. Flew to Greece for a tryout when I was almost all healed but the glory that was Greece sent me packing." She paused. I waited. "While I was there a tornado killed my parents who loved me, but not my sister who didn't. Linda was in the panhandle with one of her boyfriends."

"I'm so sorry."

"You know when I was being lonely in high school, Linda said to me, 'Well, Sis, being so tall, that's a problem you'll never outgrow.' Not really funny, is it? I found an assistant coaching job in Iowa, and that was good until the funding was cut. That's when I moved east and, well, you know the rest." She looked around. "Now I've got my own little house and a little bank account." Again the wry smile, "And a man who delivers chocolate cake. Not so bad."

She turned toward the window. "Oh, look. *Night.* You'd best push off."

And so I did.

4.

I see now that we weren't really employees at all but the employed unemployed, the useful useless.

So far as I could make out the Hesiod Corporation had no clear use for their lease but couldn't bring themselves to give it up either; and so, inertia being the most powerful force in the cosmos, things just went on month after month. I felt at ease with the *Caroline V* and mastered my charts. My rotations turned into a routine.

What did they do, the islanders? They read, painted, played solitaire; they wrote bad songs and worse poetry; they remembered and forgot. They tried gardening, knitting, carpentry, cartooning. After three months, somebody at the company thought to supply radios and three months after that televisions.

I think the islanders were mostly unaware of how this sort of life changed them, made some stronger, weaker, more or less thoughtful. Some saw their two-year contract as salvation, their island as a refuge; others felt they were serving a sentence. And some grew to cherish their islands the way of misanthrope does his dog, a chatelaine her castle.

It's not surprising that the young hermit was the first to crack up, though not the last. When I arrived one morning he was hopping up and down at the dock stark naked. He pleaded with me to take him ashore. "*Non sum dignis! Non sum dignis!* For the love of Jesus, get me out of here."

Mrs. Jackson—Ma—took a fall and ripped up her knee. By the time I arrived it had swollen up like a Dostoyevsky novel. Getting her aboard was difficult but she kept calling me "sweet thing" and never once complained. She apologized for putting me to so much trouble and said she knew they wouldn't let her back. It was like being orphaned, watching her go off in that taxi.

Mr. Glatthorn turned morose; Mrs. Jasinski whined; neither lasted out the year. What was that analogy? "Business is to wealth as . . . solitude is to inspiration"?

There are many ways of being alone, and from the outside they all look the same. Solitude can shade into loneliness and loneliness may congeal to solipsism. I doubt that any of the islanders became thoroughgoing solipsists, but several of them developed egos puffed up like poor Mrs. Jackson's knee. Solipsists are humble, despairing, lonely, disconsolate, skeptical, rare; egoists are rancorous, arrogant, gregarious, never in doubt, and common. To achieve these states of soul an island isn't required, but isolation does speed things up.

Say a woman is lonesome and longs to be married, to be half of a couple. What a preoccupation she can make of it, and how many forms her sense of deprivation can take, anything from fantasizing about her ideal mate to becoming a man-hater. Yet, even if she manages to struggle her way to resignation, her awareness of being alone will matter more to her than anything else. That would be Sheila Grillo, a plain woman of thirty-seven who replaced the hermit God spit out.

Suppose a man cuts himself off from everyone, lives alone, joins in no one's joys or sorrows and keeps his own to himself. Is such a recluse rebelling against the human condition—that of a social species, after all—or is he only being more honest about it, admitting that, at bottom and in the end, we are alone? I imagine that sooner or later, if he remains on his own, he will arrive at the latter position because it justifies him. My condition may not be a happy one, he will say to himself, but at least it is more truthful than that of those who laugh it up at a dinner party. The nothing I have is more honest than the pitiful consolations of . . . *next* to nothing. Would that, perhaps, be me?

I became a regular at the bar where I answered questions about the islanders, politely denied knowledge of Hesiod's intentions, listened to superficial, zealous opinions about politics and baseball and went home early.

In January, the *Caroline V* sprang a couple of leaks and had to go into dry dock. I was assigned a retired, charmless tugboat. It reminded me of an old stevedore who had drunk, smoked, and sworn for too many decades. If the thing ever had one painted on its stern, its name had worn away. I was surprised by how much I missed the *Caroline V* and the resentment I felt for this sluggish, lumbering tug, whose engine sounded like an elephant with bronchitis. There was no sympathy between us.

"Where's the *Caroline*?" the islanders wanted to know.

I had become a skipper, and the bond between captain and craft is the same whether the vessel is an aircraft carrier or a Boston whaler. I played with classifying the islanders as boats. This one was a speedboat, that one a tramp steamer. I decided that Cicely Weston was a tall ship, maybe a bright and graceful brigantine. Her ever-lengthening hair caught the wind like a topgallant.

I often found myself wondering how things were for Cicely out there on her island. She seemed to me to be doing all right. She told me she didn't bother with the television but liked the radio. She would sometimes give me titles of books, mostly novels and books of philosophy. She read Isak Dinesen, Charles Dickens, a lot of David Hume. Once she asked for a book of poems by a woman named Szymborska. I thought I'd read a few of them before I gave the book to her. The poems were easy to read; and one led into the next so that, before I knew it, I'd read them all. Cicely assumed these books, like the delicacies, were provided by Hesiod. It pleased me that she didn't know that I'd bought them myself.

The day I gave her the book of Szymborska poems we sat for a while on the dock. The gulls were noisy and the water was green.

"Come on up and have a cup of coffee and tell me a little about yourself," she said over the coughing of the idling tug.

It was a carefully phrased request. You may have noticed how the words, "a little," will keep you from confiding much of anything. They're a polite way of laying out the narrow parameters of one's interest. Still, you don't have to accept the boundaries. Cicely wasn't asking for my life story but, I decided, something intimate. Tell me just one thing; just make it crucial, essential.

Up at the house she sat at the table with her hands on her knees, bent slightly forward.

"Well?"

"When I was in college I dated a girl named Diane. She had a long neck and pale skin. We were both juniors when we met. That was in April. Springtime had kind of messed with my mind, my solitude. I was withdrawn and had been since I turned twelve. In college I lived alone, ate alone, studied alone. But that April, well, you know, I caught spring fever. I was bursting with ideas and hormones. I felt like my head was going to explode or just float up into the sky. So, for two weeks, I lived by a metaphor. I took to wearing a tie, to keep my head in place. I only had the one. It had been my father's, one of those old-fashioned wide ties, solid black. Diane, whose hair was nearly the same color, came up to me in the Quad where I'd been sitting on the grass trying to read a textbook on German history. I couldn't concentrate. 'Why the tie?' she asked.

"We saw each other every day until the semester ended. She was off to be a camp counselor and I had a construction job. Remember when jobs weren't so hard to get? We wrote and phoned all summer. We discovered books together, music, paintings. In September we picked up where we'd left off. We had no secrets, no unshared thoughts or enthusiasms. It was a new experience for me."

I looked at Cicely, who was leaning further forward. "It felt like love," I said. "You know, like belonging."

She nodded.

"Okay, that's how it was. That spring I took her to an expensive restaurant, asked for a table in the corner, and I proposed. She patted my hand. The one with the little jeweler's box in it. She looked embarrassed and said no."

"Did she say why?"

"She may have wanted to, but I didn't stick around to let her. I tossed money on the table, got up and left."

Cicely leaned back in her chair and was quiet for a minute, then she put her hand on top of mine, just as Diane had done. We'd never touched before. I felt something like an electric shock.

"I'm not going to re-up," she said solemnly and removed her hand. "In fact, I'm going to leave next week. I have to." She mumbled so that I heard her with difficulty. "My sister's very sick. She called last night." Cicely got to her feet, and I felt like a dinghy overshadowed by a liner.

Though my knees almost failed me, I got up too.

"Look, can we please go to bed?" she asked. "I've been thinking it over and decided it would be wrong not to."

5.

Once upon a time, philosophers set the ordered domains of their dreams on islands cut off from the foolish, corrupt mainland where some people had no jobs. These islands of sanity— old Utopia, New Atlantis—were fashioned from their creators' hearts' desires, illusions they wished would become realities without believing they could. Islands can be like that. They also make serviceable forts, penal colonies, pest houses, quarantine stations, little prisons of doom and exclusion—Swinburne and Angel Islands, Devil's Island. Once upon a time, the pious colonists of Massachusetts Bay herded the Indians they had converted out into their harbor, on to Deer and Long Islands, where most died, probably in accord with the secret prayers of the panicked denizens of the City On A Hill.

On the bright October day I took Cicely Weston off her island home I realized that the *Caroline V* had been mine. I never got her back. The company decided to junk her. Cicely leaned down and kissed me on the cheek, bravely hefted her bags, then vanished into the middle of the continent. I never saw her again, either.

There was no re-upping for anyone. Evidently, the Hesiod Corporation was never able to settle on a plan for the islands. They surrendered their leases and the legislature, after searching for a more profitable alternative, voted to declare the harbor islands a park.

After I'd helped Mrs. Jackson and her ruined knee down the gangway and unloaded her suitcases, after the taxi I'd called to take her to the hospital had pulled up on the cobblestones, she nearly enfolded me with her girth and with the hug came a warning. Holding me close, she whispered in my ear, "Remember, sweet thing. Some people, wherever they are is an island. Watch you don't turn into one of them."

Thermal

A steel-blue hammer crashed down on the anvil of the city. Leaves dangled from the trees like clusters of hanged men. Shimmering from the sidewalks; boiling up from the gratings; turning the boulevards into streams of molten tar; blistering window boxes and withering geraniums. My little room, only months before a cherished refuge and nest of freedom where I had thought to store up courage enough for a lifetime, turned into a trap, a kiln evaporating energy, reason, self-reliance. I hardly ate and slept in fevered fits. One morning I found a crowd gathered on the stairs. Old Mrs. Villiers on the third floor had died and, even though her desiccated body was little more than a wisp of flesh, the ambulance men strained and swore as they removed it. The same scene was being acted all over the city, as in the plagues of old. The weathermen, once content to wait their turn between murders and baseball scores, now led the news but nonetheless despaired. Snowstorms, hurricanes, floods always cheered them; galvanized by crisis, they began such broadcasts in a state of exaltation. Now they were using discouraging phrases like "not in the foreseeable future" and "no relief in sight," delivering their unchanging forecasts with apologetic gloom. Who cared what records were being broken or paid attention to the daily toll of asphyxiated elderly?

This heat wave had gone on too long; it did not feel like a crisis but a judgment. People still went to work but accomplished little; the indifference of the tropics had descended over the city. Blackouts, once extraordinary, grew routine. Passengers staggered out of overheated buses as if abandoning stricken ocean liners. Even after dark the once swarming, high spirited streets were vacant.

Dizzy, dazed, despondent, each day I felt myself shedding weight, surrendering more and more of what tied me to the earth. Late one afternoon while crossing a street, hurrying toward the shade of an awning, I was struck by a gust of hot wind and felt myself being wafted up into the air, saved only by the tar sticking to my shoes. I grasped at buildings and railings until I made my way back to my room, shed my clothes, lay my swimming head down on my soggy pillow. I was a child again, home from school with a fever. My mother was sponging alcohol all over me and softly singing, *I'd like to get you on a slow boat to China.*

I woke an hour later feeling lighter than ever. Even thrusting my head out the window I could get no relief; the air no longer felt like air. There was nothing else to do. I tottered down into the street. Though the sun had nearly set, stone and asphalt held fast to its heat. Two claps of thunder rattled the windows around me but no rain fell. As I passed over a grating air shot up and this time I really was lifted off my feet, only a few inches perhaps, but I was dismayed by this proof of my nothingness.

The train was thick with commuters whose eyes either drooped with exhaustion or were open wide, on the edge of panic. All the seats were filled at once and I had to stand. I deliberately wedged myself between a man in a serge suit and a stocky woman with no eyebrows, afraid that I might either collapse or float up to the ceiling.

The suburb seemed a little less hot, an illusion owing to the space between houses. Along the empty streets the moist air hummed as if a plague of locusts were eating up tidy lawns. There were breezes. My heart was already heavy but to make my body weigh more I tried pressing downwards with my knees. It was futile of course.

I found the house unchanged. The living room drapes had been drawn to keep out the sunlight; the windows were all shut tight. An overturned wading pool and a plastic doll house lay in the front yard. As I looked at the door, expectant and defeated, the humming grew louder, almost like a death rattle. Then a sudden gust from the south lifted me and I had to snatch at the hedge.

There was no doubt; the wind was rising. Holding on to bushes, I made my way around the side of the house and peered into the dining room. My father sat at the head of the table making funny faces at his new daughter who whirled a spoon over her curly head. Then he was talking to her. Perhaps, I thought, he is telling her about me. While I watched, his wife carried in a roast chicken from the kitchen. Imagine, roasting a chicken! They looked cool and dry, content, normal. While I made no part of their happiness I nonetheless felt proud of it, since I had made it possible. Fascinated, I looked on, all the while growing lighter, though I had almost stopped perspiring. The wind played about my feet, lifting me as much as six inches then setting me down, as if it were toying with me.

I glanced up at the window that for so many years had been mine. What if I released my hold on the rhododendron? Would I sail up to it and somehow float inside? My loose trousers billowed around my thin legs like wings.

The wind blew stronger though without cooling me. Perhaps a thunderstorm was building up, even a tornado, some climactic release of energy. With great pains I managed to work around to the front door. The heaving air was raising me higher and higher. Clutching the knob as tightly as I could, I knocked three times. How cool it must be inside. How glad he would be to see me. I was certain he would hug me.

I waited a long time. Perhaps no one had heard me. Using almost the last of my strength I managed to pull myself down with one hand and deliver a final knock. At last, she opened the door. I was still clinging to the knob with my fingertips.

The edge of chilled air from inside the house grazed my knees like a promise. She peered out, frowned, perhaps at me or from the blast of hot wind. I looked down at her pleadingly, opened my mouth and stretched out my hand as the updraft forced me away. She turned her head. "It's no one," she shouted and then slammed the door. With that I lost my grip and was lifted up into the heart of the fiery wind.

Romanza

Stipulations

Last July 17, a Thursday, in a basement practice room of the Rheinach Center, Rudolf Kanter (26) scuffled with Arnold Pracht (41). At the time both were composers-in-residence at the White Mountains Music Festival, then in the second of its three weeks. The younger man had the better of the brawl, knocking the older down—twice, allegedly—resulting in bruising to Pracht's cheek and jaw, a contusion on his left side, and a sprained right wrist. Kanter sustained minor scraping on his knuckles. There was a single witness to this event, Marie McDermott, a twenty-two year-old violinist.

Kanter and Pracht both remained at the Festival until their respective commissioned works were performed, but Ms. McDermott departed on the afternoon of July 17. She returned to her home in Benton, Indiana, making no formal or informal statement to anyone.

Arnold Pracht did not press a criminal charge against Kanter. However, on August 4 a local lawyer acting on his behalf filed a civil suit in a New Hampshire court demanding damages in the sum of $100,000. By then Kanter had gone back to his home in Brooklyn and Pracht to his in Vienna.

Rudolf Kanter was served with papers on August 6. He informed his parents who immediately contacted their regular firm. The case was put into the hands of Frederick Rosen, Esquire, a member of the bar of New Hampshire as well as New York. Rudolf offered no account of his actions to Rosen beyond saying that Arnold Pracht got what he deserved and that the latter's assertion in his filing that the attack was "malicious, unprovoked, and owing to professional jealousy" was false on all three points.

A Conversation with My Sister

Helena, then in the second year of her clinical psychology program at Stanford, phoned me the week after I returned from the Christmas Break. I was in the middle of my freshman year at Penn.

She started right in. "It's about this friend of yours."

"Rudi?"

"I'm talking about the one who stayed at the house last week."

"We all missed you terribly."

"Sure, I hated not being there."

"No, you didn't."

"*Disliked* then."

"How about *barely noticed*?"

She knew I was teasing, knew I knew she missed me but also that I was happy for her and the guy she called DSB—decidedly serious boyfriend—Jack from Santa Rosa with whom she'd spent the holidays, laboring at her thesis, eating California rolls, making love. I'd always vetted Helena's beaux and, to my considerable pride, she'd attended to what I said, nearly always acted on it, regretted when she didn't. Jack had made the fearsome trip east during the summer to be vetted big time. He'd earned my imprimatur, a big thumbs-up that delighted Helena. I thought Jack was a great guy, even if he was in dental school. He won me over by not trying to and because he treated my sister with a combination of adoration and irony. I also approved of the tact with which he coped with our parents. Father was stiff with him and said little, like a distracted drill sergeant; Mother, on the other hand, was as inquisitive as a prosecutor at Nuremberg. My parents had the customary prejudice against potential mates of the non-Chinese variety and the usual single-minded dedication to the achievements of their offspring. Second-generation successes, my folks: Dad, a taciturn plasma physicist, Mom, a voluble and well-paid radiologist—both with standards more exacting than those of the quality control folks at Lexus. They weren't unaware of being Chinese-American stereotypes; they simply didn't care, not so long as Helena won her gymnastics title, played Chopin without dropping a note, and got early admission into Harvard. If anything, I was even more of a white sheep, not because my grades were better than Helena's, but because I was more dutiful. In her teen years my sister cultivated her gift for being disagreeable, elevating it to high art. I admired her for contradicting Father and still more for daring to go up against Mother. To Helena's credit, she never ridiculed me for being submissive. In her early, Freudian stage she once said, "Well look, Harry, it's no fault of yours Mom implanted that super-colossal Superego inside you. You naturally think it's *your* voice insisting you press your nose against the grindstone, never talk back, and get a 4.0. Of course you think it's your very own Jiminy Cricket letting you have it. But it's not, kid. It's Mom."

I loved my big sister. Like the DSB, I treated her with adoration. With irony was how she treated me.

"So what about Rudi?" I asked.

"Just wanted to give you a heads-up."

"They've been telling you that they don't *approve* of him."

"Don't suppose you needed *me* to pick up on *that*."

"No, it wasn't exactly hard. But it all bounced off Rudi— the scorn, disdain, suspicion, the horror."

"That's nice."

"So *what* then?"

"Well, it's kind of interesting actually. Seems they can't figure it out."

"What?"

"The friendship, you and Rudi. I mean they're sure of *you*. You've never put a foot wrong; you made it through your entire adolescence without slamming a door."

"Okay. We've been over this. I didn't rebel. I admit it, which doesn't mean I like hearing about it."

"I know, I know. Sorry. Okay, so this Rudi struck them as somebody *you* wouldn't like. Mom said he wore a muffler around his neck the whole time and insisted on cooking a soufflé and then ruined the whole dinner quizzing Dad about Heisenberg. She said he even told a Chinese joke, for God's sake. Did he *really*?"

"Muffler, yes; Heisenberg query check, but no Chinese joke. He quoted a proverb; it's just that they'd never heard it before. I can't believe they thought it was a *joke*."

"So, what was it? The proverb."

"'Happiness is when the grandfather dies, then the father dies, then the son dies.' That sound like a knee-slapper to you?"

"Sounds *morbid* to me."

"You had to be there."

"She said he smokes *all* the time."

"Tobacco. Mostly. And not while he's brushing his teeth."

"And he's saving up to buy a Picasso?"

"He can afford one."

"Mom said he's wild and lazy and undisciplined. I guess what she means is transgressive."

"Oh, Grandma, what big *words* you have."

"Hey, kid. I'm in *grad* school; you're just a lowly *freshman*."

"Rudi Kanter's cool. I'd say he's the best of everything I'm not."

"Oh?"

I felt it was time to change the subject. "How's the dentist-in-waiting."

"Still waiting—usually on me. But don't evade the issue. What they can't figure is what you *see* in this Rudi."

"Oh, that's easy. He taught me about Debussy, Lenny Bruce, Piet Mondrian, Thomas Mann, Gustav Mahler, Eugene Ionesco, Le Corbusier, the Marx Brothers, and Bill Evans—and that's just the half of it, and that's in just one semester. Rudi knows Latin, Greek, French, and German. He does symbolic logic. He writes wonderful music and plays four instruments. He calls up girls he doesn't even know. He *tap dances*. I can't say if he's *transgressive* because I don't know exactly what that means. Disobedient? Irreverent? I think the puzzler is what *he* sees in *me*. In fact, I've been meaning to ask him."

My sister had the loveliest way of shutting up and she did that then, long-distance, just like when we were sitting together, a pair of over-achieving schemers who'd reached a consensus.

"I'm so lucky," she said suddenly, from the heart.

"Sure you are."

"I mean that they named me Helena. It's good they went for *visual* alliteration or I could have been Susan Hsu. Then I'd have to correct everybody's pronunciation—'Sue Sue,' and

I'd sound like one of those giant pandas everybody stares at waiting for them to reproduce. I'm glad you're enamored of your supercool friend and learning so much. By the way, Groucho or Chico?"

"Boxers or briefs?"

This was an old joke of ours, a souvenir of our comfy sibling solidarity.

The Road to Benton

I rented a red Chrysler convertible at the Indianapolis airport and played CDs of Torroba, Thelonius Monk, and Brahms as I meandered my air-conditioned way south, more or less following the Wabash's turbid progress toward the Ohio. This was flat farm country in two tones of green—soy and corn—*echt* Midwest, the heartland, and not so long ago a hotbed of the Ku Klux Klan.

When Rudi phoned me he hadn't sounded like he was in any trouble. I knew about the Festival and thought he'd called just to tell me he was back in town and how it had all gone. We'd always kept in touch and saw each other every other week or so. He'd come over from Brooklyn Heights and we'd meet at some bar or restaurant or rendezvous at Chelsea Piers. In good weather we'd walk by the Hudson or over the Brooklyn Bridge. Rudi loved Roebling's span and accounted it the finest piece of public art in America, closely followed by the Vietnam Veterans Memorial. In fact, when he phoned he'd told me a bit about the Festival—what the accommodations were like, things people had said for and against his *Pastorale*. As always, he'd begun with the same little joke, asking if I'd gotten married—or my sister divorced—since we last spoke. Rudi once explained that teasing is a fruitful method of dealing with the world if one likes the place well enough yet can't quite bring oneself to join it. Teasing he called a social attainment of the half-hearted and the whimsical, "people willing to treat anybody like a child." He certainly liked teasing *me*, so it was always significant when he didn't. This was the case when, in our junior year, I finally did ask him why he wanted me as a friend. It wasn't an easy question to pose; it could have sounded like angling for praise or, worse, the prelude to a brush-off. But Rudi seemed to grasp what I meant. He was an aristocrat, had gone to prep school, was imaginative, facile, well-dressed, cultured, traveled, a jack-in-the-box for wit, exhilarating and grueling company in the way a companionable pyrotechnic display might be. I was the obedient son of immigrant strivers, publicly educated, a plugger, always anxious and I thought myself a dull foil for the brilliant diamond he so obviously was. The foil might be excused for admiring the jewel but why should a diamond take an interest in what merely sets it off?

Rudi had lived on my hall our first year; thereafter he had his own condo. His father had been advised to buy one for him, though Rudi protested he preferred to go on living in the dorms. If absolutely necessary, he might live in the house of one of the WASPy fraternities that were courting him like mad. But he didn't want to move off campus. Rudi performed a good imitation of his father who had the eccentricity of emphasizing his nouns, as if he were speaking German: "If we've got the *capital*, son, we buy a *condo* then sell it for a nice *profit* when you graduate. Assuming the *market* keeps rising, it could pay for half of your *tuition*, maybe more. Stupid *not* to do it . . ." Rudi grimaced. "And that, *mon frère chinois*, is how the rich get richer."

So we were lounging in his off-campus living room, feet on the glass-topped coffee table. Rudi was smoking marijuana and I was sipping a pale ale when I put the question: what made him want to be my friend in the first place and then persist in it? For once he didn't toss off an epigram. He took his time, let the question hover over us like the blue smoke from his joint. Then he rather gravely said, "I see an American." I rubbed my hairless Chinese chin and tried to make sense of this. The implication was that I was closer to being the genuine article than he.

Hauling ass across the flat bosom of the motherland in my Chrysler last August I recalled this conversation and wondered if that was what he really meant and, if so, why it mattered to him. Did Rudolph Kanter, with birthrights to cash and culture, see me romantically as a Representative American, my *chinoiserie* notwithstanding? Did he see me as a bootstrap-puller, a self-inventor, a Franklin-Whitman-Emerson-Lincoln-Ford, a strait-laced, slant-eyed Gatsby? Next to Rudi I always felt slow and inadequate, and he appreciated this, allowed for it, tried to mitigate it. Was he telling me I had something he lacked and could never have? Did he actually like that I was such a Good Boy, yearned for my parents' approval, was uncorrupted either by trust funds or special talents like his flair for writing dirty poems in Latin and charming, clever, touching music?

Rudi had asked to meet and suggested the Danube, a new restaurant he'd praised. It was down in Tribeca. So that's where we got together.

There was some preliminary chit-chat but as soon as he got into the Pracht story I interrupted him.

"Give me a dollar."

"What?"

"Then I'll be your lawyer."

"I've already got a lawyer. Old family retainer. Well, not all that old, actually."

"So you'll have *two* lawyers. It's protection, Rudi. This way anything you tell me is privileged."

He took out his billfold and handed me three dollars. "You should never under-charge," he joked. "Your clients won't respect you."

I pocketed the bills. "Okay, now tell me exactly what happened."

And he did, his version of it, at least.

A respectable firm of corporate lawyers (who never under-charged) recruited me straight out of Columbia Law School saying they liked the undergraduate degree from Wharton, were impressed by the diligence demonstrated by my grades and glowing recommendations—they praised everything except my Asiatic face which, I suspected, was the real selling-point. They were a homogeneous bunch, white from the shoes on up; they needed some kind of minority or other. Now that I'd worked my tail off for two years I was entitled to a week's vacation. After lunch with Rudi, I decided to take it at once. I meant to go to Benton and talk to Marie McDermott. At least I would try.

I had a tough time persuading Rudi. He didn't seem to want the violinist approached. That, he said, is why he hadn't told his "real" lawyer about her. But I pressed him. I pointed out that the other side might subpoena her as a witness anyway.

"That's for sure not going to happen," he said wagging a finger at me.

"Well, then. Is it that you think she won't bear you out?"

He shrugged.

"There's some *other* reason?"

He twisted in his seat. "Maybe you could ask her for an affidavit or something?"

"An affidavit might not be admissible. Anyway, the other side would have to be given a crack at her. And then they'd certainly subpoena her—which, in my opinion, is what *you* should do. According to your story you're her hero, right?"

"Maybe. I don't actually know."

"Why not?"

Rudi smiled ironically. "Because she's even more Chinese than you are."

"What?"

"Inscrutable." Rudi laughed hollowly. "Besides, she never thanked me."

It's a capital error to put an unwilling witness on the stand the substance of whose testimony is, moreover, unknown to you. But I didn't say this to Rudi, who was looking more and more like he was on the point of firing me. He really was in a spot.

"Look," I said. "I'll phone her up. Just see if she's willing to talk. To me, I mean. Then we can decide. You don't have to do a thing. That okay?"

"You mean you'd go out there and interview her? She's somewhere in *Indiana*, I think. That's a long way, Harry."

"Well, I've known you a long time."

Pracht v. Kanter

It is possible that whoever was responsible for choosing two composers to reside at the White Mountains Music Festival judged contrasts piquant: an established European and an American still on the make; one difficult, the other accessible; two distinctive takes on tradition—something like that. The question of whether they would get along, much less come to blows, is unlikely to have been discussed even by a committee staffed by people well informed about how prickly and competitive musicians are. But perhaps I am doing these people an injustice. Maybe they just had a sense of humor or reckoned if some sparks flew as high as the peaks of the Presidential range it would be exciting. "An event! . . . Yes, and so educational for the youngsters." The youngsters: I'm not satisfied that the committee gave adequate consideration to them.

In our senior year, while I was sweating out my LSAT score, Rudi announced his decision to study musical composition and to do so in Paris. He cast his choice to me—and very likely to his family—in terms of historical inevitability.

"They say, and persuasively too, that every great fortune is founded on a great crime. Well then, assuming the family manages to hold on to it, the money gets laundered in a generation or two and the family turns law-abiding. The robber baron's succeeded by the banker and the surgeon, then come the academics and philanthropists until, at last, we descend to the artist. I've decided to be that artist. Painting's messy, writing's tedious, sculpting requires muscles, acting demands both exhibitionism and talent. So I've decided to write music."

Never mind that he'd been writing music since he was nine. Still, it was a novelty to think of Rudi actually *wanting* something, bracing to witness this brilliant but languorous dilettante contemplating the rigors of professionalism.

So after graduation Rudi and I went our separate ways, both determined to work hard and make our ways in the world. We kept up with each other by email and phone and whenever Rudi flew home to New York we'd get together. He'd tell me outrageous tales about European women and tease me about my own anemic social life, which was arranged exclusively by my mother.

Rudi returned from Paris after two years, buoyant as a fresh cork and with a quantity of finished work. He had some early success, not all of it due to family connections, though his relatives probably wanted to manage his career the way mine did my sex life. His first big break was the premiere in Baltimore of his *Piano Concerto*. Typically, he sent me his own review.

"Young Mr. Kanter's music inclines toward the tuneful and witty rather than the daunting or deep. Imagine Poulenc without the Catholicism or Rossini at twenty-three. All the same, it's not just a matter of smooth surfaces. The *Andante* is built on a melancholy melody that moves in both senses. The composer seems to have been promiscuously influenced. The dissonances of the *finale* are redolent of both be-bop and Bartok. Regarding tradition, young Kanter expresses his regard for it, broadly defined, in an inverted way, via a sort of affectionate irreverence. This boy may have promise but so far seems more concerned to please with glossiness than to abrade or delve, preferring to juggle with what's been done rather than take the risk of originality, assuming he's capable of any."

The actual reviews were more glowing, but less interesting and also, I thought, less perceptive. The fact was that Rudi did crave immediate success. He claimed his *Concerto* was the result of calculation rather than inspiration. In my opinion this was true in a way and false in a way. Rudi can't help writing playfully, wittily, ingratiatingly, because that is his character. And he is sufficiently romantic never to pass up a good melody, especially in his slow movements, which are the places where he permits himself to dip his toes in the abyss. The *Sarabande* of his *First Quartet* made me tear up when he first played it for me on the piano. I told him the music made me think of a dying man recollecting the happiest Sunday afternoon of his childhood. He hooted, of course, but with delight.

Over our post-prandial espressos at the Danube Rudi discoursed at unnecessary length, and with an acerbity excessively relished, on Arnold Pracht and his *oeuvre*. According to Rudi, listening to Pracht isn't a thing one undertakes casually, or even on purpose.

"Maestro Pracht," he said, "thinks exceedingly well of Maestro Pracht; in fact, I believe he thinks of little else. Pracht cultivates his reputation the way Nero Wolfe does orchids. He writes articles which, no matter their titles, are invariably about his own work. They all sound like old-fashioned manifestoes. He loves being interviewed and comes over as a cross between a film director and a designer of women's clothes. He yearns to be admired not only so as to prop up his *amour-propre* but because he wants women. He wears a lot of leather and is beginning to turn leathery himself, what with all the time he spends sunning himself on other people's yachts. I ran across him in Paris and he was just the same. Fifteen years of phony iconoclasm and genuine debauchery take a toll; the guy's starting to look wasted. It almost goes without saying that he's contemptuous of everything American. *Amerika, du hast es schlechter.* Except for the greenbacks, of course, and except for the girls. The man plays things two ways: he can set himself up as the sole legitimate heir of the Viennese tradition, as if he used to hang out with Mozart and Mahler, and at the same time he's the *enfant terrible* smashing every worn-out convention, a mad Calvinist in a cathedral. Pracht's the most *theoretical* of composers. His insecurity shows up in the way he insists on how complex and profound his intentions are. When you actually listen to his stuff it's hard not to think of what Twain said about Wagner. You know—that he knew the music was much better than it sounded."

"Wow. You *really* don't care for this guy," I said superfluously, just to make it seem that what we were having was a conversation.

Rudi blew his nose into his napkin, folded it up. "Say you stuffed everything I can't stand about so-called serious contemporary music and the pretentious people who write it into a centrifuge and ran it for an hour or two. The scum at the bottom of the test tube would be Arnold Pracht. The guy adores being called difficult and challenging and edgy, even *ugly*—anything but *academic*. This insistence on always doing 'something new' betrays his slavish obsession with tradition, which, of course, he vehemently denies. His latest fad, by the way, the one about which he lectured the girls in the mountains, is testing the limits of music. I can still hear him holding forth in that ludicrous Wienerschnitzel accent."

By now Rudi had worked himself up to unstoppability. He delivered the following in the voice of a Gestapo officer in a second-rate WWII movie.

"On ze left hand you have, ja, noise, nicht wahr? Was ist *noise?* Ze rattling radiator, ze infernal traffic, ze collapse of an apartment block? Zen, on ze right you have monotony, yes? Ze dial tone, ze buzzing door bell, ze drone of a Tibetan monk. Verstehe? Yes? You follow? Well, ze one ist all variation und ze other all repetition. Was den ist ze music? Tradition insists ze music must be so to say an aggregate, a compromise; zat is to say, repetition und variation also. Zat ist was has been thought always. Not too much ze one nor again too much ze other. But why, I should like to ask? Why zis prejudice? To seek out ze harmony in one single tone, ze melody hidden in random rattling—zat ist was I have set out precisely to accomplish in zis new piece I have composed for zis grosse Festival, ze work which you will so much honor me by performing."

Rudi snorted. "Intentional drivel," he declared, striking the table, "one long Teutonic pick-up line. Pracht's one *real* talent is disguising lechery as music theory. Marie was the only female who didn't melt, didn't respond at all in fact; so naturally she was the one he had to have: that red hair, the green eyes and milky skin, that coupling of loveliness with silence, the provocation of her seriousness and total indifference."

This final, unexpectedly lyrical outburst of Rudi's aroused, as they say, my suspicions. But then, a lawyer's trained to be suspicious, to check all the angles. I couldn't help but notice, for example, that he mentioned milky skin and auburn hair but not Ms. McDermott's surname. As to his professional distaste for Pracht, I was reminded of one of the few Chinese proverbs I knew, had remembered, in fact, because of Rudi. Now I laid it before my agitated friend.

"A bird does not sing because it has an answer. It sings because it has a song."

"Exactly," he growled and hit the table so that the little cups jumped.

The McDermotts

The population of Benton, Indiana is pretty much what you'd expect. The staff at the Ramada didn't actually stare at me; in fact, their exaggerated politeness made me wonder if they mistook me for a Japanese businessman looking to open a Honda plant. The reception clerk even made a funny little bow as he handed over my key-card, uncertain but willing to practice oriental etiquette. I couldn't have been more amused if he'd come out from behind his counter and kowtowed. "Mr., uh, *Hi-Sue?*" he ventured. "It's pronounced *Sue,*" I said for the ten thousandth time in my life. When he heard the New York accent he didn't appear embarrassed, only stupefied.

Ten minutes on the computer had yielded a few data on Marie McDermott. She was a violinist, held a bachelor's degree in music (*magna cum laude*) from Indiana University and was a candidate for an M.F.A. at the same distinguished institution. She had performed fairly widely, albeit in small local venues, both as soloist and in chamber groups. Her notices ran from more than satisfactory to inappropriately adoring. She had won a place among the first violins in the University's symphony orchestra. Her high-school graduation picture was online: Catholic uniform, long red hair, straight little nose. If there was a smile there you'd need a magnifying glass to find it. At seventeen she looked as solemn as a fugue in B-minor. There was also a more recent picture, a professional portrait. In this one she was holding her violin by its neck and had on a dress of what looked like green velvet—Maid Marian with a string instrument depending from her delicate hand like a defunct swan. The earnest twelfth-grader had grown up to be a knockout but she still wasn't smiling. Even on the computer screen I could see what had turned Rudi lyrical. Ms. McDermott was an ideal illustration of what Kierkegaard—a philosopher I'd had to read for a required humanities class and never forgot—called "The Interesting." He'd defined it as "a border category," something that's two things at once: beautiful but also meaningful, aesthetic yet ethical too—combining the qualities of a physics textbook with those of a Roadrunner cartoon. That is, your average supermodel isn't as interesting as one with a 160 IQ who can play Bach. Ms. McDermott was gorgeous; she stuck me as untouchable yet put together in such a way that, assuming you were alive and male, you'd want to touch her.

I gave the timing of my initial call to Ms. McDermott some consideration. If I tried her during the day there was less chance she'd be home, but a night call, outside office hours, might come off as unprofessional, which was the last thing I wanted. According to my sources (Rudi and a garrulous female Festival official I'd managed to get hold of) Ms. McDermott—homesick? disgusted? traumatized? —had fled after the incident to her parents' home in Benton. Assuming I'd gotten the right McDermotts on the search engine, Marie's father, James Michael McDermott, was an executive with Archer Daniels Midland; her mother, Margaret, was active in executing the good works of Holy Cross Church. Marie had two younger sisters, aged eighteen and fourteen. I noticed the spacing—one girl every four years, one tuition at a time—which suggested an admirable mastery of the Rhythm Method. I recalled a poster I'd once seen from The-Family-That-Prays-Together-Stays-Together campaign of the 1950s: standard-issue white family in their Sunday best standing at reverent attention in a pew—Nelsons and Cleavers and Father Knowing Best. Would such people even open the door to a Chinese lawyer from the fleshpots of the East wanting to talk about what I wanted to talk about? Still, I could hardly justify making the trip without first convincing Marie to meet me. But why should she? What reason could I give? Her father would hardly let me see her alone, if at all. James Michael probably kept a shotgun around the house.

I called in the afternoon and, as it turned out, one of her sisters picked up the phone and did so as if it was in an old British film, albeit one with Caller ID.

"McDermott residence. Maureen McDermott speaking. How may I help you Mr. . . *Hi-Sue?*"

I made the usual correction and hurriedly identified myself as an attorney who needed to speak with Ms. Marie McDermott. I said *needed*, not *wanted*, by way of appealing to the little sister's charitable nature. If she felt anger toward me it was well swaddled in schoolgirl courtesy.

"I'm afraid my sister's not here at the moment." Then the voice suddenly turned sincere, a decibel louder and a decade younger. "Oh," she said, "is this about what happened in New Hampshire?"

I admitted it was.

"Then can you *please* tell me what happened? Marie won't tell me *anything*."

So Marie wasn't talking to her sister, maybe not even to her parents. Why would she talk to me?

"I regret I can't do that," I told Maureen.

"Shoot," she exclaimed. "Well, Marie'll be back in an hour. Want to try her then?"

"I will."

"Should I tell her?"

"That I called?"

"Yep."

"Sure, Maureen."

"Okay. Goodbye, Mr. *Hsu*."

Meticulous pronunciation of my name was my reward for remembering hers. I just wasn't sure if she was the fourteen- or eighteen-year-old.

Marie did take my call, though almost the first thing she said was that her parents hadn't wanted her to do so.

"You told them what happened?"

"Not in detail," she said curtly but without conspicuous hostility.

I pressed the point, perhaps unwisely. "They must have been distressed for you. They'd have wanted to know the details."

Pause. "They did. Yes."

This told me that Marie McDermott had a strong character, was keen about privacy, and probably wanted to put the nasty episode behind her and get back to fiddling full-time.

I started over. "I want to thank you for speaking with me," I said.

"I can't have you phoning here and talking to my sisters. Or my parents. It would upset them."

Or send you to a nunnery, I speculated, and plunged ahead without much hope. "Would you be willing to talk to *me* about the details?"

She didn't say no. She said, "Why?"

I explained that Arnold Pracht had filed a civil suit against Rudolph Kanter, my client. Though her name was not mentioned in the complaint, should the case go forward it was possible she might be subpoenaed.

"Subpoenaed by you, Mr. Hsu?" Her pronunciation was impeccable.

"I can't rule it out. Perhaps by the other side."

"I would prefer not to be subpoenaed."

"I appreciate that, Ms. McDermott. Of course. I too would prefer to avoid it. Would you consent to meet with me?"

Pause. "I can't come east."

"No, of course not. I'd come *there*, naturally."

"It's that important?"

"I think it is."

Pause. "You believe what I have to say would help your client?"

"Certainly."

"I see. And if I refuse?"

"You were the only witness, Ms. McDermott. In the event of a refusal, I'm afraid the likelihood of a subpoena would increase."

Pause. "How do I know you're who you say you are?"

"You can look me up on the Internet." I gave her my firm's web site.

Pause to write, then, "Did you Google *me*?"

"I did."

Another pause, a long one. Impatient sigh. Then grudging consent. "But I have two conditions: I won't meet with you at my parents' house and I won't meet with you alone."

"Not a problem," I said airily. "How about over dinner at Benton's best restaurant? My treat."

"I don't like the best restaurant in Benton," she said without irony.

I ventured a laugh. "Well, *your* favorite, then."

She told me its name. Marengo. Chicken, I thought, Napoleon's Italian victory. We fixed a day and time. And so I had, if I cared to look at it that way, a dinner date.

Dinner With the Violinist

I was early. She was right on time. I wore contacts. She wore glasses. I had on a tan sport coat and a tie. She had on a blouse about the same color as her eyes, a knee-length white skirt, and a blue cotton blazer. I smiled when I saw her, which was before she saw me. When she saw me she didn't smile. I tried to comport myself professionally. She actually did.

I was nursing a tonic water at the bar while she looked around uncertainly at the door, the way people do, but she didn't do it the way other people do. I stood and raised my arm. What, I wondered, must I look like to her? Exotic? A lawyer? Yet another man from the decadent East?

There she was, milky skin and all. Those pixels were a joke, really. As she walked toward me I saw that she moved awkwardly; she had the slightest limp. Rudi hadn't mentioned that. It was, I think, the limp that floored me. And the glasses. Well, we learn: human perfection is never perfect. And then there was her impregnable seriousness, of course. The way she didn't smile. Ever.

I introduced myself. She nodded but didn't take my hand. It was a week night and the restaurant, not being the best in Benton, only her favorite, wasn't crowded. We were shown right to a table.

Marie didn't give me an opportunity to pull out her chair. She was dauntingly brisk. She sat right down and touched her hair—didn't fool with it, just fingered the ends. I thanked her again for seeing me.

"You didn't leave me much choice," she said factually, without resentment.

I glanced over the menu. She didn't need to. It was her favorite restaurant, after all.

A waitress was there at once and smiled familiarly at Marie. I ordered veal verdicchio, Marie the lasagna. When I suggested a glass of Chianti she declined. Either she didn't drink or she wanted to get down to business.

"Arnold Pracht is suing my client, Rudi—"

"Excuse me. You call him *Rudi*?"

"He's an old friend as well as my client."

"Ah, I see," she said, as if this solved a riddle that had puzzled her, perhaps why I would come all the way to Benton, Indiana.

"Arnold Pracht is demanding a considerable sum of money for damages. In his complaint he claims that Rudi's attack on him was unprovoked, malicious, and prompted by professional jealousy."

"And what does your friend say?"

I saw no reason to be anything but candid. "He's said nothing officially. He's said nothing at all, except to me."

She looked impatient. "And what has he said to *you*, Mr. Hsu?"

"He told me that he was defending you, Ms. McDermott. He said Arnold Pracht was physically assaulting you in that rehearsal room, that he happened to be in the adjacent one, heard you cry out, and came to your rescue. Is that true?"

She *was* inscrutable. I wondered if she were wondering if I believed my friend.

"Pracht offered to go over a Beethoven sonata with me, a difficult one. The *Kreutzer*."

"Yes, I know it. And what happened?"

"He did make," she hesitated over this crucial choice of words, "advances."

"Good."

Her stillness remained undisturbed; not an eyebrow raised. "Good for your client?"

"Did you cry out?"

"I suppose I did make a noise, though I wouldn't describe it as a cry. I was surprised, that's all."

"So you didn't raise an alarm, call for help, nothing like that?"

"Certainly not. Nevertheless, your client did tear open the door. He rushed in and started hitting Pracht."

"Pardon me, Ms. McDermott. I have to ask these questions. Are you saying you were *not* being molested by Arnold Pracht?"

She paused. "Did *I* use that word, Mr. Hsu?"

"What word would you use, then?"

"I believe I said he made *advances*."

"An ambiguous word—a weak one, legally speaking."

The waitress interrupted us. We fell silent as she set down our food and encouraged us to enjoy it.

Marie forked about a gram of lasagna into her mouth. "It's as good as ever," she said, but even the good food didn't merit a smile.

"Excuse me, I have to put these questions. It's my duty."

"Yes, your duty to your client. Your friend."

I leaned back defensively, brushed my mouth with my napkin. "Ms. McDermott, what would my client have *seen* when he came into the rehearsal room?"

"Hasn't he told you?"

"He did. But I'd be obliged to have your opinion."

"I can't tell you what another person saw."

I took a deep breath, hating myself, hating Rudi. "Let me rephrase. When my client came into the rehearsal room was Arnold Pracht in physical contact with you?"

Another pause, another measured answer: "Possibly," she said.

"*Possibly?*"

"You've had your answer, Mr. Hsu."

I almost expected her to add, "So do you still want to subpoena me?"

"Very well, then."

I thought that was all she was going to say but then she surprised me. "There's more."

I didn't really want any more.

"Your friend, Rudolph Kanter, had been annoying me ever since he arrived. Did he tell you that? Also, did he tell you what he was doing in the basement?"

"No," I admitted.

She nodded demurely and spoke to her plate rather than to me. "This isn't pleasant for me, Mr. Hsu. I feel, I feel intruded on by you. No, I know it's not your fault."

"Thank you. I'm grateful you said that."

"All right, then. I don't mean to sound immodest but I got the idea they were competing. Isabelle said so too. My roommate. Also Alan, a cellist. *Vying.* That was the word Alan used. He said this sort of thing happens all the time at festivals, that

225

it was a sort of game between them, that they were making me
another object over which to compete."

"*Another* object?"

"Everyone could see they despised each other and hated
each other's work."

I cleared my throat. "Did my client ever attack—pardon
me—*make advances* in the same way Pracht did?"

"If you mean did he touch me, then no. But I don't think
it was because he had any scruples about it. In my opinion he
thought he didn't *need* to. I'm sorry, but your friend struck me
as conceited. Entitled."

"You didn't like him?"

Here Marie revealed some annoyance. She put down her
fork and again began to finger the ends of her hair—that auburn hair which she still wore long, with bangs—and answered
me with steely dignity. "I wasn't there to *like anybody*, Mr. Hsu.
I was there to study, to *work*."

I drove out of Benton the following morning.

Taking his orders from Rudi's parents, Frederick Rosen
negotiated an out-of-court settlement. Rudi told me he'd have
preferred to win but didn't really care.

I've written to Marie McDermott three times. I've tried
to call her four. So far.

A Laurel Greener

It was a summer wedding, one of those festivals of the wealthy that can go on for two or three days, the climactic oaths squeezed between brunches, cocktails, and dinners. Even when ferociously tasteful they are gaudy, with guest lists toted up in hecatombs, enacted in resort hotels, municipal libraries, on wooded islands, aboard cruise ships, with credits as thick as Hollywood's: caterers, musicians, florists, dressmakers, bartenders, décor consultants. For the exalted perfection of a few regal moments—intensively recorded if not really memorable, also like Hollywood—fortunes are as gaily spilled as the champagne. Life's few sublime moments are brief as a matter of course, no less so at prodigious weddings. The small calamity is that in most cases they are not lofty enough to escape the weight of orchids and damask, that they briefly twinkle then dissolve into soiled napkins, crumpled carnations, indigestion, hangovers. But perhaps I'm being too critical, since excess is the least dispensable feature of these nuptial dramas, and the solemn exchange of vows must be followed by a ruinous and raucous aftermath, like a satyr play. I've read that there are still villages in Europe where peasants scrimp meanly for twenty years then blow every sou and dinar on a daughter's wedding; and if the show succeeds in raising a neighbor's eyebrow they will live contentedly in squalor ever after, comforted by an album of fading photographs or, these days, a discolored videotape. It's simply not true that the rich never count the cost of these affairs, that money is no object. On the contrary, every item is carefully priced, not only by the hosts but by the guests. A figure is set on each perfect rose and labeled bottle, and a ghostly tag hangs even from the bridal gown itself. I've heard how the rich talk, keeping the books. Well, after all, what use is flaunting without accounting? These carnivals are planned the way great powers prepare for war, and, overlooking the remains of the day, one almost believes that joy can wreak as much devastation as combat. I've seen mothers of the bride surveying reception like victorious generals. Perhaps all this grandeur is a bribe, a propitiation offered up to Fate, in the hope that the sheer opulence of the launch will guarantee the safety of the voyage.

This particular shindig happened to be an island wedding. It was also a reunion, thanks to our old and prosperous friend, the father of the bride, who invited us on a sentimental whim at $180 a plate. The rush of surf, never far off, marked time, and time, best defined by its depredations, was bound to occupy the thoughts of the half-dozen of us who had, with a few exceptions, not seen one another for thirty years. When we had all been graduate students together, we and the father of the bride, before he married into an empire. Official reunions to which, with a mixture of affection and avarice, the University invites its undergraduate alumni at regular intervals never included graduate students. They do not have official reunions. Perhaps in this way the University means to deny responsibility for the souls of its masters and doctors, though more likely they reckon we would be as likely to show up as to swell the endowment. We grad students went our own ways with unmothered souls.

It was getting to be late on Sunday but the celebrations were by no means over. Handsome young couples, chiefly Manhattan friends of the plutocratic newlyweds, twenty-somethings accustomed to this sort of bash, still danced boisterously on the terraced lawn, trudged from the beach glowing with excellent prospects, grinning in the faith that the business cycle had been quietly lobbed on the dust heap of history. To us they seemed at once innocent and jaded, as we probably did to them. As usual, the young and the old were both right.

We had bunched together, the six of us, in a little circle on the broad porch that skirted the hotel. This venerable pile—you couldn't look at it without thinking "white elephant"—had been built in the years before air-conditioning. We sat on the west side, out of the Atlantic wind. In a while the sun would set behind the headland. We looked across the bay at a scene so determinedly picturesque that it too might be a commodity with a brand name. The water coruscated with silver highlights about to be transmuted.

We had begun catching up hours before, of course, in the shorthand way people do after too much time has passed. Those who had them introduced their spouses; each of us presented the others with a sort of mini-c.v., radically abbreviating our lives, foreshortening here, expurgating there. We knew we were being superficial and none of us really liked it, but what were we to do after thirty years of knotty divorces and circuitous career moves? On the other hand, while skimping on ourselves, we recalled defunct professors, archaic seminars, and ancient parties in such nostalgic detail that we drove the spouses into a provisional and defensive bond of their own. Hoarding up their resentment for later, they moved off to the outdoor buffet.

We had all started out wanting, even yearning, to be historians, as if to be an historian were an existential achievement rather than the mark of a certain kind of painstaking labor. Children of the sixties, the most romantic of us had begun by envisioning ourselves as heroic revisionists, riflers of the past, intent on lighting up the world with explosive, liberating truths. It was, after all, a time when sipping a Pepsi rather than a Coke was a political act. No doubt we terrified our professors with our hair and revolutionary rancor. Heaven knows we wanted to. We had all heard the vocation. Each had his or her idols and nurtured glorious dreams; but in those days even the humble aspiration to a dull career in some liberal arts backwater became a glory beyond reach. The job market collapsed well before the '73 recession and aspiration collided with demography. Baby boomers and draft evaders had swollen the Vietnam-era graduate programs whose directors gave no thought to the imponderable question of whom we would all teach. Or, with the casual indifference of people with tenure, four percent mortgages, and cozy cottages on northern lakes, our mentors simply didn't care. They held fast to the convenient fiction that they were training scholars, not schoolteachers.

"Remember Louie?" somebody said. "Whenever he heard somebody got pregnant he'd say 'Good for business.'"

We all recalled funny, wild Louie with his ironic optimism, dead of an early glioma. There was a somber moment.

"Hey! What about *Gradstein?*"

We all groaned and in chorus pronounced the old judgment via his sobriquet, "Oh God, *Gradgrind.*"

Even after that famous afternoon when we were assembled and rather gleefully told by the department chairman that we could look for nothing but unemployment Gradstein had been infuriatingly undismayed.

"What was that thing he used to say over and over again?"

"There's always a job for the best."

We broke up. "That's it!"

Gradstein's Emersonian boast was invariably delivered without any redeeming tinge of self-doubt; his arrogance was of the impregnable variety. He relished being detested; he thought it a distinction.

No one was able to say what had become of Gradstein. Nobody cared. Three decades had done nothing to soften our antipathy, and recalling it, feeling it afresh, drew us closer, obliterating lives which, there was no need to admit, were not the lives we had once sought—except for one of us, except for Vasary. The rest of us had accepted the situation, renounced a foolish dream, had mostly prospered too, in hi-tech, insurance, law. Vasary alone had managed an academic career, served his time as an exploited adjunct, cobbling together part-time jobs here and there. Then he caught a break, a tenure-track assistant professorship, turned his dissertation into a well-received book, dazzled in the lecture hall, volunteered for all the department's scut work while pumping out a second book. We knew the story without his having to tell it. In the fullness of time, he was tenured. No one resented him and, what's more, no one envied him either. It may do us no credit but the truth was that we were all satisfied with our lives; we may even have sensed that we had been saved from something toilsome and petty, as if that post-adolescent disappointment had really been a narrow escape. Moreover, I suppose we had become cynical enough as people, and sloppy enough as historians *manqués*, to believe that among choice, necessity, and chance it's the last that does the heavy lifting. This is a convenient way of judging lives and easy enough to support; but in the end it's not chance but choice that fixes character. Where you work and whom you marry can be put down to happenstance, but not the way you labor, not how well you love.

Vasary had never been either sloppy or cynical. What absorbed him were not the accidents of history or the constraints of fatality. Character was what he liked to contemplate, in its way an idea as antiquated yet substantial as the huge white hotel whose porch we occupied. Yet Vasary was no anachronism; he understood very well that, even if we ignore the process, character is forged between the hammer of luck and the anvil of inevitability. His métier was biography; it was the individual that roused him and this he demonstrated to us that late afternoon on Wedding Island.

The raised voices and resounding bass of the amplifiers seemed to quiet down as the gabled shadow of the hotel lengthened over the terrace. We had arrived at the point in our conversation where mere recollection was no longer gratifying. There was a silence, as if we had agreed on a transition even if no one knew to what.

Then one of us asked Vasary to tell us a little about the life we'd missed, the snare we'd escaped. "But don't talk about your books, for God's sake; we've all read them."

Vasary squirmed, I think out of embarrassment both for the gratuitous rudeness of the speaker and also for himself, for having made good books while we had merely made good money. Or perhaps he was simply surprised that any of us had read his work.

Vasary had always been subtle and, I now realized, the only real moralist among us. Oh, we were all moralistic aplenty once upon that time, certain of our goodies and baddies, having properly lined up the ducks of politics and the geese of ideology. But Vasary had been different, some even called him suspect. He had the skeptic's infuriating reluctance to assent to collective conclusions, even obvious ones, and he could not conceal his disgust with slogans. It seemed to some that Vasary could be pedantic; in class he would turn a fact over like a jeweler appraising the facets of a diamond while most of us were happy to see only one side. Even at twenty-two he lacked impatience. Maybe that's why he persisted when we did not.

Why then did he choose to tell us just this particular story? Was it because he sensed hovering over our little circle some middle-aged scruple about untaken roads? Did we attend to him because the tale was emblematic, an obscurely rueful response to questions nobody had the nerve to ask? Maybe Vasary had no such purpose at all, was simply suffering from a shock of which he was made mindful by our indulgent sentimentality and the lightly borne pain of yet another generation that relished the self-pity of thinking itself lost.

"There *is* a something I'd like to tell you about. It's a story, actually. But I want you to know in advance that I really don't understand it, I mean personally, for myself. Institutionally, so to speak, it's as plain as a pancake. In cases like this there's always some kind of unofficial official explanation and I can't honestly say it's wrong, only that it's . . . that it's crude." This was the Vasary of old, the one who had always resisted bluntness.

"You make it sound portentous," somebody said lightly.

Vasary laughed. "I'm sorry. It doesn't portend anything at all. It's all over now, like Caesar's assassination."

"We can take it that this isn't about *you*?"

"No, not about me. I suppose you could say it's about a book—or two books. But mostly it has to do with a young colleague. I call him colleague though now he isn't and he wasn't even in my own department, which means that, unofficially, my responsibility doesn't amount to much. Still, he was worth watching, worth helping too, and since I did both I can't help feeling it. Helping is always a way of being responsible, a sort of vouching . . . . Don't you think?"

Nobody answered Vasary.

"Well. Maybe you can imagine him: a political scientist, mid-thirties, hard-working, intelligent, level-headed, decent, a good listener but with views of his own as well—if not a paragon then as good as. At least that's the way he looked for six years and five weeks. His name—though I suppose I can't be absolutely sure of it—is Alexander Brach. He came with an Ivy League degree and, I was told, references well beyond solid. Brach's chairman called the recommendation from his thesis advisor *an intellectual love letter*. That was the phrase his chairman used, and nobody would accuse Ralph Marburg of being effusive. Brach was an expert on Central Europe which is where he came from, apparently. Story is the family moved from Slovenia when he was twelve. He preserved a slight accent, exotic but intelligible, exactly the kind that impresses Americans."

Somebody chuckled "Like Kissinger's."

"The first time I saw him was on the tennis court. I still play a hacker's game once in a while. I guess it was September of his second year. Brach was hitting with the school's top scholarship-grade singles player, a lanky Floridian—a pro now. Colossal serve. When they began a set my partner and I decided to watch. Brach didn't have the kid's power but he had a lot more than you'd expect, and he was faster on his feet. He disguised his shots and he kept hitting lines. The kid got frustrated, especially by all that line-hitting. He started to make bad calls. It was interesting, seeing how Brach handled it. He just smiled and nodded. Of course he knew the kid was cheating but he never called him on it; in fact, he *helped* him. Brach called balls in that were clearly out on his side. It was, well, a remarkable thing. You see, he shamed the kid without saying a word."

"Did he know you were watching?"

"Oh, we weren't the only ones. There was a regular little knot of us, seven or eight, and behind the fence a couple girls who probably followed the stringbean hero around."

"So, who won?"

"I don't remember; anyway, that wasn't what interested me. A few weeks later we were introduced by Phil Marsh, a modern European specialist. Apparently they'd become pals. Marsh told me later he was thinking of asking Brach to collaborate on a textbook. He called Brach brilliant, said he knew all kinds of amazing stuff, inside dope on Eastern European politics, juicy anecdotes. Apparently he'd gotten some terrific interviews for his dissertation which was due out in a year from one of the top presses."

"Real golden boy, eh?"

"Not to look at. Short and muscular, built more for soccer than tennis. Apparently, he'd been a star forward on his college team. He smiled all the time, not in a silly way, but as if whatever you happened to be saying to him was just about the most wonderful thing that could ever be said. He looked a good bit older than he was thanks to a little goatee and heavy glasses. But despite the facial hair and horn rims Brach had a peculiarly open face. He'd hold his head a little to one side and look up at you while you talked. Easy to see why those interviews went so well. Not handsome, but a real charmer. You could tell he liked being where he was, loved his work. He looked as if he adored every statue in the quad. And he really did have the goods. I sat in on a couple of his lectures. No notes, walked around the room, plenty of humor, engaged his students by name and knew his stuff. I still remember his lecture on Metternich. He brought that old monster to life, like Dracula rising from the crypt at dusk, gave him his due, and then talked rather nobly about amorality in policy, the limits of Realpolitik, the long-term demands of justice. 'Next time,' he told me afterwards, 'we get to 1848. And so the whirligig of time brings in his revenges.' That's right, a political scientist from Slovenia who nonchalantly quotes Shakespeare and, best of all, assumes *you'll* get it. As I said, a real charmer.

"His department loved him. I think it was the one thing they ever agreed on. Brach offended nobody, deferred to everyone, avoided every tincture of pettiness, steered a safe course through rough waters, and all that's no easy thing in any department, but in Political Science it's unheard of.

"The students went for him too, but quietly, without the sort of hero-worship his elders would have resented and found suspicious. No invidious contrasts, no easy grades either, nothing facile or pyrotechnic. Brach wasn't a comet—comets burn out fast. No, above all, Brach was steady. You could see that he was already mature and would stay that way. You could see it in the way he taught and in his articles—solid, thoroughly documented things. I read a few of them. I had to ask him for them. He wasn't the sort to impose himself on senior faculty, especially if they could do him some good. On the contrary, he preferred to ask if there were anything he could do for *you*. I wouldn't call him a flatterer but, as I say, when you talked to him he managed to make you feel good about yourself. I asked for those articles because he dropped me a note about one of mine. It was on the Mortara case. I was surprised he knew of it—not just my article, I mean, but the case. You see? Of virtue all compact. Not too unlike what we all wanted to be, but without the aggressive hair, the apocalyptic posturing and all that Oedipal pugilism. Actually, Brach was going prematurely bald and, what with the goatee and the glasses, he had a really substantial air about him; in fact, he looked about a decade older than he was. You'd never guess at his athleticism, his agility. When you looked at Brach you thought things like four-square and solid through . . . .

"I suppose he was in his fourth year when the Dean appointed us to sit on a committee together, a tribunal actually. I was to chair the thing. Now, in our day these situations were handled differently—"

"What situations?"

Vasary made up for the euphemism. "Cheating," he said.

"Am I wrong or in the bad old days wasn't it guilty even if proven innocent?"

Someone laughed, but, like the evening sky, Vasary wasn't about to lighten up. "The case was complicated and the Dean had good reason to know it was going to be trouble. I suppose his putting Brach on the panel could be interpreted as a test, to see if he could have confidence in him. But deans don't go in for risks, especially when there's litigation in the air. I think he already had confidence in Brach."

One of the two lawyers among us had perked up. "Litigation?"

"A common threat nowadays. Students sue over grades, lectures that offend them, harassment. You don't dare close your office door during conferences and, if a student's liable to be hostile or amorous, you'd better stow a witness around the corner. Insurance companies have found a good market for academic malpractice policies. As I remember it, in our day protests were often silly but at least they were collective; we thought about social change, solidarity with the vaguely imagined masses. Now the protests are all private, sometimes aimed at private rights but just as often at personal advantage or revenge. No offense to you, counselors, but our generation spawned a lot of lawyers, and they need work. Any kid in trouble these days is likely to have one, or to be the child of one, and lawyers have transformed the system. The ones with kids tend to love the child more than justice. Well, maybe that's unfair. Let's just say any doting parent can be easily persuaded that the original sin was perpetrated by small-minded professors with paltry incomes and profound prejudices, never by their offspring. Those who like the new procedures call them constitutional; those who don't say they're ridiculously bureaucratic. Either way, what's the result? Cheating's more common, but that's mostly because students often don't see cheating as cheating. They mix it up with what the experts call collaborative learning. Anyway, cheating's hardly rare but its prosecution is. The disincentives are hard to overlook. Unless you can get a signed confession, preferably notarized and in triplicate, you might have to devote most of a semester to the matter and you could wind up being sued for three of four times the value of your pension.

"All right, no sermons. Our little court had to rule on an accusation of plagiarism. The case was brought by a senior man in the English department, not as big a shot as he thinks himself but an institution all the same, name of Sarnoff. And Sarnoff had fouled things up.

"The student's name was Melissa Wasserman and, to start off with, under the title on the paper she gave to Sarnoff was the name Melissa Wasser*stein*. This title page was also in a different font from the rest of the essay, a term paper on Tennyson, by the way, whose name was spelled correctly. And there were other things that bothered Sarnoff. You should know he doesn't like teaching introductory courses and that's what this was. He'd been roped into it when somebody had a bike accident and went on disability. It's also why he assigned only the one paper, to minimize his own work. He couldn't get the grader he asked for because of budget cuts. Grad students today cost a lot more than we did—which, I think, was next to nothing. Sarnoff isn't good at suffering fools gladly and—at least as regards English literature—Ms. Wasserman was a dunce. She'd never gotten above a D on any of his quizzes and she flat out flunked the midterm where, according to Sarnoff, she referred throughout to a poet named Coolidge and his good buddy Wadsworth.

"The Tennyson paper was too good. Sarnoff didn't recognize any of the obvious sources, though. It was getting to the end of the first semester and I guess he was rushed. This is where he made two mistakes. First, he didn't file the four required copies of the form for reporting unethical practices—one for his department chairman, one for the Dean, another for somebody called the Coordinator of Student Life, and, of course, the one for Ms. Wasserman. The second goof was giving Wasserman an 'F' for the course. Her father, the attorney, was on the phone with everybody starting January third. He demanded to know how his lovely and talented daughter about whom all the English teachers at her private school used to rave could possibly have flunked English 125. He said she'd told him that 40% of the grade was for a term paper she'd never gotten back but on which she'd worked very hard and knew was pretty good. Had Professor Sarnoff, who wasn't answering the phone in his office, failed this paper and if so why? Oh, and was the Dean familiar with the case of Freed versus the Regents of the University of California?

"Well, these days deans are a little like summer camp directors. Around the turn of the century Stephen Leacock—the economist and comedian—observed that universities would be all right as long as they believed students needed them more than they needed the students. Elitist and arrogant, just the sort of sentiment that rubbed us the wrong way, I know, but I have to tell you, not altogether false. Anyway, the Dean phoned Sarnoff at home. Sarnoff wasn't pleased to be called at home, even by the Dean, and said he was pretty sure the paper wasn't the student's work and that she'd flunked the midterm and got a D on the final anyway. I'm not sure what the Dean had to say about being *pretty sure* but whatever it was it got Sarnoff's back up. He said his grades were nobody's business but his own. Which, of course, isn't true any more, especially if said grade has to be defended in a court of law. The Dean pointed out that Sarnoff had never confronted Ms. Wasserman, never accused her, never returned her paper, and neglected to file the requisite form before the semester ended. He just went ahead and flunked her, and the Dean explained why all this was wrong in the way that deans do.

"But this is beside the point. The point is that by the time the case got to us in March Wasserman père was loaded for bear and Melissa had put together a story. She said that she knew she did poorly on Professor Sarnoff's tests—well, on most tests actually, because she 'tested badly.' So the paper was going to be her salvation. That's why she worked so hard on it, and that's why the night before it was due she took it to William Whitmarsh, a pal of her boyfriend's, a computer science major. Whitmarsh helped her, she said, but only with grammar and spelling, nothing else. They worked from her disk on his computer and then printed out the final draft. The following morning, when she was on her way to hand in the paper, she realized it didn't have a title page, that her name wasn't on it. She didn't want just to *write* her name on it, she said; it wouldn't look *neat*, and there weren't any computers available except at the library at the other end of campus. So she phoned Whitmarsh and asked him to run off a title page and bring it to her before nine o'clock when the paper had to be submitted. They met outside Sarnoff's classroom at five of nine and, in her rush, she just clipped the title page on without looking at it.

"Well, there were more details but this gives you the idea. Sarnoff didn't back down. He'd finally filed the forms in February—backdated—basing his case on the title page and the high quality of the paper relative to Wasserman's dismal other work. He wound up his statement rather pompously, I remember. Stuff about 'stretching credulity' and 'beyond the bounds of reason' and the improbability of a student, 'even one who couldn't tell Coleridge from Coolidge,' misspelling her own name. The Dean wasn't delighted but Sarnoff forced his chairman to approve the charge and so a formal hearing had to be called. Procedures, you know.

"We met in the Dean's conference room. Present were three tape recorders, Brach, a chemist named Dolores Murray, and me; then there was the proofreading computer major Whitmarsh, Wasserman, her father, who bullied the Dean into letting him sit in, Sarnoff, and a young colleague of his named Bright. Bright was Sarnoff's third mistake. He's a flashy sort, the kind people used to admire for telling students to call them by their first names. I had no idea what he was doing there until after Sarnoff finished restating his case. He turned triumphantly to Bright and asked him to tell the tribunal something he believed highly pertinent to the case. Bright claimed that he'd been told in confidence by another student that Melissa Wasserman had bought a paper for Professor Sarnoff's course. Daddy turned the color of a mandrill's bum and sputtered. I asked if this student was willing to come forward and Bright said no. When he heard that Wasserman just about went through the ceiling. I had all I could do to get him under control. For a minute it looked as if he might actually go for Bright, and I can't say I blamed him much. I thanked Bright and told him to leave. Sarnoff looked daggers at me, but also—you couldn't miss it—scared.

"It was at this point that Brach asked me if he might pose a couple of questions to Whitmarsh. I told him to go right ahead.

"He was great, though I didn't realize it until later. We'd only had the file for a couple of days, you see, and the chemist hadn't even read it before the hearing. Not so the diligent Brach. He asked Whitmarsh if he was indeed a junior majoring in computer science. Whitmarsh, who hadn't said a word so far, answered yes, with a British accent. Brach asked if, being a Brit, he had studied English poetry much before becoming a computer science major. Whitmarsh didn't hesitate; he was upper-crust, supercilious and brazen. No, he said, he'd pretty well managed to avoid studying poetry. He really didn't care for the stuff.

"'So then it wouldn't be possible for you to have written the paper Ms. Wasserman submitted to Professor Sarnoff.'"

"'That's right,'" said Whitmarsh.

"'Final question,' said Brach with that endearing smile and upturned face of his. 'Since Ms. Wasserman is the girlfriend of one of your closest friends and you knew her well enough to do her this favor, why did you type *Wasserstein* instead of *Wasserman* on that title page?'

"Whitmarsh missed maybe half a beat before he said that, after all, she'd just awakened him with her phone call and he had to rush to get the title page to her before nine. So he'd made a mistake. No big deal."

"Brach thanked him and looked over at me. I was on the point of summing up, saying that we would deliberate before reaching a decision, when Wasserman broke out again. 'Look,' he said, actually pulling one of the microphones closer, 'to find my daughter guilty you not only have to believe *she's* a liar but that Mr. *Whit*marsh here is lying too. I just hope you Ivory Tower bastards don't try to cover each other's asses because it's obvious that the good professor screwed up royally and got that other jerk in here to save his rear end and I want you to know that if you try to punish *my* daughter for *his* mistake I'll sue your asses too.' Or something along those lines.

"Nice fellow," somebody whispered.

"Concerned parent," someone else replied facetiously.

Vasary continued. "I thanked him for his candor, adjourned the hearing, asked the witnesses to leave, and switched off the tape recorders.

"As soon as they were out of the room Brach took a computer printout out of his briefcase and laid it in front of me and Dolores Murray. He didn't say a word. Instead he stuck his hand back in his briefcase and took out the *University Bulletin* and laid that beside the printout. On top of these, still without saying anything, he laid his copy of Wasserman's paper, turned to page 17, where he had highlighted two words. One was honor spelled *honour* and the other was civilization spelled with an *s* instead of a *z*.

"'It's obvious Whitmarsh wrote this paper,' he said, 'and here's the proof.' Dolores Murray, looking only at the paper, said that a couple of Anglicisms didn't actually prove Whitmarsh had written the paper since he might, in checking the spelling, reasonably have spelled like the Englishman he was. Brach didn't reply; he just removed the paper and the *Bulletin* and pointed to the printout. It was Whitmarsh's university record, and it showed clearly that, while the young man was indeed a junior computer science major, he'd only been one since January. For his first two years he'd concentrated in English literature. Among the courses he had taken in his first year was English 125, then taught by the cyclist for whom Sarnoff was filling in. Brach—and this is my point—was conscientious. Later, he said to me that he felt Melissa Wasserman's dishonesty, her impudent persistence in it with Whitmarsh's assistance, was a betrayal of the trust on which all our work depended. He knew Sarnoff had fouled up, but he also saw the old man was suffering, and that the Dean wouldn't mind hanging him out to dry. Brach grasped the whole situation and the strangest thing of all is that I believe he really meant what he said about trust."

By now it was growing dark. Inside the hotel someone switched on the porch lights, then, thinking better of it, turned them off again. Perhaps they noticed us and didn't want to attract insects. In the few moments of illumination we could see that the expression on Vasary's long face was grave, even morose. Nobody interrupted him.

"Brach was a married man. I had him and his wife to dinner a couple times. Oh yes, we became quite friendly after that hearing. Well, I was bound to be impressed, wasn't I? The wife sold real estate. One of those short intense women whose vitality can be a little irritating. I think she was very proud of Brach, her husband The intellectual. Around her he was quiet, content to let her do the talking. She wasn't a frivolous woman, just one with more words than knowledge. I suppose you'd call her ambitious. As I remember the evening, she talked about a great many things the way children sometimes do, not asking questions but trying out answers to see if the grownups will contradict them. I had the impression that Brach never contradicted her. She laid out their plans, or rather hers, where and how they would live once 'Alex got his tenure,' as she put it. The big Victorian house they would buy, the two perfect children she was going to bear, the trips to Europe they would take for the sake of his research. She asked me quite a few questions about the tenure process and made it clear that she would have liked to hear how secure his chances were, as if I had a say in the matter. I learned that they had met when she was a senior and he was in graduate school, finishing up his dissertation. She wanted me to know how terribly hard he had worked on it, as if no one had ever struggled with a thesis before. Well, you know." Vasary shocked us by raising his voice. "And he smiled, even at that!"

He paused then asked us elliptically, "You don't mind?"

No, we said. Go on. We didn't mind.

"Well, of course his chances were good, could hardly have been better, really. No natural predators, adoring colleagues, a proud chairman and, after the Wasserman affair, a grateful dean, not to mention five years of sterling evaluations from his students, and the book from the good press. There were plenty of encouraging noises in the corridors too, where these things generally get decided, including, as you've probably guessed, some from me.'

Vasary sighed. "'*This laurel greener from the brows/Of him that uttered nothing base.*' That's Tennyson by the way. Well, I had gotten to know him and that's what he was like, *nothing base*. As I saw it Brach more than merited the single gift academics have it in their puny power to bestow, the right to cross that bar and join the fleet outside the harbor. Brach had been scrutinized as sharply as anybody else, you understand. Oh, we were sure of him, sure that what you saw was what you got—that he was indeed solid through and through. And he was happy to be among us, which counts for more than you'd think. He told me once that he could think of nothing else, could love nothing more, than what he was doing. I wonder if you know how rare that is? I wonder whether, if you hadn't escaped yourselves, any of you would feel that way. Academic talk sometimes seems to me to consist in nothing but idealism expressed in a context of cynicism or the reverse, of complaining doubly distilled like cognac, backbiting and the gasps of a baffled will to power. There was absolutely nothing of this in Brach. Nothing. He wanted to teach and study; the furthest his ambition went was perhaps to contribute a little to the future happiness of a melancholy people and to inspire a handful of students. Even after five years of probation his laurels were still as green as the grass on that terrace over there . . . .

"Laurels?"

". . . Well yes, that was our judgment. And I sometimes wonder if we really were fooled."

"Fooled?" somebody said in the dark.

"Oh yes, that's what everyone said, of course. Huge deception. A humbling lesson, terrible thing. Shake your head and then forget it or, worse yet, turn the whole mess into some general principle or future prejudice. In a year or two people might recall the lesson but they'd forget the man. Alexander would be cast into a nice deep oubliette loaded down by his mortal sin. That's what it was, completely lethal, and it left us breathless. For weeks those of us who knew him just looked at each other and, if we spoke at all, did it in whispers. It came down as suddenly and irrevocably as the guillotine . . . ." Vasary stopped, perhaps to catch his breath.

"*What* came down?" somebody asked impatiently.

Vasary chuckled bitterly. "I suppose it was the whirligig of time," he said, and again paused for a moment or two. "If we tried we could probably see a shooting star," he said in a dull voice, then went on.

"During that last year I thought I came to know him— well yes, I *did* know him, which is the worst of it. It was just a fact I didn't know, a secret. But not all secrets are consequential. Not knowing where somebody was born is trivial; not knowing they have a terminal disease is another matter."

"Brach died?"

"Yes and no. That is, like many other people, he's gone on living after he died, or became as good as dead. I don't feel confident enough to say exactly what happened; all I can tell you is the facts. You've been very patient with me and I appreciate it, truly. It's not so much like old times as it is therapy. I'm sorry."

There's nothing like being congratulated on your patience to make you lose it. "Come on, Vasary," somebody said with exasperation. "So what *did* happen?"

"What happened I can tell you, but not why. All right, Brach's tenure review began at the appointed time, last September. It took about five minutes for his department to record a unanimous vote. Then his chairman composed the requisite encomium and sent the file on to the Dean, who was to make his recommendation and pass the dossier on to an all-university committee, after which it would go to the provost, the president, the trustees. It's set up like a steeplechase, as you know. Jump the hedge, leap the water, then there's the brick wall. But Brach was golden. When I ran into him the first week of classes he seemed to me humble enough but altogether confident, justifiably too. I suppose his wife was already keeping her eye peeled for that big old Victorian.

"It was the beginning of a new year and everybody was busy. I didn't think about Brach for a couple of weeks. Then one afternoon I ran into Ralph Marburg, his chairman, in the parking lot. Marburg looked as if he were the one who'd just gotten the terminal diagnosis. 'Have you heard yet?' he asked me. And then he told me what had happened the previous afternoon. That's all it took; not even a whole afternoon really.

All over in an hour, a little longer than a guillotine takes, but not if you count the ride from the prison.

"When Marburg got back from his eleven o'clock class there was a message waiting for him; the Dean wanted him in his office instantly. Poor Marburg, the Dean sat him down and laid everything out. That morning he had gotten a call from the graduate dean of the university that had proudly conferred on Brach his doctorate. He thought the Dean ought to know they were withdrawing the degree. This decision was taken after the University Counsel received a fax from the press that had published Brach's book. The publishers had heard from a lawyer representing a certain Croatian scholar who taught out in the Midwest. This man claimed, and what's more proved, that nearly forty pages of Brach's book—pages which had likewise appeared in his doctoral dissertation—were lifted straight from a monograph he had published eight years earlier in Holland. The press was calling in all unsold copies of Brach's book and notifying every library that had purchased a copy to remove it from their shelves. It was a non-book. I still have the copy he gave me, by the way. On the flyleaf he wrote 'The first of many things I hope we can share.' The Dean informed Marburg that obviously Brach's tenure case would be terminated immediately but, on top of this, he wanted Brach off the campus by the next day. He didn't give a damn how his classes got covered.

"Marburg told me he was deeply upset and had staggered over to Brach's office but he wasn't there. He was still hoping for some explanation, some words that would undo everything the Dean had said. Brach had no classes that day, so Marburg telephoned him at home. Marburg said, 'I had to tell him it was all over.' I asked if Brach had put up any kind of fight. He said that's what he had expected, but there was no such thing.

It occurred to me that Brach wasn't surprised, that he'd probably been waiting for the guillotine all day. By then he would
certainly have heard about his degree and he'd doubtless have
heard from the press as well, or their lawyers; very likely the
Croat's as well. I imagined him sitting by the phone waiting
for Marburg's call, like some marquis in his cell waiting for
the tumbrel. According to Marburg the only thing Brach said
was 'All right.'

Vasary paused, tapped on the arm of his rocking chair,
leaned forward.

"... It really is *the* mortal sin, you know. Academics insist
on their property rights as fiercely as any rancher with a Win-
chester. Professions draw lots of lines around behavior—from
sexual harassment to how colorful your language can be in
a meeting—but these are all, in a sense, negotiable, flexible.
Allowances are made, excuses can be found. But no one could
ever forgive what Brach had done and he knew it. So he said
'All right.' Just like that. Nothing more. Marburg thinks he
must have been relieved, glad to be caught, but I can't make
myself believe it. I think he had contrived to put it behind him,
absolved himself, simply forgot about it. After all, he didn't
even need those ripped-off pages. They weren't crucial. So, why
did he steal them? What could have pushed him? Did he even
need a push? His wife's ambition, the pressure of time, some
idiotically misplaced wish to perfect the thesis, the insanely
hubristic notion that he'd never be found out, revenge on Cro-
atians? Or did he somehow delude himself into thinking that
what he was doing, the sin he was committing, was, to use
his own horrible phrase, *all right*? Like Wasserman .... Was
the sin just some awful lapse or rooted in him, a momentary
desperation? Was it a crack in the foundation?"

"What happened to him?"

"Oh, I never saw him again. Nobody did. The Dean got his wish. The next day Brach was simply gone. Those of us who knew him best, liked him most—and there were quite a few of us—were floored. Much worse than a death, to tell the truth. How could we have failed to see such a flaw, we, the professionally . . . perspicacious? We looked at each other with a kind of shame. The truth is we didn't feel so much betrayed as humiliated. For him we felt, well, we felt a lot of things, all unmentionable. When we met and whispered together about Brach we'd ask if anybody knew what had happened to him. It was painful to ask, actually. There was a rumor that his wife had left him which I can't think of any reason to doubt. But that was it. Brach was more than dead. Even Marsh hadn't heard from him or been able to get him on the phone. The line had been disconnected . . . ."

"This still bothers you, the not knowing?"

"What bothers me isn't the not knowing or even that I misread Brach—that hurts but it's only vanity and I can accept it. What disturbs me is that I might *not* have. Your professions all have their ethical standards; their unpardonable sins too, no doubt. Imagine one of your own young colleagues, a steady and reliable one full of promise who'd been nothing but decent for half a decade; imagine such a person not merely crossing some line, but violating the one rule that can't be broken without being forever branded, doing the one thing—*having* done the one thing—beyond any possible forgiveness or redemption. Can you imagine the *finality* of it?"

The question was rhetorical. Vasary fell silent. Perhaps he had terrified himself in trying so hard to make us feel that Brach's disgrace was a tragedy, evoking horror beyond remedy so as to draw us together, middle-aged people on a dark porch watching young couples meandering over green lawns, leaning on one another, privileged, expectant, happy, just a little drunk.

"So? Nothing else, then?" someone asked at length.

"A couple weeks ago I had a doubles match. Marsh was on the courts. He called me over and told me he'd discovered that sometime during the winter Brach had found a job a few towns over managing a newly opened tennis club. According to Marsh's source, the owners fired Brach in May when they discovered he'd been embezzling. He said Brach had given the money back, most of it anyway, and no charges were filed. Then he disappeared."

One of us rebelled, spoke up indignantly. "Disappeared is too kind a word, Vasary; worse, it's a *romantic* one. I'd say your friend went on the lam, looking for his next scam—maybe his next wife."

"That's what I meant by the unofficial official view, that Brach was a cracked egg from the first. It doesn't matter that he was born elsewhere, may have had some trouble in childhood—no, it really doesn't. The unforgivable sin is. . . unforgivable, I know. What I wonder about is whether redemption was what he was after all along."

"You mean tenure, not redemption. If I'm a good boy and make nice to all the heavy hitters then it'll go away and I'll be fixed for life. *That* sounds more like it."

"I don't know," sighed Vasary. "It sometimes seems to me that if he put up no defense it's because he'd already convicted himself. I really don't know. But other things are certain such as that Brach's beyond the pale for good, outside the gates. In a sense, he really *is* decapitated."

By now the island was dark. On the porch we fell quiet, no longer straining to hear Vasary. Instead we listened to the party that was still going on and, below that, the insects calling to one another and, underneath everything, the waves breaking against the rocks.

Last Poems

Coincidence

"Coincidences always come in pairs." So reads the fourteenth iambic pentameter line of Armin Ritter's "Duetta," a sonnet that means a great deal to me. It sounds as if he's being ironic or deliberately stupid and might as well have written "String quartets always come in fours." But the line isn't a tautology. Two simultaneous events aren't enough to make a coincidence. A coincidence is a coupling that can be all velvety and seductive, sleek as a couple of inveigling aristocrats; a coincidence can stand right in front of you, chin out, hands on hips, shouting. Coincidences are inward things; the incidents are outward but the *co* transpires between the ears.

For our senior year my two best friends, Nimala and Valeria, and I rented a house together three blocks from campus. Our landlady, Mrs. Ardekian, was a widow whose husband had for years been the University's bandmaster. She herself created the position of "Mother of the Marching Band," a role she kept up even after her husband died. Mrs. A. loved her tuba players, tradition, the University, its students and alumni. When they were flush, she and her husband bought a small, second house as an investment and the lease on this house passed each year to a group of seniors. For a time Mrs. A. gave herself the pleasure of personally interviewing all prospective tenants, serving juice and cookies in the living room of the Victorian pile in which she and her husband had lived together with several generations of female German shepherds. When Mrs. A. had to give up her home and the dogs, she moved into a retirement community and held on to the rental property. She let it on generous terms to seniors recommended by the previous year's renters, whom she trusted to choose successors who not only wouldn't trash the place but would keep it up. My friends and I got the coveted place thanks to Valeria's being lab partners with two of the three women who had rented it the year before.

It was a neat little house, white with green shutters, on a small lot, garden in the rear, living and small dining room, three bedrooms, two baths, a full cellar. The kitchen appliances were old-fashioned and, perhaps for that reason, reliable. So was the furnace.

Nimala, Valeria, and I came back from Christmas Break in varying degrees of emotional turbulence. Mine was conventional enough: what to do with graduation staring me in the face. Nimala's was more serious; she hadn't gotten on at all well with her family. What had been merely tricky a few years before had now swollen, she said, to impossibility; that is, negotiating the contradictory injunctions to stick to her own kind and Americanize; to be independent while carrying out all her parents', aunts', and uncles' advice; to live both in Baltimore and Bengal. Valeria's emotional tumult was of an entirely different character. Chip Stauffer, the third-year medical student she'd been seeing since the middle of junior year, had asked her to move in with him and she'd agreed. Chip already had a one-bedroom apartment which Valeria said was plenty big enough.

"My parents didn't make anywhere near the fuss I thought they would," she said joyously.

Nimala rushed over and gave Valeria the kind of hug one hunter might give another who's just brought down a twelve-point buck.

"So, you told Elyse and George." I said. When Valeria had me to stay for a week at the Minetti mansion the prior summer, her parents had insisted I use their first names.

Valeria said primly that the secrets she kept from her parents were only little ones. The Minettis were rich and, it seemed to me, easygoing; yet they neither spoiled nor alienated their kids.

"Of course I told them. They'd have found out anyway."

"Well, I don't see why you expected a fuss. I mean, Chip's a six-foot third-year med student," mused Nimala. "My mother'd put on bangles and dance down Washington Street," her voice fell "—if only Chip were Amartya."

Valeria was radiant and feeling generous. "Look, I'm not going to stiff you guys. I'll pay my share of the rent for the rest of the semester. A deal's a deal."

"If things don't work out—" I began to say.

"Shut *up!*" screeched Nimala and tossed a toss pillow at me.

"Chip's coming to pick me up in an hour or so. We'll be taking most of my stuff tomorrow. Come on, Karen, be happy for me."

I was happy for her, in a melancholy way that pleased her. When the estimable Chip showed up to bear her off she hugged us both tightly. It felt like the start of a honeymoon and, in fact, within the week she was showing us the ring. Gigantic stone.

So far no coincidence, I know. Be patient. They come in pairs.

Back in September, Valeria, a stalwart citizen, had ordered delivery of the local paper. I glanced at it over coffee late on the Saturday morning after she left us. This is where the irresistible coincidence comes in.

Because of the recession one of the reporters had begun a misery column, one story per diem, to put, as he unfortunately said, a human face on the statistics. The column was even called *Human Faces* and each awful entry was topped by a picture of someone looking frightened or defeated.

That morning, however, the photograph was quite different. It was a formal portrait, obviously out of date, of this fortyish man with close cropped salt-and-pepper hair, wearing a tie, a jacket, and wise smile. His name was vaguely familiar.

Armin Ritter, a local poet with a national reputation, is losing his home. Mr. Ritter, 67, explained that he had paid the original mortgage off but seven years ago, when his wife became ill and the cost of her care exceeded his coverage, he took out a new mortgage, "one of those adjustable-rate time bombs," as he puts it. Ritter retired three years ago, at the mandatory age, from his job at the Registry of Deeds. A year later his wife passed away. The monthly mortgage payment doubled last year. The bank has given Mr. Ritter until Friday to vacate the premises. "Ever let the fancy roam," Mr. Ritter rhymed gamely, "Pleasure never is at home." The Ritters were childless. Mr. Ritter's brother died several years ago. "I've been too settled for too long. Haven't published a poem in a decade. Time to move on, I guess." When asked what he planned to do, Mr. Ritter recited a nursery rhyme. I asked him to write it down for me.

> There was a naughty boy
> And a naughty boy was he,
> For nothing would he do
> But scribble poetry.

Armin Ritter has won two prizes for his poetry. Eighteen years ago the University conferred an honorary Doctor of Humane Letters degree on him.

Now, like so many others, he has joined the army of the homeless.

I remembered. In high school, in the days when my feet always hurt and I still dreamed of becoming a prima ballerina, I had been struck by a poem of Ritter's in an anthology. I felt he had written it expressly for me—even *to* me—and that it was about a bond between us. Perhaps my old romantically ambitious self wasn't so wrong. Anyway, I've never felt the urge to scoff at her. I put down the paper and went straight to my laptop and found the poem which is just two quatrains long.

Poet, Dancer, Tree

> The poet aches just like the dancer's toe.
> Who knows of that broad gnarled beech
> the agonies of its growth, what blisters,
> what strained heavings through dirt, towards sky?

> All beauty's born of pain. Nothing strides
> into the grace of form without labor.

And still, when words and limbs are tightly tuned,
who remarks the ground over which they glide?

I still liked what Ritter had written, though in a different way. I liked the way *strides* is echoed by *glide*; I paused over *strained heavings* and the ontological grandeur of *through dirt, towards sky*. Would any pubescent dancer disagree that beauty is close kin to pain? On top of this, the copper beech was still my favorite tree. So here was Armin Ritter, the poet who understood me when I was sixteen, with no place to lay his head. And here was I, a half-dozen years later, barely a mile away in a house with a spare bedroom. It felt more like a syllogism than a coincidence.

The idea took hold in me like a harpoon. When I laid it before Nimala she was flabbergasted and had a slew of practical questions.

"Would we be responsible for him if he got sick? Would we have to cook for him? He probably goes to bed a lot earlier than we do; what if we have a party? Wouldn't we have to clear it with Valeria? With Mrs. Ardekian? And, you know, he is, you've got to admit, a strange man—I mean a stranger *and* a man . . . though I guess poets can be pretty strange in all kinds of ways. In fact, the whole idea is just weird." She didn't press me on any of these imponderables because she felt certain that Ritter would reject our offer even if we made it.

"He's probably made plans," she said. "Wouldn't some poetry society rush to his aid? Publishers? *Some*body?"

"Well, if he's going to the Home for Homeless Poets, he'll just tell us."

I couldn't have answered all her questions. I simply insisted it was the obviously right thing to do. I made a big point of the coincidence itself. "Don't you think it's significant?"

"What?"

"Valeria leaving and . . . you know."

At which bit of superstition Nimala smirked.

"Come on. It might be fun," I thought to add.

"Fun? We're twenty-one and he's, what. Seventy? Eighty?"

"Only sixty-seven."

"Oh *well*, then." She laughed her best laugh, showing every one of her exceptionally white teeth, none of which had ever required a filling.

An Indian dental student she dated a few times to make her parents happy said to me pompously and in her presence, "It's obvious Nimala is a very sweet and virtuous girl, impervious to Western decadence."

We phoned Valeria who was still in the supra-lunary stage of her engagement and would have agreed to anything. "Go for it!" she more or less bellowed.

Invitation

When Nimala suggested we phone Ritter I raised my finger and affected a Shakespearean tone. "No, noble deeds in person must be done or not at all. We have to go to his foully foreclosed house, and betimes."

Nimala made a face. "Middle of the afternoon would be best. Unless he takes endless naps like Uncle Prasad. It would give us some time with him. I think we should get a sense of him before we, you know, make the big offer. Also, we don't want to get there just when he's sitting down to dinner."

"Maybe you're right. We should call first."

"Generally speaking, I am right. You haven't noticed? But you have to make the call."

"Why?"

"Because I was right and because it's your whacko idea."

I felt suddenly nervous. Maybe the whole thing was absurd. But I was determined and tried to think what I'd say to Ritter.

"How's this? *Mr. Ritter, we understand you're about to be homeless and we have a proposition for you.*"

"Well, it's certainly direct. But then we wouldn't be able to get a feel for him. Don't you think we should at least *see* him first?"

"How can I call him without explaining why?"

"Okay, then I was wrong."

The force of the coincidence wasn't completely dissipated. I really didn't care about getting a look at him. Caution was cowardice. "Then let's just call and tell him what we have in mind."

Nimala shrugged dismissively. "You know he's just going to laugh and say he's moving in with some nephew."

"Then it's okay with you if I just come out with it."

"*We have a proposition for you*? Makes you sound like a Mafia guy—or Lady Bountiful," cracked Nimala.

"The *we* wasn't lordly. Or criminal. I just wanted to include *you*."

Nimala, impatient, tossed her head. "Oh, whatever."

I went looking for the phone book. Somehow it seemed more fitting than using the computer. Didn't matter, though. A recording said the line had been disconnected.

"Poor man," said Nimala. "No phone."

"Okay. Back to Plan B. I'm free at three-thirty today."

"No can do. That's when my seminar's supposed to end. Make it four-thirty. Okay?"

Around three a steady rain began. We put our umbrellas in Nimala's Honda.

Ritter's was a nice residential neighborhood so parking was no problem. The street was deserted in the rain, everybody working, in school, or lying drugged behind the drapes.

Ritter's about-to-be-former house was a fair-sized Dutch colonial with an attached garage. There was a sign on the lawn with a blunt tone.

Armin Ritter opened his door wide, not just the suspicious, shamed crack I expected.

He looked his age—balding, thin, face lined, dressed in old man's slacks and a plaid shirt—but there was something youthful about him that you noticed right away. Most old people seem to have slammed the door and settled in with their certainties; but Ritter's door was wide open in every sense. He didn't look at the two of us suspiciously, but with expectation, almost with pleasure, eyebrows up, mouth forming a welcoming smile. I had the odd feeling that Ritter thought there might be something wonderful he could do for us. "Did you notice his eyes?" Nimala asked later. "Sharp as thorns, my auntie would say."

"Mr. Ritter—" I started.

"It's pouring," he said as if a catastrophe had befallen us. "Come in, come in."

He continued talking as we shuffled into the tiny foyer. Ritter held his arm out, pointing to the living room. "When your parlor looks like the Golden Horde has blown through it's customary to apologize. So, sorry." In fact, the room didn't look ransacked but about to be evacuated. There were books, cartons, papers, plates, rolled-up carpets, old record albums and newer CDs, curtain rods, a lot of black plastic bags. There was a couch and two armchairs. Ritter cleared the couch by dumping everything that was on it behind it.

"Please," I protested, not liking to see him exert himself.

"I've been foreclosed, you see."

"Yes," said Nimala. "That's why we're here."

"Oh, and here I was thinking you just wanted to come in out of the rain." Our first taste of what one critic called "the sly Ritter irony."

"If we might just—"

"I could offer you some Dom Perignon and beluga on toast points," he shrugged, "but even if you accepted. . ." He shrugged. "Well, there's some tea. Would you like some tea?"

"No, thank you. But—"

"Now, now, please sit down. It's a pleasure just to look at the two of you and I intend to go on doing it while you say whatever you want. Not interested in buying the house, are you?"

"No, Mr. Ritter, it's not the house.""

"Good, let the bank eat it, I say. Mit sauerkraut. Okay, then what?"

"It's *you* we're interested in," said Nimala.

He kept his eyes on us as he backed his rear-end into one of the armchairs. "Now that's flattering. You're students?"

"Yes, we—"

"I used to get a lot of letters from students. You'd be surprised how many. You know I wrote poems?" We nodded. "They'd usually been assigned a paper on some poem I wrote and wanted me to explain it to them so they could explain it to their teachers. I never explicated things very clearly. Still, it felt nice to be regarded as the horse's mouth—as opposed to the other end." He smiled with satisfaction.

I could tell Nimala was enchanted; I was becoming exasperated.

"It's not about a poem, Mr. Ritter. We have a proposition for you."

His eyebrows shot up again. "Proposition?"

"An offer, I mean."

Nimala chimed in. "It's just an idea we've had." She turned toward me. "Well, Karen did. I'm Nimala, by the way."

Ritter rose and held out his hand for us to shake. "Delighted to make your acquaintance, Nimala. Karen."

"Karen saw the article in the paper. And. . . well. . ."

I leaned forward to signify I was taking over the floor.

"Where are you planning to go, Mr. Ritter?"

"Go?"

"You have to leave here. According to the article, by Friday."

"Um. Yes. Well, I'm not quite sure. Probably a motel for a few days, until I get my bearings."

"Nothing . . . longer term?"

"So nice of you to be concerned, Karen. And unexpected." He crossed a leg over his knee, a movement that seemed at once nonchalant and defensive.

I pressed on. "Then you have no *real* place to go?"

"Oh, *real?* A notoriously elusive concept. A Frenchman once wrote about being 'at the disposal of life'. Of course he said it long before they invented garbage disposals."

"Nowhere, then," Nimala murmured with a moue so sympathetic Ritter might have been a kitten.

"Well, since you ask so kindly, I've applied to a few of those places they call artists' colonies—you know, nice cabins all over the woods, a composer or novelist behind every third tree. A long-shot, but still."

I was as relentless as a car salesman. "But nothing *now?* Nothing this *week?*"

Ritter glanced up at the ceiling. "The reporter thought Keats wrote nursery rhymes."

Nimala gave me a pleading little nod, the high sign.

"Mr. Ritter, we rent a three-bedroom house near the University, about a mile from here. Yesterday our roommate moved out—or rather, she moved in with her fiancé. She's going to continue paying her share of the rent. We'd be delighted if you'd move in with us—until, as you say, you get your bearings. Rent-free. I'm afraid it can't be a long-term offer because the lease runs out when we graduate at the end of May. So, what do you say? Us, or the Bide-A-Wee?"

When I finished I looked over the room and thought of what power time and familiarity confer on objects. All this detritus must have been precious to him. But there was far too much for the "naughty boy" to bear on his back when he "let his fancy roam." I supposed that, unlike memory, fancy travels light. Was this why he quoted Keats to the reporter and not Yeats or Tennyson—Keats who never aged?

Nimala dropped a silken net over his astonished silence. "I think," she said slowly, "it would be an adventure to live with you, even for a few months." If she didn't sound like a Mogul princess at least she looked like one, especially when she lowered her gaze. "More of an adventure for us than for you, perhaps." She looked up. "I've never lived with a poet."

Ritter began to laugh and when he stopped took my left hand in his right one, Nimala's in his left. "So this is what it means to be at the disposal of life. All right. Yes, yes, I gratefully accept your most generous offer. But on one condition. I've lost my house but I'm not entirely destitute. There's what's left of my pension and Social Security too. I insist on paying my way. Oh, a second condition: you let me cook for you once in a while. Oops, and one more: you won't be annoyed if I write verses under your roof. You see, I'm trying to finish a book."

"That's wonderful," exclaimed Nimala.

"We'll see," he said solemnly and released our hands. With a little groan he stood up straight so we were looking up at him. "The working title 's *Last Poems*."

Installation

We found a self-storage place outside of town—bottomland with a sort of necropolis of concrete oblongs, metal doors with huge padlocks. We rented a van for a day and called in a couple of boys to help move the stuff to which Armin Ritter was unprepared to bid adieu. To the house he brought only clothing, one carton of books, another of towels and linens, minimal toiletries (Nimala: "Did you get a load of the shaving mug and brush?"), his sound system and quite a number of CDs, more classical but also some jazz from the 50's and 60's. Of a wooden lamp he said, "I made it myself. For writing under." There was also an old Cutty Sark box with "MSS." inked on it. ("Figure maybe one poem a month worth keeping, for a dozen years.") For writing he had an antique Smith-Corona portable, but his prize possession, which he kept in a special box and held on to tightly in the van, was a big black German fountain pen. "Poems ought to be hand-made; every word should have weight," he explained when he let us look at it. Fountain pens and shaving brushes. "The peculiar beauty of the obsolete," as he says in "Yawls and Spitfires."

"Cute," said Nimala later, shaking her head. "No cell phone."

"And no computer," I added.

"Oh, my God."

When everything had been set down in Valeria's old bedroom we had our first dinner, volunteers included. Even though it was under forty degrees, the boys grilled burgers and kielbasa on our old hibachi. Ritter wasn't exactly voluble but what he did say was charming. Mostly he let us talk. After the boys left the three of us went upstairs. He stood in the middle of Valeria's bedroom looking both lost and found; Nimala and I lingered just outside the threshold.

"You'll be comfortable?"

"Need anything?"

He sat down at Valeria's little oak desk, ran his hand over the green blotter he'd put on it, and started arranging things.

"The art of our necessities is strange," he said, musing and quoting, while toying with his talismanic pen. "But you've placed me in no hovel on a heath. This is a palace. A mansion. No wind, no rain, no cold—not even the chill loneliness of a widower. Karen, Nimala, let me thank you with tomorrow's dinner. Right now, though, I need to write. To *try*, I mean. You shouldn't ever keep her tapping her toe. It's risky. Ungrateful."

And so we left him feeling luckier than Lear. As for Nimala and me, we felt like two revised daughters.

The music began near midnight. A late Beethoven quartet played low, diffidently.

Presents

The dinner was French so it required a lot of cooking and a load of ingredients. While we were in class, Ritter walked four miles in the gelid January gray to buy what he needed at a specialty shop. Wine too—Nuit St. Georges the label said. Neither of us had ever eaten so well or so much, certainly not in our little house. He'd even typed out a bill-of-fare and drew curlicues around it.

> Salade fraicheur avec crabe
> Andouillettes (delicious miniature sausages)

Terrine des tomates avec poivrons et basil
Souris d'agneau
Fromage St. Marcellin et Citron Sorbet

Ritter took such obvious pleasure in our pleasure over his offering that we fell into a sort of positive feedback loop: Nimala and I going "Mmmmmmm," Ritter beaming and dishing out gut-busting seconds.

Afterwards, he insisted on doing the washing-up.

"Don't you have studying to do?"

"Alas," sighed Nimala, rubbing her tummy.

"I have to finish *Northanger Abbey*. Gothic Lit. Can't imagine why I took it."

"Astringent and corrective," said Ritter. "Always made me think of *Don Quixote*."

I'd forgotten that he'd probably read everything.

"How?" I asked.

"The ills that come from reading too much of the wrong thing."

I picked up the sauté pan he'd just rinsed and began to dry it, but he shooed me out of the kitchen. "Go, go. Read, read."

With all those calories français inside me, I fell asleep over *Northanger Abbey*, which isn't a patch on *Pride and Prejudice*. I woke on the couch, or half-woke, yawned and dragged myself upstairs, leaving the novel where it had fallen, spread-eagled on the floor. There was light under Nimala's door; Ritter's was open. He was seated at his desk, apparently looking over items from his carton of mss. Which was next to the desk. No music.

"Good night," I said drowsily. "I'm turning in. Austen and andouillettes are soporific."

He chuckled and wished me good night. "Good digesting, too. Nietzsche claims it's the origin of philanthropy."

In the middle of the night I detected whispers of Mozart and Smith-Corona.

I was up at eight. Nimala, with her late class schedule, slept in. Ritter wasn't in the house, but he had set the table before leaving. Laid next to one plate was *Northanger Abbey* with a sheet of paper inserted between its pages. Here's what he'd left for me:

Going to Bed with Jane Austen

> I imagine her fluttering as I clamber in
> like a dove disturbed in her cote, cranky
> but interested, black agate eyes missing nothing
> of the comedy of pose, of sheet, of weight.
> Then, propped on one elbow I'd pronounce, "This is
> what happens after all the novels are over,
> Jane—what you, knowing everything in
> miniature, didn't ever know . . ." But then
> I'm sure she'd laugh—and what a laugh!
> My pompousness explodes like a wineglass
> spilling amour-propre all over the queen-sized bed.
> I am discomfited, delighted; I am
> ashamed, amused; while she, she is at her ease.
>
> Rational conversation and sublime gossip
> fill the remainder of our night until,
> like that famous sultan, I finally fall
> asleep, putting matters off yet another day.

Ritter had written this poem just for—just to—me. No doubt about it. "For Karen Krauss" was typed under the duplicitous title.

I wrote him a thank-you note and slipped it under his closed door.

Loved the poem. Thank you, thank you. I'll prize it always.
K.
p.s. Do you often fantasize about defunct female authors?

Over a more conventional dinner that night Ritter and Nimala got into a discussion of religious restrictions on women. It began when she complained to him about her parents, how they wanted her to Americanize and, just as much, not to. I didn't pay close attention to what she said, having heard her on this topic dozens of times. But I did listen to Ritter.

"It's not that unusual," he said. "I've often thought that what matters for immigrants in America isn't what year it is but which generation they're in. It's second that has it toughest."

"That's me. Generation Deux."

"Should be some comfort that millions have gone through it. . . . Here's a story. Once I was helping this fellow I knew study for his citizenship exam. We got to talking about the meaning of the Declaration and he said, 'I think what our Founding Fathers meant. . .' That pronoun! *Our.* I could almost have cried."

"You're a patriot!" I exclaimed. "I thought you'd be a citizen of the world. I thought that's what *all* poets were."

"Not all. No. But I do think of myself as a patriot. In fact, I love my country too much ever to be a nationalist."

There was music that night, also the next. Bach, *The Well-Tempered Clavier.*

The following morning it was Nimala who had a poem to digest with her late breakfast.

Caro's Table

Beneath the immaculate linen and
those cotton socks two comely ankles swell.
Is to think of them to be led astray?
To contemplate how the bones flow so, to
wonder what is bone, what flesh, stroking
with one's mind the unrepeatably dear
concavity between shin and calf, a
triumph of trillions of contingencies;
to caress even the curt yet tender words, the
firm Teutonic nouns—ankle, thigh, throat,
knee, brow, breast—into which a body can
be butchered or beloved? Nudity,
is vast, he warns, particularly woman's,
albeit Solomon himself seems to
crawl like some besotted beetle hopeless
of the whole so seeking mastery of parts,
anatomizing desire with
analogies—breasts like twin fawns, teeth
like shorn ewes—a pastoral, goatish lust
born of a mind that likewise conceived the
Temple cubit by cubit. Is her hair
naked, her contralto nude only because
their tones are beautiful to beguile
and divert, because all that is unclothed
even in imagination must distract
us from our joyless prayers and loveless
commandments, thwarting the profane
redemption of modest metaphor?

Even "the voice of a singing woman,"
the sage chides, is nudity, naked sound
that dissipates thoughts of his jealous
God whose table must be primly laid,
no ankles touched beneath its spotless cloth.

Ritter watched her read it in almost the same way as he had watched us down his souris d'agneau.

"I love it," she said enthusiastically. "But who's this Caro and why the table?"

"Joseph Caro was a medieval rabbi. He wrote down a bunch of laws which he titled *Shukhan Arukh*, which means *the set table*. He was afraid that women would distract men from thinking about God all the time, because of what he called their nudity. By Caro's logic their nudity was anything that might distract a man and so he considered the voice of a singing woman to be the same as nudity. It's not just the ankles."

"Such erudition!" said Nimala, delighted.

"Such transparent repression," I chimed in.

"Patriarchal religions are all suspicious of women, especially their effect on men, of course. Projection's what Doctor Freud called it."

"You're a feminist?" I asked, still looking to slap labels on Ritter.

He laughed. "Back in the early 70s, when Women's Lib gushed out of the Civil Rights and Anti-War movements—just the way Women's Emancipation did from Abolitionism a hundred years before, by the way—a woman poet demanded to know my position on sexual equality."

"And you answered. . ?"

He shrugged. "Of course I said 'of course.'"

"No fool you," said Nimala evenly. "But I love that you dedicated the poem to me. Is it going in your book?"

Ritter raised his palms. "Oh. The book. Maybe. You think it's good enough?"

"*Good* enough? It's *splendid*. I want my parents to memorize it."

And so a pattern, like Caro's table, was set.

Obsequies

When I was a sophomore I took a Victorian Lit course with Professor Morse. It was a solid course and Morse was a good professor: prepared, knowledgeable, articulate. Only passion was lacking. At the time I figured that it wasn't surprising that an expert on Matthew Arnold should seem staid, serious, diligent—in short, Victorian. Morse was admirable but not lovable and he really did seem to embody the earnest spirit of the age about which he lectured.

Then, in February, a janitor discovered Morse dead in his office and the campus went into shock. His students had no explanation. Everything had seemed perfectly normal in his senior seminar. The topic was Tennyson's *Enoch Arden*, a sad tale but not one anybody was going to kill himself over. The University President put out a mass email so clogged with clichés it sounded like a form letter. I was terribly upset. Pillars like Morse aren't supposed to collapse. Stability isn't supposed to be precarious.

"I knew Morse," said Ritter when I told him the news, which I did as I walked in the door.

"You did?"

"Not all that well, but yes, we got together a few times. He was a good man and a brilliant reader. Did you know he loved jazz?"

"No, I didn't know that." It was hard to put the earnest, controlled Professor Morse together with jazz.

Ritter sighed. "Played a little piano."

"You don't seem all that surprised."

Ritter rubbed at his chin. "No? Maybe it's my age. After sixty no death is as much of a shock as it is at twenty."

I looked at him more closely, sitting there on the couch. "So, nothing more?"

"He was a depressive, Karen."

"You mean—clinically?"

"I don't know clinical, not clinical. He kept up a good front but Morse was like a dog's ear in winter—even colder on the inside than out. He once told me he felt like he'd fallen down a well with stainless steel sides. But I didn't expect this. No."

Then he got up, went to his room, and shut the door.

Nimala didn't know Professor Morse but his death was all she could talk about over the turkey breast and red potatoes Ritter had roasted for us.

"The funeral's Thursday. In the Chapel. I can't go. Organic midterm. You going?" she asked me.

I looked over at Ritter, who had said nothing at all.

"Are you?"

"I don't know?"

"Will you go with me. Please?"

"Wouldn't you rather be with your friends? Classmates?"

I thought it over. "No. I'd rather be with you. Please?"

And so we went together to Morse's funeral, to the Chapel and even to the cemetery where Ritter briefly put his arm around me. It was thin but felt like a cable. It was freezing and there was snow on the ground but that wasn't why he did it.

As I drove us home he suddenly said "February."

"Excuse me?"

"Longest month of the year, isn't it?"
That night it was Bill Evans and Miles Davis the next.
On Saturday morning Ritter put two sheets of paper
under my fork, an elegy à la Ritter.

How About You?

After the chaplain finally shut off
the dripping faucet of his oily words

in which sense he felt was nearly made; after
his sister read his allegedly favorite

poem, three of his musician cronies
tramped up to the drums piano bass

secreted behind the pulpit and
rendered a loose and lachrymariffic

Someone To Watch Over Me, riffing with
eyes half closed though, given he'd hanged himself

in his office, no one there supposed he
believed anybody watched over him;

in fact, the Gershwin was a request from
his wife over whom he'd lovingly watched,

a truth featured in several eulogies,
who looked as though she'd endured successive

catharses after watching all the lost
plays of Sophocles and Euripides,

so drained of pity terror blood that she
scarcely noticed her two daughters, over

whom he'd also lovingly watched, one to
either side of her, fiddling with her skirt

staring across her at one another,
their perpetual war suspended by

this rude truce. He'd also watched, it seemed,
over colleagues, not all of them younger,

and students who looked at the wife as they
jokelessly spoke; the jazzmen played well

but we listened the way you do when the
music isn't meant for you. After the

song a minute of disquieting quiet
before the provost stepped up to declare

official sorrow, the sadness of the
secretaries vice presidents trustees

then suavely announced the scholarship fund
and where our contributions should be sent.

Maddening morning traffic, we made the
slow-motion drive to the cemetery

whose ashes maples sycamores copper
beeches looked as if they'd live forever.

"Why 'How About You'?" I asked when he came downstairs.
"Don't you know the line? Cole Porter," he said dryly. "*I
love a Gershwin tune—how about you?*"

Sirens

Nimala and I decided to throw Valeria a party. What we had
in mind was a sort of engagement/bridal shower/girls' night
out/spring festival/pre-graduation shindig. We set the date for
a week before Spring Break.

When we told Ritter about the party he made an awkward
joke about Pentheus and the Bacchae. I'd noticed that he'd
been getting more and more classical that week.

"Don't you worry," he assured us. "I'll make myself scarce.
I'll be spending the evening with another of the spouseless.
Nice lady, very good cook."

So far as I knew, Ritter had never been invited anywhere
before.

"She invited you for *that* Saturday?"

"Well, actually she invited me to dinner a couple of
months ago. I just plan on accepting now. The bus goes almost right by her place. Look, I'll probably be back in medias
your saturnalia but I'll just tip-toe upstairs. You won't even
know I'm here."

Nimala crinkled up her eyes. "Ah you're shy, aren't you?
We'd *love* to introduce you."

"Shyness doesn't enter into it," he said brusquely.

I teased him. "I'd think by now young women would've lost all their mystery."

He raised a finger. "Let me tell you something about the terrifying power of young women—even little girls. You're dangerous. You can shatter any man's ego—Olympic champions, truck drivers, Presidents of the United States, makes no difference."

Nimala showed him every one of her lovely teeth. "And how do we do that?"

"Simple. Here, I'll show you."

He pushed us across the kitchen into the doorway, shoulder to shoulder. Then he retreated to the living room.

"Now," he shouted, "when I come back into the kitchen put your hands over your mouths, look at me, at each other, then—giggle."

Ritter could crack us up whenever he wanted to.

I once got up my nerve and asked him why it was that nobody from the poetry or academic worlds had offered him any help.

"I'm not a joiner."

"A joiner?"

"That's what my mother said of me—with disapproval, you understand. She was of the it's-not-what-you-know-but-who-you-know school. Poets and academics love conferences, societies, associations—things to join. They network like spiders. I never networked. I found a quiet, undemanding job that wouldn't interfere with my writing, assuming I could do any. Some poets know my work, I guess, but hardly any know me. I did get acquainted with some academics—poor Morse, for example—but I never had the chutzpah to teach."

"Rather publish than perish? Well, did you ever do a public reading."

"*Once*," he growled.

I don't know if Ritter was an unusually wise man for his age but we felt he'd do. Of course he had habits and eccentricities that annoyed one or the other of us. The late-night music and typing were okay; we'd gotten used to that in the dorms. But Nimala could be exasperated by the moodiness that sometimes made him laconic and by what she called "an old-man smell" wafting from his room. I never noticed it myself. But I have some trouble with his constant literary allusions and the way he'd throw foreign phrases into our chats: *und so weiter, succès d'estime* and, once, *medio tutissimus ibis* (my least favorite). I felt as if I were being tested and I didn't think he had the right. Of course, we did things that set his teeth on edge too. He'd wince if we split an infinitive or used a crude word. I soon realized that Ritter had some illusions about women, at least young ones, and that Nimala and I were inadvertent iconoclasts. To tell the truth, shocking him rather pleased me. "The way you talk about your boyfriends!" he once burst out over dinner. It was quite gratifying. I never cared for being romanticized and told myself it was good for him and for his writing to get over his creaky, Tennysonian notions. If he loved us, well that was all to the good, but he should love us as we were.

Ten girls came to the party. There were presents for Valeria, including some crude gag-gifts I'd have liked Ritter to see, plenty of beer and wine. Nimala and I baked a cake and cooked up a ton of finger-food. It was a raucous affair and, though we kept one ear cocked, we didn't hear Ritter let himself in and creep up the stairs. We played loud music, sang along karaoke-style, and laughed like maenads. The party didn't break up until after two and after midnight we forgot all about him. If he was playing Handel or Sonny Rollins up there, we never heard him.

Late the next morning, staggering into the kitchen with our hangovers, Nimala and I were presented in the usual fashion with this long poem:

The Entanglers

*The best tight harmony since the Everly
Brothers*, said Rolling Stone. *Rapturous, the
audience's mouths fell open.* Sure, sure.
Rapturous. We know about rapturous,
starvation too, can recall the reeking
hairy men pissing over their gunwales
hooting polyglot filth, watched them forget
their mothers and their whores, grow thinner and
waste away. Those were the days. Their empty
mouths fell open too. Slain by rapture.

Oars we could cope with but not steam, surely
not submarines. And our hair, these scaly
warbler's feet. *Get with it, girls,* our agent
yelled. *Times change. Cut the tresses, get some Doc
Martens, then we'll see what we can do.*

They say he sang more sweetly than we, waves
and wind contending, song washed by song as
the heroes rowed like bats out of hell. They
claim we fled, offed ourselves in frustration

when the truth is we never heard a word,
not one note. Ligea's lethal soprano
was blown back against the wrack and rocks,
his tenor gulped by gulls and whoosh of wave.

Now we've gone electric, amplified sugar,
fishnet stockings, minis, beaucoup cleavage.
Parthenope vamps, Leucosia sighs,
and in *Euxine Honey* Ligea soars
above high C. Our hugest hit so far.

You'd think he'd have noticed we're a trio.
Beeswax in their ears? Roped to the mast? Sure.
Some guys you just can't reach; duty hardens
their souls or music is just a cage to
them or they can't get into voices that
are nude, cool, humid, smooth, round, inveigling
with words beneath words, sound under sound,
who never go beyond sandy shallows
to the bottom of green forgetfulness.
He was one you couldn't tie down. That's all.

Sex and drugs ensnare, marriages, contracts,
love—these are our trade, our constant themes.
Hands held high, they sway through noisy surf,
boys and girls wrapped up in our strands of sound,
starving, drowning in eager ecstasy.
Swimmers in seaweed. Victims of harmony.

Commencement

Nimala sucked up the expectations of her parents with her mother's milk and built her life on a disjunction: good grades or worthlessness. So when she got a C on her microbiology final, she tumbled into an abyss that had long been prepared for her.

"You've been accepted by *three* med schools," I reminded her. "There's going to be a *cum laude* after your degree. I'm proud of you. It's only one test, a meaningless one at that."

I didn't see that it was useless to console her in this way because the crisis wasn't academic but existential. And it was only sharpened by the panic all seniors feel but only admit to in jest.

It was Ritter who pulled her out of her funk. One rainy May afternoon I came home and heard his faint voice coming from upstairs, evidently from Nimala's room, in which, so far as I knew, he had never set foot before. He had never been in mine, either.

Ritter was delivering a fanciful lecture about how human societies had originally been matriarchal. He piled on the evidence, everything from the Venus of Willendorf to Ishtar, Isis, Astarte and the White Goddess, from Mycenaean queens to the Old Religion of North Europe with its witches.

"Of *course* men bowed down to women, magical creatures with the power to bring forth life. If God is a cosmic parent, then which parent came first? Thus the big hips and boobs and vaginas on the earliest cult artifacts. Couldn't be more obvious. So why did things change? When did the earth goddess who threw parties and wanted everybody to be fat and happy, get displaced by the stern, legalistic sky god who wanted everybody to be behave? It happened over and over again. The Bible has just one version. But why? Well, my dear, my hypothesis is that some particularly bright troglodyte figured out how babies are made. He must have been a genius. After all, it's hardly obvious. In the last century you could still find tribes who thought women got pregnant by walking by spirit abodes or when the recently deceased dove in their ears. Impregnation and gestation aren't self-evident. I never knew a kid to figure the business out on his own. So it was a big achievement, figuring it out. Now, imagine how this new theory would have hit the men, what it did for their amour-propre. *She* didn't do it, *I* did it. She's the *field* but I'm the *husbandman*. She *is*, but I *do*. In no time it's pyramids, ziggurats, skyscrapers; it's purdah, burka, no votes or property rights. It's primogeniture and chastity belts. You mean they didn't teach you any of this? Nobody explained why new daddies hand out cigars?"

By now Nimala was giggling. "Sometimes a cigar is just a cigar," she burbled.

"Well, not *this* time."

That night Ritter's Smith-Corona was accompanied by a Brahms' sextet and in the morning Nimala found this poem under her cereal bowl:

Against Discouragement

You know it's mere vanity, this wishing
to be told you've been a swan all along,
needing a license to breathe someone else's
air; yet the want of a nod or some smudged
stamp has left you stateless, a refugee
tiptoeing through your shattered globe,
forlorn and feckless and unshod.
I see you, conquistador of deserts,

wandering your room, charting each square and
minim of its narrowness: warped walls, the
unexpansive ceiling, two dismal lamps.
Have you done your uttermost then, pushed
self to self's last frame, where it says The End?
Have you forgotten that—for such as you—
it's the inside of the camera that
shadows forth the warrantless world?
The best runner outstrips her exhaustion,
ignores the finish and forgets the start,
moved, not by the wreath, but inside her heart.

The week leading up to graduation was bittersweet. I was
eager to move on yet reluctant to part with anything or anybody. Our families would be coming to make a fuss and take
pictures and weep and then bear us away. Nimala and I had
to consider which juniors to recommend to Mrs. Ardekian.
There had been no lack of supplicants: wheedlers, pleaders,
bribers.

"Don't you think we should give the guys a turn?" Nimala
said.

"They might trash the place. Guys are so messy."

"Not all of them. Ritter's neat as a needle."

"A pin."

"Pin, needle. Whatever."

"But Ritter's not twenty-one."

"True, but. . ."

And that's how we finally spoke about the taboo subject
that had been eating at us, Ritter's future.

The letter came that week, telling Armin Ritter he
had been granted residency at Rheinach Artists' Retreat

in Wisconsin from June 15 through August 31. Food and lodging included. "Congratulations. We shall be honored to have you with us."

"On Wisconsin," he said after reading the letter to us. He wanted us to be proud of him, I think, and not worry.

A celebration was required. Nimala and I baked another cake and followed an online recipe for *coq au vin*. We played sixties golden oldies, the music of Ritter's youth, and made him sing along. We both bought presents for him. Nimala gave him two reams of paper and a disk of Scarlatti sonatas. I gave him Busoni's transcriptions of Bach and a bottle of black ink.

"The stationery stores don't even carry bottles of ink these days," he had once complained with that querulous indignation the elderly can suddenly feel about change. A bottle of ink could stand for a lot of things, I guess.

That night, almost our last, he played both his new disks; there was some typing at midnight, and in the morning we had our final poem from Armin Ritter:

One Consolation

As I grow older so the world grows
more complex, and more forgetful too,
as if wisdom and ignorance joined hands,
pressed cheeks, and staggered through a clumsy dance
to time's swift jigs and slow sarabandes.
Life's banal days and undistinguished nights
must not be despised since they're all I can
return to from my odysseys, my flights
through the exotic latitudes of my dreams.

Though quotidian tunes weary our ears
with routine rhythms punctuating years,
such music's always sweeter than it seems.

We gave it a formal reading, Nimala and I alternating lines. We applauded; Ritter bowed. Then we both gave him a kiss on the cheek and Nimala burst into tears.

The following January I was in New York being a graduate student at Columbia when I received a package from Ritter. It contained his book, *Last Poems*, in which he had included all the verses he had written for or because of Nimala and me. On the flyleaf was an inscription in German. "It's the native language of my Pelikan," he'd once joked when I'd asked him about his talisman. "My chief link to tradition. A present from Amanda. My wife." I remember realizing that this was the only time he had mentioned his wife's name, or even spoken of her.

With his big black pen he had written *Eine Muse ist wo Sie sie finden. A. Ritter.*

An enclosed note informed me that the book won a minor prize and, on its strength, he had been invited to join the faculty of a creative writing program in Colorado. "I accepted and begin my new job this month. I'm to teach poetry but I doubt poetry will learn much. So, I've got a new home."

I would like to have known where he lived from September through December. I hate to think of him in a motel.

That was two years ago. Two days ago I read Ritter's obituary in the *Times*. It wasn't long but it was dignified, the kind a respected minor poet—a poet one reads chiefly in anthologies—would receive. There was, of course, no mention of his semester in Mrs. Ardekian's little house.

I phoned Nimala in Los Angeles. She had received a copy of the book too and, of course, we reminisced.

So I suppose I am filling in a blank in his biography with this little memorial, my tribute to our noble, homeless knight, the poet Armin Ritter.

About the Author

He was supposed to be a lawyer, like his father and maternal grandfather. As his vocation was settled at birth, he didn't have to give it any thought. It seemed inconsequential when he was assigned to a tenth-grade Honors English class and fell in love with a reading list of long books by Cervantes, Flaubert, and Dostoyevsky. Apart from wanting to read everything he could—as an adolescent he devoured lots of good books in a bad, escapist way—he didn't suppose this immersion in literature had anything to do with his future. In twelfth grade he contributed two short stories to the school's literary magazine. When his teacher asked him what he intended to do with his life, he replied that he was going to become an attorney. Mr. Hill smiled. "Read Franz Kafka," he said. "Kafka was a lawyer."

In college, he majored in English and took philosophy courses for fun. He studied everything from religious thought and music history to economics. It didn't matter as there was no pre-law curriculum. Then, one bright morning in October of his sophomore year, he woke to an aural hallucination. A resonant voice asked, "How would you like to get up and be a lawyer all day?" Before he could reflect on either the hallucination or the question, the answer burst from him: "No!"

Law school having been eliminated by his suddenly verbal subconscious, an abyss gaped before him. What to do? He never decided; that is, he kept on doing what he was doing. He stayed in school and, in the fullness of time, found himself with a doctorate and sitting at the front of a classroom. He had painted himself into an academic corner.

But through those years, the urge to write something other than seminar papers and lectures simmered away like a half-forgotten stew. Once secure in his job, writing took over his summers and winter breaks. He began to turn out stories, poems, and essays and so forged a double life as teacher and writer.

That he felt a drive to write, and the misery of not doing so, doesn't mean that writing has ever been easy for him, no more than teaching. He took comfort from Thomas Mann's reply when was asked how he'd define a writer. "That's easy," Mann said. "A writer is a person for whom writing is more difficult than it is for other people." The same might be said of professing for professors.

Some facts:

Robert Wexelblatt is a professor of humanities at Boston University's College of General Studies. He has published five collections of stories; two books of essays; two short novels; a book of poems; essays, stories, and poems in a variety of journals, and a novel, awarded the Indie Book Awards first prize for fiction. A collection of Chinese stories, is forthcoming.

It is his good fortune to have one daughter and two grandsons, all perfect.

www.ingramcontent.com/pod-product-compliance
Lightning Source LLC
Chambersburg PA
CBHW031338020726
47499CB00005B/1324